Tainted Rose

Carissa Barker-Stucky
& Kimberly Glassco

Dedication

To my one, my Christopher. Somehow, you continue to put up with me and our four-legged kids.
— Carissa

To my wonderful mother, Pamela Glassco. You've always been my #1 fan. You encouraged me to spread my wings of creativity and soar.
— Kimberly

Table of Contents

Acknowledgments	i
Map of Nocis	iii
The Secrets of Nikko Mori	1
Words of Wisdom	21
Pirate Knives and Emerald Eyes	39
Fate's Tempest	61
Of Damsels and Darkness	87
Rainbows and Rampages	105
Trust	127
Broken Bonds	137
Fireside Shadows	161
Joy in the Midst	181
Full Bloom	201
Bitter Reunions	231
Ruin and Reckoning	249
About the Authors	285

Acknowledgments

Fluffcake:
Reading your feedback both helped with the production of this tale and encouraged us to continue. You helped us see that our characters could make an impact— and that a certain villain was good and awful. Thank you for sharing this journey with us. The sweets through the years also helped. ;)
Carissa

Chris:
I already gave you a shout out in the dedication, but that really isn't enough. You've been my bastion from the moment I realized there was more to you than a funny way of sitting in the cafeteria. You've been by my side through this adventure of life and lived up to every word of your vows— even when I woke you up at all hours or downright ignored you for this project. I love you.
Carissa

Maaura:
Look! Your crazy roommate and suite-mate actually published this hot mess! You were our first official fan, even when we really should have been studying. You've continued to encourage us as the years have passed. We promise the next story won't take another decade...
Carissa

Mom:
I can't tell you enough how much your support for me over the years
has meant. You have always encouraged my creative spirit and nurtured
my writing talents even when others said that it was a waste of time.
If it weren't for you, I never would have discovered my love of writing
stories. It all started with you chronicling in a notebook—a notebook
I still have twenty-two years later—the adventure my six-year-old self
regaled you with while sitting in the bathtub. Thank you for being my
first and always number one fan. You've inspired me as I've pursued
my dreams and throughout my walk with Christ. I love you so much. I
thank God for blessing me with such a loving, creative mother.
Kimberly

Dad:
Thank you for all your hard work throughout the years. You provided
for and protected our family. If not for all you've done, I wouldn't have
been able to go to college and meet my wonderful friend and coauthor.
Thank you for supporting me in all my endeavors and helping me learn
to stand on my own feet. I'll always be grateful to you and grateful that
God blessed me with you. I love you so much.
Kimberly

Megan:
We finally did it! You finally get to read the story I used to talk your
ear off about. Thank you for the excitement you always had in hearing
about the book and characters— not just this book either. I've always
appreciated your enthusiasm and patience in being my sounding board,
even when you'd give me grief for telling you all the twists and turns
before you ever turned the first page. You've been a great friend and
morale support throughout my writing development. In the paraphrase
of a certain actor we both love, I am richer for having you in my life.
Kimberly

Katie:
Thank you, dear sister, for taking an interest and the time to read our
wonderful adventure. I appreciate how you've supported me and been
my close friend throughout my life. Even though our ages are a fair
distance apart, you've always been game to go on adventures with me
and shared my love of reading. I'm glad I got to finally share with you
the world and characters and adventure that has been close to my heart
for years. And don't worry, there's more to come!
Kimberly

NIKKO MORI
ep Shadow Veil
Talon
Thorn-Drake
Hawk Glen
Howsergale
Caer Albright
N O C I S

The Secrets of Nikko Mori

The hem of the traveler's cloak hushed over the faded path. She ghosted through the forest, her boots making neither sound nor mark as she walked. The forest seemed to burn as brilliant rays testified the sun slipping away; the woman was eager to mimic the sun's actions. She was unsure how much farther to the border. Hopefully, the next village would house a mapmaker. A mapmaker and fewer soldiers. She needed a path beyond that which lay before her feet. A plan. A destination. Would she go to Andor? To the enemy of her country? She dare not call them her people. Not anymore. Perhaps she could slip further west, aiming for neutral Regalia. Time would tell. Hopefully, with a map's assistance. For now, all she could do was continue forward.

The forest itself seemed strangely serene and yet watchful. The leaves rustled slightly despite the lack of wind, and the animals kept their distance. This place was one of the few territories outside royal influence. People whispered of a fierce guardian deity that protected the forest with a fearful vengeance, though none had ever actually seen such a persona. And yet, as the traveler wandered under the trees, the sensation of being watched followed her. At first, she attributed the feeling to paranoia for her pursuers. They had been tracking her for so long, it was hard to think of anything else. Part of the reason she needed a plan. She wouldn't let them catch her; she couldn't. She refused to go back. As the watchfulness seemed to persist, she paused.

The woman turned a slow circle, gazing deep into the trees and boughs, searching for the presence. Her black cloak concealed almost all her features, and a thick scarf beneath concealed the lower half of her face. The cloak's hood was pulled forward to shadow the rest.

Nowhere did the presence seem to manifest. It was as if the forest itself watched her. As she watched in turn, bushes moved aside to reveal a path while some others seemed to close tighter together. People from neighboring countries and towns not far from the borders of the trees often told tales of how the paths in the forest changed, rendering maps useless. The cursed forest of Nikko Mori was alive.

And yet a gaze not quite so intent followed the traveler's movements, curiosity glistening in innocent eyes. A slight rustle in the bushes attested to the smaller, less pressing presence moving to another spot. More rustling came from the bushes before a blue rubber ball rolled into the open along the path. The presence stopped, hesitating.

The traveler turned quickly, her legs automatically slipping into a defensive stance as the bow in her cloak showed her arms had moved as well. She hesitated upon seeing the blue ball, straightening and watching it calmly. Were there children here? She had heard tales of those who sought sanctuary in the forest; it was part of the reason she had traveled this way. She hoped the forest may help her evade the king's men. But a ball hardly spoke to the presence of soldiers. It was only a matter of steps before she knelt before the toy and picked it up, gently proffering it to the bush.

"You needn't fear me," she offered in a hushed tone.

Silence stretched for several seconds. Then, slowly, a child— no more than seven years of age —stepped out of the thickened brush. The fair skinned little girl watched the traveler warily, her blue eyes staring with curiosity at the strange person. Someone had pulled her mop of brown ringlets up into two pigtails on either side of her head, while bangs covered her forehead. Slight freckles dotted her cheekbones and the bridge of her nose, testaments to her time in the sunlight. She wore a simple, dark green frock and small leather boots. At first the girl made no move to approach the traveler. After a bit longer of staring, the child cautiously closed the distance and reached for her ball.

The woman smiled gently beneath her coverings, plopping the ball in the girl's outstretched hands. It wasn't often she got to spend time with children. In her armor, they were frightened by her presence; in the castle, they overlooked her as they were taught. Having a child before her, unafraid, curious, was a welcome change. And all the more proof that she had made the correct decision in fleeing. How many children like this one would suffer under the king's current plan? She knew all too well the part she would play in his violence had she stayed.

The girl's cautious expression lifted into a bright smile of gratitude. Hugging the ball to her, she held her hand out to the stranger. Now that she knew the stranger wasn't dangerous, she could give a proper greeting. Behind her, a figure rose and carefully stepped clear of some taller bushes. The drawn bow in his hand gave a clear indication that he'd been ready to shoot the stranger if she'd tried to harm the child. Keeping the nocked arrow pointed to the ground for now, the young man relaxed his pull on the string, though he didn't release it. Sapphire blue eyes watched the stranger from within a green mottled hood.

The fabric reached down and around his shoulders in a sort of shawl. His brown leather trappings looked of elven design with the patterns etched along the material. The dark green tunic under his gauntlets and leather jerkin matched closely to the little girl's dress. Dark brown pants and boots matched the rest of his outfit, allowing him to blend easily with the forest. A black leather belt crossed his chest, with another branching off and around the other side of his waist, securing a sword across his back as well as his quiver. A sheathed dagger adorned one hip while a leather pouch hung over the other. He didn't speak at first, simply watching the newcomer. Even with the hood concealing most of his features, the woman could see his fair complexion matched that of the Nocium people, same as the child, though both showed signs of their skin tanning from frequenting the outdoors.

"You were pursued into the forest," he stated matter-of-factly. "We wish for our presence to go unnoticed."

The cloaked woman watched him calmly from where she knelt before gracefully standing. "Then go," she advised quietly after shaking the small girl's hand. "You need not trouble yourself with my affairs. I hope to be through the forest soon." Her voice was smooth and resolved as she stood. This was the path she had chosen, and fate would show her consequences in time— be they for good or ill. She was moderately surprised that the tracking party had been brave enough to follow her into the infamous forest, but then again…she knew who led them. The king's best knight would not stand for what he considered superstitious nonsense. She had all the more reason to be on her way.

Something flashed across the young man's eyes for a

moment but was gone as quickly as it came. Glancing at the trees a moment, he seemed to consider something. "I can guide you if you wish. It will make the passage easier. And I can help throw off your pursuers," he offered calmly. "With the 'strange' aura of this forest, very few dare enter here. You're either very brave or very desperate."

The woman's cowl dipped slightly as she inclined her head. "I would not wish to inconvenience you. I can find my way. Besides," she chuckled, nodding to the young girl. "Your sister, no? You should see her home. Your presence will not remain unnoticed if you aid me."

He nodded almost imperceptibly. Finally, he returned his arrow to his quiver before stating, "I ask that you be quick. Shaddai be with you." He touched the little girl's shoulder. The child glanced up at him. Before taking his hand, she waved farewell to the stranger, smiling cheerfully as she did. She beamed all the brighter when her brother's hand lightly ruffled her hair, the girl laughing silently. Beneath his hood the woman could barely make out the slightest of smirks ticking the young man's mouth. Taking his sister's hand, he led her back into the cover of the trees. The traveler watched them for a moment before turning to continue down the path. She pulled her hood tighter over her features and sped her pace.

*****

A small contingent of soldiers had entered the forest a few miles behind the woman. Most of them seemed to be more along the lines of hunters and trackers, dressing in thick leathers as opposed to the armor of the knights. Their trek was slow, the woman's trail nigh impossible to determine. But they were confident because of their leader. The knight walked with the confidence of years, the salt-and-pepper hue of his hair a testament to his experience. The man almost seemed to follow a sixth sense to track the fugitive. In reality, it was one of the original five. He could smell her quite distinctly.

The young man now stood behind a tree as he surveyed the trackers. He'd taken his sister home where he knew she would stay until his return. Then he had doubled back to find the rest of the intruders. He planned to watch the proceedings to make sure they caused no harm to the forest or its inhabitants, but otherwise he would not intervene. The forest hid his presence and all traces of it, but still he remained cautious. His eyes studied the leader of the group as the young man's gaze sought the man's true essence to gauge these intruders. He frowned when he saw it. Something seemed off about this man— his essence was unlike the others. The sooner they were gone, the better. Even as he watched the group, the forest began working to lead the trackers away. A strange aroma now covered the woman's scent. It was as if the flowers had started giving off their fragrance with irritating potency.

The knight scowled, narrowing his eyes. "What witchcraft is this?" he growled, glaring around. He had heard the stories of this supposed-dark forest, but in a land where peasants could aspire to wizardry, magic did little to dissuade him. He sighed, relaxing and running a hand through his short hair. "Keep moving forward. If this forest wants us gone, it can help us find the fugitive. Come on."

The young man— Tristan was his name —frowned at the knight's comment. A fugitive? What had she done, he wondered, for them to pursue her here? Then again, he himself had come from an area where the master could brand a subject a fugitive simply for looking at him wrong. The woman hadn't seemed evil, and if she had been, the forest would not bother to protect her. The forest's presence took on a darker feel and slowly became oppressive and hostile. Tristan silently surveyed the trees, noting the change. If the woman really proved to be a mere fugitive, why would the forest go to such lengths to protect her? While the leader didn't seem to pay the hostility any mind, his men grew cautious. One of them caught up to the broad man.

"Sir Jeremiah, perhaps we had best—"

"If the next words out of your mouth, soldier, are 'turn back,' then rest assured the fugitive is not the only one who will face the king's wrath upon our return," Jeremiah responded, turning to meet the man's gaze. "This woman is dangerous, both to others and to our country. She cannot be allowed to escape. She must be brought to justice."

Tristan glared at the man. However, just as he moved to retaliate in some way, a sharp pain constricted his chest. Collapsing back against the tree, he silently cursed at the noise the impact caused. And now pain paralyzed him to the spot. Tristan gripped his jerkin over his chest, biting his lip to keep from crying out. His whole body trembled with the intensity of the agony erupting through him. *Not now.*

Jeremiah had frozen as the small thump reached his ears. He frowned in Tristan's direction, cautiously drawing his sword. He held it upright, defensive. His attention snapped sharply to his right, however, when the cloaked woman snapped a twig. All he saw was the hem of her robe vanishing behind the trees, but that was all he needed.

Don't just stand there!" he growled at the others, spurring them to chase her.

The woman, for her part, could not decide whether to curse herself or feel proud for acting impulsively for the sake of another. It was slightly exhilarating, making that choice. She wondered why the young man from before had been there; had he been following the soldiers? Why? She had taken to hiding amidst the trees when the forest seemed intent on helping her, but the forest dweller's distress had not escaped her. He wanted to be unknown, and unknown she would keep him. Besides, she could run faster than most of the king's men. Jeremiah was the only one who concerned her; she wasn't sure of his true origins, but he certainly wasn't human.

Tristan waited to see if the soldier would head after his men. He tensed slightly when Jeremiah hesitated. However, the man then followed the trackers, leaving Tristan alone in that part of the forest. As the pain finally began to subside, the young man slowly released his jerkin. That was too close. And yet, thanks to his blunder, the woman's pursuers managed to gain an edge. He hesitated, not wanting to get involved any more than necessary. Then again, he couldn't just let the woman take the fall for his mistake. Once he regained enough strength, Tristan pushed off the tree and raced after the trackers. He didn't engage them yet, letting the forest handle most of the men for now.

One by one the trackers ahead of Jeremiah fell. They never saw the branches until they impacted their heads. Some of the other men tripped on thick tree roots and tangled in them. Jeremiah hissed as the forest continued to work against them, but he pushed ahead.

"Stop involving yourself," he growled as he ran. "You know nothing of our conflict." As he spoke, he reached into his waistband for a small dagger. He quickly drew it and slung it at the running woman. To his satisfaction, it embedded itself just below her knee. The woman dropped but turned the motion into a roll, standing to face him with a long, slender blade aimed towards him. Another peeked out from beneath her cloak, pointed at the ground. What could be seen of her outfit was unlike anything Tristan had seen before. Silver fabric that seemed to shimmer in the sun and shadows alike fit tight against her, with deep red filigree drawing designs along her figure. She was grateful for the enchantment on her cowl and scarf; her face remained hidden. Jeremiah stopped running as he reached the woman, though he drew his own blade in response.

"Cryso." Despite his harsh words to the soldiers, he was surprisingly calm addressing her. "You do not need to resist."

"I refuse to return. What other option have you presented to me?"

"So be it. Be grateful you are needed alive."

Tristan crouched in a patch of thick bushes where he could see both the knight and the fugitive. For now, he watched and waited. He'd rather leave them to settle their affair, but at the same time he couldn't bring himself to leave. He was the one who put the woman in her current plight— the least he could do was help. If she needed it. He frowned when he smelled blood in the air, and not from the soldiers the forest had downed. Tristan peered through the bushes and focused on the woman, searching her body to make out where she might be wounded. When he found it, his concern deepened. However, she didn't seem fazed by the injury. Tristan sighed. He'd let her fight for now, but he remained in case she needed him. His vision sharpened once more as he studied the man's essence, trying to place it. The air seemed to shimmer around the woman, this 'Cryso', as she faced the man. Knowing what Tristan did of languages, it was most likely only a part of her name in its original tongue. The calmness of her stance, the way her sword seemed an appendage as opposed to a burden, proved her a warrior by experience.

And yet, she did not want this fight. It felt as though fighting was all she was good for these days. But if it meant her freedom…well, one more fight it would be. She tossed aside the knife she had pulled from her leg, letting it land with a soft thump in the leaves.

Jeremiah was the first to move. His sword was larger, broader by far than the two blades Cryso wielded, yet he had the power and speed to move with ease. The base of Cryso's first blade intersected with the base of his as she forced it aside and to the ground before bringing forth her second blade; Jeremiah released one hand on his hilt, catching the blade of her sword with a gloved hand. The blade sliced through the leather he wore, yet it stopped against his flesh. With one hand holding her sword and the other gripping his locked-up blade, Jeremiah resorted to using an armored boot to try and kick her leg out from under her. Cryso dislodged both of her swords as she leapt back to avoid the strike, hissing slightly as she landed hard on her injured leg. She needed to heal, but she didn't have a free hand. She doubted Jeremiah would give her a long enough pause.

True enough, he was charging at her. She lifted her blades,

crossing them to catch Jeremiah's sword between. He may not be human, but neither was she. Her arms shook as she held their blades steady, meeting Jeremiah's glare. She planted her feet, ignoring the warning beneath the back of her knee as she shoved against her blades, uncrossing them to force Jeremiah's away. She dropped and spun quickly, aiming to cut his legs out from under him. Jeremiah turned the swing of his sword to plunge it quickly in the dirt, cutting off her swing. Cryso used the contact to push herself away from him, once more avoiding his follow-up strike. She landed on one knee, the other upright, and touched her fingers to the wound. She didn't have enough time to heal, but she did have enough time to call on her ability for something else. Drops of blood swirled around her fingers as she pulled her hand away and flung it towards Jeremiah; the droplets crystallized into small daggers. Jeremiah hefted his sword to block the shards, but Cryso was right behind them. She leapt as Jeremiah brought his sword around, landing on the flat of the blade and jumping again as he jerked it to knock her off. She landed in a crouch behind him, spinning as she rose and swiping her blades at his back. Metal met cloth, scraping through his armor and clothing again… yet leaving his flesh untouched. She could almost swear something had been coating him a moment ago, catching the diluted light of the forest. Cryso stared as Jeremiah turned, smirking.

"Is this all the great Scarlet Swordsman has to offer?" he taunted. "All your training, all of our sparring— you cannot even mark me."

"What manner of beast are you?"

Jeremiah scoffed. Instead of answering, he hefted his sword around and swung it in a horizontal arc. Cryso snapped out of her stunned posture, leaping up and back; she caught herself on a hand, springing upright a few feet away. She staggered slightly as her leg throbbed from its injury. It shouldn't ache this much. Her head shouldn't be spinning, not yet. What was on that dagger? Had he poisoned her? Before she could conquer her thoughts once more, Jeremiah was in front of her. He swung his sword about, shifting it so that the flat of his blade connected with her injured leg. Cryso cursed, trying to use the momentum to dodge to the side. She managed to gain control of her fall and spin a bit away, cursing more mentally as her vision swam slightly.

Tristan had a feeling he knew now what the knight was. Again, he was tempted to intervene, but he didn't want to insult the woman by taking her fight. Her skill with her blades proved rather mesmerizing, making it obvious she was a professional fighter. Scarlet Swordsman. He'd heard the name before when he received news of life outside the forest. People called the fighter the best in the kingdom, young but talented. He'd championed tournaments and showed the best skill on the battlefield, too. His name came from the legend that the Scarlet Swordsman's blades were stained with the blood of his enemies. As Tristan watched, he studied what he could see of the woman's odd clothing. The Swordsman, he knew, typically wore crimson armor. He almost laughed with learning the celebrity fighter was, in fact, a woman. Why did people always assume a man to be the best fighter? Then again, the title proved rather misleading as well. Tristan shifted slightly where he crouched. If this really was the Scarlet Swordsman, then she more than likely didn't need his aid. And then there was the matter of his staying hidden, not drawing attention to the fact that he resided in the forest. However, he had a feeling the knight wasn't fighting fair if the fugitive's reaction to her wound proved anything. Silently, Tristan prayed to

Shaddai for guidance.

Cryso scowled beneath her cowl as she stood, putting most of her weight on the non-injured leg. She closed her eyes, taking a deep breath. Even as Jeremiah charged at her once more, a glistening field of silver came to life between them. Jeremiah paused before he could hit it, reaching a hand out and testing the now-solidified air. He could see through it, but he could not pass. He frowned; magic should have no restrictions for him. How was this ability different? For her part, Cryso knelt and touched a hand to her wound, using her magic to draw out the poison and heal the injury. The effects were already there, but at least they wouldn't worsen. She stood again, shaking her head as if to clear it before facing Jeremiah again. The soldier was as he had been, hand against the barrier, but there was something… something in his mouth. A purple and green mist seemed to hover as if attached to his very breath, puffing out in a cloud like warm air on a winter's day. His eyes had changed as well, the pupils slitted. As she watched, the knight breathed some of the strange miasma against the barrier, though it stood solid. It only flickered when Cryso's vision swam again.

Jeremiah took the opening, bashing against the weakened barrier with all of his might. It shattered in a rain of starlight. Cryso gasped painfully with the sensation; it felt like her soul shattered into a million pieces. Jeremiah reached her easily, gripping her throat and slamming her back against a tree. Cryso choked as he lifted her feet off of the ground. The enchantment around her hood at last gave way, the cloth tearing away against the bark. Darkened gray skin like slate contrasted sharply with shimmering silver hair tied back in a practical braid. Her pointed ears quivered slightly with her tension; she forced her eyes open to glare at Jeremiah, inadvertently revealing her strangest feature. While one iris was the deep crimson of her people, the other was a startling blue. Even for a Drow she seemed young, perhaps no older than Tristan himself.

"I was rather hoping to simply sedate you," Jeremiah growled, "but it seems something stronger is needed." He took a deep breath as though to blow his poisoned air in her face. Cryso quickly closed her eyes and concentrated. A shining mark, a circlet stretching across her forehead before filigree surrounded a multi-pointed star in the center, appeared as the silver barrier flickered back to life between them just in time to block the miasma.

A dark bladed dagger suddenly sliced Jeremiah's wrist, causing him to drop Cryso in surprise. Faster than the eye could follow, Tristan caught the Drow maiden and kicked off the tree to dodge around the man. Backing away several paces, Tristan set Cryso on her feet before readying his bow, his arrow aimed for the knight. "Leave this forest, dragon," Tristan ordered calmly. "It has given the Scarlet Swordsman sanctuary, and not even the king has the authority to oppose that privilege."

Jeremiah snorted as he rubbed his wrist, checking the wound. "Sanctuary? It's a forest, boy. And anything within the bounds of Nocis grants the king jurisdiction, so I suggest you bite your tongue and step aside." Despite his calm words, a muscle in his neck twitched. Who was this lad, and how did he know what Jeremiah was? What business of his was the woman? His curiosity only grew when he caught the lad's scent. The one who had escaped his attention when Cryso revealed herself. Cryso remained silent, down on a knee to finish healing the effects of the poison and to catch her breath. She eyed Tristan sharply as she situated her cowl and scarf back over her features. Why was he interfering now? Had he not wished to remain unnoticed? Such conversation would have to wait until Jeremiah was dealt with.

"By divine law, any who seek shelter in the Sanctuary forests and are deemed worthy are placed under the protection of Shaddai until such a time as the person leaves. The king knows this. His authority means nothing beneath the branches of Nikko Mori or Sylva Arae," Tristan countered evenly. "Besides, for the Scarlet Swordsman to flee, it makes me wonder what exactly the king was doing. Is it truly that he wishes his superior warrior to return? Or is there something more to this hunt?" His own hood had fallen back. Medium brown hair— reminiscent of his sister's hair color —cut short lay in haphazard layers close to his scalp, looking as though the young man had tried to cut it with a knife. Sapphire eyes watched Jeremiah with a calm intensity not unlike a wolf. "And even if the king won't acknowledge his lack of authority here, I will still lend my aid. What kind of person would I be if I let someone else take the fall for my mistake?"

"The king is the king, boy, and no peasant superstition is going to supersede his authority," Jeremiah stated with a growl. "Royal business is really no business of yours, but the woman is a deserter, a dangerous one at that. She could put the whole kingdom at risk with the things she knows. Her life belongs to the king, and to the king it will return." He clasped his hand around his sword, lifting the blade and pointing it towards the pair. "Step away or stand and fight. This is your last chance."

"The forest sought to protect her. That's reason enough for me to take her side. Even so, she risked capture to help me. Now, I will repay that debt," Tristan answered. He let his arrow fly, but before it even reached the knight, Tristan seemingly appeared behind him, slashing at the man's back with his dark blade. The tip sliced through armor as well as the black, hardened scales that formed beneath, barely cutting the knight, but cutting him all the same.

Jeremiah grimaced with the unexpected pain, pivoting and aiming his blade at Tristan's. The black scales did not vanish from his skin this time, spreading to cover his torso and racing down his arms— or that is what they saw. For all the pair knew, Jeremiah was now coated in the ebony armor. As Tristan moved to block Jeremiah's swing, Cryso stood and grabbed her blades once more. Now that she was healed, her mind was clearer. She wasn't going to let the forest-dweller face her opponent alone. Especially not now that she knew what he was. "Dragon," the lad had named. Jeremiah had not denied the claim.

Eluding the swipe, Tristan displayed his dexterity. He pulled out another dagger of the same material as the sword and engaged Jeremiah, dodging and countering swiftly. As he moved, it became clear the lad had trained extensively. His bearing resembled that of the nobles, and yet his grace seemed more elven. As he met Jeremiah's blows, the younger man's strength and speed proved to be more than that of an average human.

Jeremiah's eyes narrowed as they battled. He had been hoping the kid was all surprise and bravado. So much for a quick battle. And with Cryso now joining, swinging her blades and adapting to complement the young man's style…well, his task was becoming more arduous. Still, after that first surprise, he had managed to prevent any damage. The cut would heal easily enough. After exchanging blows for some time, Jeremiah pushed his sword in a full swing so the pair would dodge away. His eyes sparked with frustration and annoyance. This was supposed to be a simple hunt; these two were proving tiresome.

"You have had your fun," he growled, rolling his shoulders and seeming to stretch. But instead of relaxing back into his battle stance, he continued shifting. As the pair watched, his skin stretched, split, blackened, and reformed. Muscles tore and rebuilt, adapting to his changing bone structure. Where they had been facing a soldier, now they faced a full-grown dragon with scales of truest black. Purple smoke rose from his nostrils, tainting the air with a putrid stench. Cryso took a half-step back, her eyes examining the massive creature. She flexed her fingers, adjusting the grip on her swords. This would not be the first dragon-kin she had battled; it would be the first with only one ally at her side. Still, the young man had proved his mettle. Tristan regarded the knight as he took in his larger, more deadly form. He hesitated when he noticed the miasma. That wouldn't be good to have spewing into the forest. Unfortunately, their fight happened to be in the middle of Nikko Mori; he'd have to minimize the damage as much as he could. A branch of dark crystal seemed to form from nowhere and wrapped around the dragon's muzzle in an attempt to keep him from using the poisonous gas. Sheathing his blades, Tristan drew his bow once more, nocking an arrow. He aimed and released, seeking to hit the dragon's eye.

Jeremiah gave a dark laugh, the sound echoing through his chest. He took in a deep breath, shifting his head so the arrow flew harmlessly to the side, and then exhaled through his nose. The putrid smoke condensed into a heavy miasma. The murk seemed to suck the life out of anything it touched. Before it could reach Tristan, however, Cryso was at his side. Her cloak flared back in the breath, but the brilliant silver energy arced from her and swirled around the pair, forming a new shield. Her eyes watched the poison, calculating.

"Is there some way to contain it?" she asked the forest-dweller without taking her eyes from the beast and his poison. "I can only create shields centered around myself, and I would have to bleed the dragon dry to contain this much substance with my other abilities."

"Perhaps," Tristan replied. He didn't necessarily wish to display more of his power lest he gain unwanted attention, but what the dragon would report would no doubt bring more of the king's men anyway. Stretching his hand out he concentrated, his eyes never leaving the dragon's. Translucent hues of twilight swirled through the crystal that spread from his hand and out over the forest for several kilometers, covering the ground and trees without killing anything. When he reached his limit, the crystal formed between the trees as well to create a barrier and keep the poisonous cloud inside the containment area. Once that was done, more crystal branched up from under Jeremiah to spiral around the dragon's hind legs to keep him from moving. Tristan drew an arrow once more, the tip made from the same crystal, and aimed to pierce Jeremiah's chest. The blow wouldn't kill the dragon, but perhaps it would slow him down enough they could escape. Exhaling softly, Tristan loosed the arrow.

Jeremiah reared up and thrust a scaled arm forward, deflecting the arrow before slamming his hand against the silver orb containing the two fighters and shoving down against it so that they risked being crushed were

Cryso to drop the barrier. Jeremiah pressed against the shield, testing the limits of the young woman's power. She stretched her arms as if to reinforce the shield, though she did not touch its surface. Cryso grimaced slightly, her breathing growing heavy as she strained to keep the barrier up. The silver flickered slightly but did not falter. The dragon then turned his attention to the crystal containing him. He twisted his neck around, taking in another deep breath and heaving a dense blast of corrosive miasma against the crystal in an attempt to weaken it. At first nothing happened, but eventually the crystal binding the dragon's legs slowly began to melt under the gas until Jeremiah could break it. Spikes thrust upward from the crystal beneath them to pierce the dragon's underbelly, but they suddenly stopped short. Tristan grimaced. His heart thumped loudly against his chest as pain shot through him. He could feel his energy slipping away— the earlier throbbing returning with a vengeance. Still, he pushed himself. Gritting his teeth, he summoned a large spike to form before piercing it into the dragon's hand. The spike pushed even as Tristan paled and grimaced with the effort. Gradually, he forced the dragon off the shield.

"It might be wise for us to retreat," he told his ally through gritted teeth. Pain filled his determined gaze. Cryso nodded. She slid one of her blades back into its sheath beneath her cloak before using the other to cut open her palm. Once the second blade was sheathed, she reached her cut palm out and swiped it to the side. A large arc of red sprayed from the wound as her eyes stained pure crimson. The arc crystallized into several long spikes before shooting towards the dragon. As the slice in her palm healed, Cryso spun on her heel and grabbed Tristan's arm. The barrier dropped, and the Drow ran. She could hear Jeremiah roaring in anger behind them, but she didn't stop.

As they neared the crystal barrier, the hardened substance parted just enough to let them through. She let Tristan overtake her, the young man knowing the forest more than she. She was surprised at how little she needed to slow to have him lead; Drow and elf-kin usually outpaced even the most stalwart humans, yet the young man dashed ahead at incredible speed despite seeming worn. The scents and sounds of the forest sprang up around them, covering their trail and hiding them from the dragon.

Words of Wisdom

After traversing a random path through the forest to throw off any pursuers, Tristan slowed to a halt at a small clearing. He waited a moment to get his bearings and make sure the dragon wouldn't find them.

"Well, that proved a rather invigorating battle," he remarked casually. Locating a nearby spring, he stopped to clean his blades of any blood. "I must say, I'm a bit surprised to learn the Scarlet Swordsman is actually a woman. I suppose that goes to show that people are fools to assume that the only strong fighters are men." As he cleaned his blades, the twilight crystalline material receded, revealing the weapons to be of elven make. He'd coated them with his crystal while fighting the dragon to give them better strength against his scales, but now he left them in their original elven steel form. Sheathing the blades, Tristan turned to face the Scarlet Swordsman. His vibrant eyes still held a pained look, but his posture remained straight-backed and noble. "If you don't mind my asking, why are you running from the king?"

"War is brewing," Cryso answered quietly, staring at the water. "Our 'good King' Arden has challenged Andor as of late. King Traiborn has not taken kindly to it; rumor has it only his wife Queen Corianne stands between them, citing her duties as High Priestess of Andor to try and keep the peace. And now I learn that Arden seeks to undermine her efforts— and wishes to use my power to do so." She sighed, reaching up to rub her temple. "I am tired of being what I am. I found a way to break the bond placed on me and left at first opportunity." She chuckled mirthlessly. "You think you are surprised at hearing I am a woman? Imagine the shock of the multitudes if they learned the strongest knight in the kingdom was little more than a slave." She turned away from the water, eying him. "Are you injured? Or is there some illness that causes your pain?"

Tristan waved his hand dismissively. "More like the price I pay for guardianship over something the world is better left without," he answered, sighing softly as the pain began to subside. "I know that feeling of being trapped. Why do people harbor greed and let it blind them? It's one of the many questions echoing through the universe." Shaking his head, he stepped away from the spring. "I doubt the dragon knight will give up the chase so easily." He watched the forest as he contemplated something.

"Unlikely. And also unlikely that he will leave you in peace." She did not move. "Why did you help me?"

Tristan paused before turning his gaze to her once more. He remained silent for a bit longer before finally speaking, "As I told the dragon knight, you helped with covering my mistake earlier. I felt it only right to return the favor. Though, I waited to make sure you actually needed any help. I didn't want to offend you by seeming to presume you couldn't fight him yourself." He hesitated. "That's not the only reason, though. I can see essences and yours holds a uniqueness like mine, something setting us apart. I was curious as to what that might mean," he added softly.

Cryso sighed. "I shouldn't have needed the aid. I've bested him in spars time and again. And yet, all it took was a little poison." She folded her arms, glancing away. Jeremiah had shamed her, and her weakness had endangered the young man and his sister. "I know not what an essence is or why ours may be similar. I have no answers for you. But you have my thanks."

"Poison can fell the strongest of warriors regardless of race," Tristan remarked. "You should feel no shame. Despite his tactic, you fought well." He studied her a moment, his eyes sharpening before reverting to normal. "As for the meaning of an essence, it is the embodiment of the most important traits that make things what they are in the world around us: characteristic traits, ethnic origin, etc. Everything that makes that person what they are. In other words, I can see a person or thing's true form. However, though I can see your true form, I don't understand it. I've never seen an essence like yours. The only thing even remotely close would be my own." He glanced through the trees at the sun, gauging its position. "If you wish to stay the night here, I can lead you to a small elven village farther inside the forest," he offered.

Cryso was quiet for a moment. "I would not wish to imperil them...and the elven-kin do not look kindly on most Drow. Even when one is only half."

"Half?" Tristan asked but then he nodded. "I suppose that explains your eyes." He fell into quiet contemplation, weighing his next decision carefully. "Come with me then. I'll shelter you for the night." He wasn't completely sure he could trust her, but he knew even with the forest protecting her it would be only a matter of time before the dragon found her again. At least with him, she had a better chance of staying hidden. Holding out his hand, he offered, "My lady." Cryso hesitated, eying his hand. He and his sister would be in danger. But the young man was curious about her, and…she had to confess, she was about them as well. She could cover more ground, or she could learn more of this forest-dweller and the little girl he guarded.

She was tired of thinking like a soldier. She took his hand.

Despite his rugged appearance, the young man guided her through the forest as a gentleman would a lady. He led her deeper and deeper, the trees drawing closer together the farther they ventured. Eventually, Tristan led the way to a certain, more closely-grown grove. At first glance, nothing seemed remarkable about it; however, as Tristan guided Cryso between the branches, they came out into a clearer space with a tree fashioned as a cabin at its center. The elves in the village Tristan had mentioned were the ones who sang the dwelling from one of the giant trees making up the forest. From one of the branches billowed smoke, the limb acting as a chimney. A few windows allowed natural light into the abode and, along with the small, arched door, gave the tree a rather homey appearance. A brook trickled nearby, supplying fresh water for the siblings. Runes had been cast onto the trees surrounding the dwelling to provide a barrier that camouflaged the interior of the grove to passersby and gave an added layer of protection. It was meant to keep travelers from stumbling upon the dwelling and to keep Arianna from wandering off without Tristan's notice. Outside the treehouse, the little girl played with her ball near the water. When Tristan and Cryso entered the grove, the child looked up as though she sensed their approach. Grinning brightly, the girl ran to her brother, clutching her ball in one arm still. Tristan released Cryso's hand so he could scoop the girl up in both arms.

"Good girl, Anna," he praised. "You stayed here like I asked. See? I'm all right." He let the child touch his face and shoulders as if inspecting for any wounds. Then he pointed to Cryso. "This is the lady you met earlier today. I brought her here to stay the night, so she'd be safe. Is that okay?" He smiled when the girl nodded excitedly. Propping the ball between her arms she started moving her hands in a series of specific patterns. Tristan watched her a moment before speaking to Cryso, "She's introducing herself. Her name is Arianna, and as you guessed earlier she is my sister. The gestures she's making are part of a signing technique that allows her to talk to people who know it. 'Language of the Silent' as the elves call it." He bowed slightly to Cryso, "As for me, I am Tristan Nightshade."

"You need not concern yourself with translating; I am versed in this language." Cryso smiled as she released the enchantments on her scarf and hood, lowering the garments. "While you are aware of my calling, I should tell you my full name is Comson Cryso. In your tongue, it means Crimson Rose." She dipped her head slightly in greeting.

Tristan nodded at her comment about the language. His eyes took in her features. "I can see why you hide your hair. Beautiful, but you'd stick out like a tree on the ocean." Her slate skin could be mistaken for a dark human or some such, but her hair and her eyes were the giveaways. "I've never met a Half-Drow before, and I've seen even fewer folk with eyes as lovely as yours." He blushed slightly when he noticed Arianna grinning at him. "What? I'm stating facts; no harm in that," he remarked dryly. Turning once more to Cryso he hesitated before asking, "May I call you Rose?"

The Half-Drow smiled. "Rose would be wonderful," she

confessed softly. She was used to being referred to by whatever the generals chose; it was nice to decide for herself. And it would help reclaim who she was to change what others called her. She wasn't entirely certain how to react to his compliments— she wasn't used to others noticing her appearance. "In truth, I am aware how most view Drow-kind. And I knew Jeremiah's men were attempting to track me."

"I don't mind the Drow. The forest's guardian is one. He's helped me look after my sister and taught me a lot of things. I assist him with guarding the forest from those who slip past its initial defense, and I consider him a friend," Tristan told her. He turned and motioned for Rose to follow him as he led them inside the treehouse.

Inside, the dwelling seemed smaller, cozier. A fireplace sat in a bit of an alcove. A stone hearth and half wall laid into the dirt floor and up part of the alcove kept the fire from spreading through the wooden structure. Wooden dishes and utensils lined shelves set into the wall on one side of the fireplace while spices filled the ones on the other. A little from the hearth stood a small sofa and a reading chair. A table with four chairs— two for the siblings and two for guests —was behind the sofa. Another alcove served as a bedroom with a bed jutting from the wall near a set of stairs leading to a loft. A smaller bed lay not far from the bigger one. While windows allowed for natural light, there were also lanterns with magical light crystals hanging in various parts of the dwelling. Everything had elegant designs chiseled into the woodwork, even the walls. Some dishes and furniture appeared more rugged than others, the dwelling attesting to the progression of a woodworker.

Setting Arianna down, Tristan moved to the fireplace and

began preparing some tea. The little girl ran to a chest at the foot of the smaller bed and rummaged inside for a moment. When she emerged, she clutched a carving in her hand. The child scampered to Rose and held up the carving for the woman to see, Arianna beaming proudly. The carving depicted a small faerie in flight.

"It's her favorite toy," Tristan supplied, glancing at his sister with a fond look.

"It's beautiful," Rose praised softly, smiling at the little girl and patting the top of her head. She gazed around at the rest of the dwelling. "Did you carve all of this?"

"Yes. With my sister to look after, I can't very well leave the forest. Carving relaxes me. It didn't look very good in the beginning, but I've reworked some of the furniture and dishes over the years." He motioned for Rose to sit at the table before pouring tea for them both. As they sat, Arianna played with her carving in front of the fire. Tristan watched her for a moment, his eyes calm but sad. "Arianna's social experience is limited mostly to me and the denizens of this forest— though she's more trusting than she should be with strangers." He motioned to Rose as an indication. "Then again, perhaps she's simply a better judge of character. She seems to know when someone's intentions are good or bad; I don't know how she knows. She likes you, so I figured whatever your reason for running must be good. Seems Arianna was right."

He fell silent as he thought for a moment. Why did Rose's essence look similar to his own? It couldn't be a racial trait; he wasn't a Drow. And yet he did have powers similar to hers. Though, he had his own secret to keep. He drank his tea, his eyes darkening as he mused. "I know blood manipulation is common to Drow, but what about your other power? The forcefield. Were you born with the ability or were you taught?"

Rose took a quiet sip as she contemplated his question. "I have always had the ability," she answered softly. "Though I do not understand it. I know not from where it came; I merely discovered it on instinct. I have since trained myself on how to summon it when needed." She shook her head. "I cannot imagine it played much in Jeremiah's furor for finding me."

"Perhaps it had more influence on the king's decision than you realize. Your essence isn't like most people's I've seen, and I can't help wondering if your mysterious power has something to do with it," Tristan commented. He met her gaze, debating. Should he reveal his own secret? He didn't know her, really, so why should he trust her? Yet Arianna's reaction to her coupled with Rose's essence gave him the distinct feeling he should. "Markings appear on your skin when you use your power," he remarked slowly. Were their secrets connected? Coming to a decision, Tristan reached his arm out, stretching his hand towards where Arianna played. Along his skin, markings appeared and glowed with a soothing light— warm and softly golden. From his fingertips, up his arm, over his shoulder, and across his collarbone the markings took the form of filigree resembling swirling wisps of fire. They shone brightly enough that they remained visible even under his clothes— though the light only shone dimly through the fabric. Particles of light floated through the air like a banner of dust and swirled around Arianna. The girl smiled brightly, leaping to her feet and having her faerie follow the stream. She danced in circles, looking all the world like a child playing with a real faerie.

Rose watched the dust, fascinated. "Like the particles of my barrier," she commented softly before shaking her head and looking back to him. "But yours are golden, and mine silver," she added. "I suppose there could be a connection; it makes more sense and less sense. A true puzzle." She took another sip of her tea.

"I was born with mine, as well," Tristan told her. He released the power, much to Arianna's disappointment. However, the girl didn't pester him. Instead, she returned to her earlier play. "My mother once told me it was a gift from Shaddai. That He meant for me to do great things in His name. I'm not sure what she thinks He intended for me to do, but I wait for His call."

Rose chuckled mirthlessly. "When is His plan ever so obvious?" She shook her head. "Then again, perhaps it was His guidance that led me to this forest. If this forest is of Shaddai, perhaps we were meant to meet."

Tristan hesitated, dropping his gaze. His eyes looked sad once more but also distant and full of pain. "Your venture into this forest is similar to mine," he voiced softly. Taking his empty cup to a basin, he pumped some water from a built-in fixture and washed the dish. As he dried it, he tried not to let his mind wander into sorrowful memories. However, he didn't turn around even after he replaced the cup on a shelf. His hand trailed down the wall slowly. "Our mother brought us here to protect us from pursuers," he tried to explain, clearing his throat when his voice thickened with emotion. "She…poured her remaining energy into a barrier that surrounds the forest as added protection." He trailed off in a whisper as tears stung his eyes. He didn't look down when a small hand clutched his pant leg, though he did set his own hand onto the child's head to comfort her. He knew Arianna could sense his emotions, so he tried to keep them in check. However, the memory of his mother always brought forth a raw grief that never healed. "Arianna...doesn't remember her. Our mother d-died...not long after Arianna was born." Why was he telling this to a stranger? She didn't need to know. "I'm sorry." He ruffled Arianna's hair before finally moving back to the table and sitting. His sister pulled one of the other chairs around and up against his before sitting and snuggling into his side, trying to comfort him in her own way. "I'm all right, Anna. I promise," he assured her gently as he looped his arm around her.

"I did not mean to stir sad memories. I apologize," Rose commented quietly. She glanced down at the table. With the scene before her, she felt even more an intruder. What place had she witnessing another's grief? "I lost my own mother when I was young. My father and brother, as well." What was it about Tristan that made her want to trust him? Was she so desperate to make her own decisions? Perhaps she was. "My grandmother is the one who sold me."

"I'm sorry," Tristan remarked sincerely. He hesitated as he stroked Arianna's hair. He studied the table for a bit as he worked to get his emotions under control once more. Finally, he asked, "Why would your grandmother sell you? You don't have to answer if you'd rather not; I'm just curious." It sounded as though her situation wasn't so different from his.

"I do not mind," Rose assured him. "My father was human, and my grandmother believes I am a stain on our bloodline. She has always believed the Drow superior to other races; the fact my mother ran away to marry a human infuriated her." She pressed her hands to the teacup, though it was growing cool. "She hunted us down to cleanse the bloodline. I know my mother stayed to fight her, and I know my brother escaped with me. I was very young. Our grandmother eventually found us hiding in a stable. I vaguely recall my brother being taken away. My grandmother was going to kill me, and I used the barrier for the first time in my memory."

"I'm sorry. That must have been heartbreaking," Tristan sympathized. "It seems we two may be kindred spirits of a sort." He glanced down at Arianna when he noticed how still she'd become. The child slept against her brother's side, oblivious to the sad tales. "I at least had Arianna—though being eleven, I had no idea how to care for an infant. Thankfully, my friend found us and helped me learn."

Moving carefully, Tristan gathered Arianna into his arms and moved to the smaller bed. He proved the truth of his words by getting her changed into her nightgown without waking her and tucking her into her bed. He let her hair down, combing his fingers gently through the curls. After watching her sleep for a moment, he moved back to the main room. "You may have my bed for the night. I have some business to address, so I'll be up a while longer." He hesitated to leave Arianna with Rose. Normally if he needed to leave his sister, he would take her to one of their elven friends in the forest, but he hated to wake Arianna now that she was asleep. And it would take him even longer to complete his errand if he left to get one of their friends—not to mention he'd still be leaving Arianna in Rose's care during that time. He thought about his sister's reaction to the woman. For whatever reason, Arianna seemed to trust Rose, and, strangely, he felt he could, too. Perhaps it was Shaddai encouraging Tristan to trust Him.

Rose watched him, a smile touching her lips as he tended his sister. She stood and moved her cup to the washing area. Should she really stay? She was tired. Her body demanded rest from her long journey and the earlier fight. So, rather than protest further, she thanked Tristan for his offer before moving to sleep.

Tristan watched her for a bit, still debating. Finally, he left the house and ventured back the way they had come. He moved easily through the darkness, his eyes accustomed to day and night alike. And he knew this forest. Without having someone to guide, Tristan found his way back to the battlefield quickly. He slowed, making sure no one was still there. He knew the soldiers and the knight were still alive—the forest hadn't killed them, and he hadn't slain the dragon. But he wasn't sure if they'd continue their search or not. Once he was satisfied no one remained, Tristan gradually removed the crystal wall.

Inside, he found the area sick and dead or dying. Grass and trees alike stood withered and gray from the miasma. Such a sight pained Tristan's heart even as his anger rose towards the dragon who would dare poison the forest. The markings along his arm began to glow once more as he stepped into the area, the light encompassing his body to protect him. Even as he walked, the grass revived in the wake of his footsteps. When he reached the center, Tristan held his arms out to a comfortable position and closed his eyes, letting his power flow. Golden light swept like snow over the damaged earth and flora. Everywhere it touched, the poison dissipated and the forest revived healthier than ever. Warmth and light radiated throughout the area, restoring all from the damage rendered. His work done, Tristan gradually retracted his power.

As the night returned to its natural darkness, he opened his eyes and surveyed the healed patch of the forest. As he studied it, he sensed someone approaching. At first, he feared the dragon or his men had returned, but the forest remained calm. Still, Tristan's hand touched his dagger. Turning in the direction he sensed the presence, he spied a familiar figure emerging from the trees. An elder Drow approached in gray and charcoal attire akin to what his people usually favored, though he wore a brown cloak to better blend with the forest. The front of his long, silver hair was twisted back in two braids and tied behind his head while the rest of the silky strands draped his shoulders. His build was broad for a Drow and yet slender, a hidden strength belying the man's nimble movements. His face still appeared rather young if not for the few accented lines near his eyes and on either side of his mouth. A single twisting shell earring adorned his left ear. The Drow's crimson eyes met Tristan's blue ones.

"I sensed the battle that took place earlier," Clovestein told him calmly. Glancing around at the newly healed area, he nodded. "I came to see what had transpired and to aid if I could, but it seems you had no need for me."

"Intruders," Tristan explained. "Well, one refugee and a hunting party." Clovestein regarded his charge for a moment, studying the young man sagely. Tristan sighed with the look. "The Scarlet Swordsman has deserted the king's army. He didn't take kindly to it and sent a knight and trackers after his prized fighter. Turns out he's a she. And she is Drow," he explained further.

Clovestein inclined his head approvingly. "You sheltered her." It wasn't a question. To anyone else the man sounded as though he'd simply stated a fact, but Tristan knew Clo was praising him. The younger man didn't trust others easily after the events that brought him to the forest, so it said something that Tristan not only allowed the woman to stay with him but also left Arianna in her care.

"She's...her essence looks a lot like mine," Tristan confessed, his expression perplexed. "I've never met someone else with a similar uniqueness. And she brings news that Nocis and Andor may go to war." He didn't say outright what really troubled him.

Clo spoke for him, "You sense a change. Seven years you've lived in this forest with time flowing smoothly while the peace of your sanctuary has remained undisturbed. But now, a pebble has dropped into the water, and you know the ripples such an event creates."

Tristan sighed, running his fingers through his hair. "Seven years. And yet my grief feels as raw as though my mother died just this morning," he murmured. His eyes studied the forest as the familiar ache constricted his chest. "Her barrier around this forest and her grave are all that's left of her." He felt Clo's firm hand grip his shoulder comfortingly.

"No," his deep voice corrected the young man. "There is you. There is your sister. Her most precious treasures walk alive in this world as a testament to her time here." He grew quiet for a moment, simply watching his charge. Shortly after Tristan arrived in the forest, Clo had found him and helped him with Arianna. He taught Tristan many things, always a guide and guardian to the young man and the girl. But Tristan was growing; he didn't need a guardian so much anymore. And yet uncertainty filled him. Clovestein's hand slid from Tristan's shoulder to grip the young man's chin and guide him to face the Drow. "When the change comes,

Luadril, do not fear. Shaddai will be with you always, and He knows the future. Let Him guide you. Even if it means your time has come to depart from your mother's protection."

Tristan's eyes widened slightly. "I...I can't just leave. I have duties here to help you protect the forest. I agreed to assist you, its guardian. And I have to think about Arianna's safety," he rambled as he started to pull away from Clo. But the old Drow kept his grip firm.

"You cannot remain here forever. Your father will come for you, protection or no. Besides, as the years progressed, your mother's barrier has been slowly diminishing. It was never meant to stand forever, and soon it will fade entirely. I know you feel it, too," he told Tristan. Then he added cryptically, "There may be another reason aside from your and your sister's safety to leave, as well."

The young man frowned at him. "Clovestein, what do you know?"

However, Clo shook his head and released Tristan's face. "It is not my place to say. You'll learn soon enough if what I spied on the tides is any indication." He watched Tristan as the young man gave him a perplexed look. Clovestein smiled softly. "Others can step up to aid me in protecting the forest, but Shaddai is calling you to your purpose. The greatest help you can give me is by following the path He has laid before you."

As the Drow turned to leave, Tristan took a step after him, reaching his hand out. "Clo," he called. When the man stopped and faced him once more, the younger met his gaze. "Thank you for everything you've done for Arianna and me. You've helped us a great deal, and I appreciate your friendship. We both do."

"It has been my pleasure and honor. You are a good son and brother. A most loyal friend. Your sister is blessed to have you, and I for knowing you both," Clo told him. Gently, the Drow guided Tristan into a reassuring embrace, squeezing him tightly as the younger man returned the hold. Once they pulled away, Clovestein gestured for Tristan to walk with him through the forest if he desired. The young man smiled softly and fell into step with the forest's guardian. They combed over the area a little more to make sure everything healed properly from the battle before venturing their way through the trees.

Soon, Tristan began the trek back to his home, splitting off from Clovestein with a word of farewell. When Tristan reached his home, he knelt by the stream and washed his face before moving inside. After deactivating the magic illuminating the crystal lights, Tristan settled in front of the fire, watching the flames as he contemplated Clo's words. What wasn't the Drow telling him? And what had he seen on the coast? Even as these thoughts tumbled through Tristan's mind, his eyes slowly closed as he succumbed to sleep.

***

Rose woke with the sun. She paused as she took in the soft mattress beneath her and the enclosed wood above. It was a bit disorienting after her nights under the stars. Steadily, her waking mind remembered Jeremiah and the forest. Tristan and Arianna. She sat up quietly, noting the still-sleeping little girl in the other bed. Her feet barely made a sound as she stood and crept to the door. Tristan still slept by the fire, so she continued to slip out the door. They had given her shelter; she could repay with food. The forest had allowed her to hunt the day previous, so she saw no reason to abstain.

Pirate Knives and Emerald Eyes

Pain surged through Tristan's chest, jolting him from the deep confines of slumber. He blearily opened his eyes and gazed at the glowing embers in the fireplace. He grimaced from the pain still lancing through his chest, but lifted his head a little when a small hand touched his shoulder. Blue eyes peered down at him with concern. Tristan reached up and touched the little girl's soft face, tracing her cheek. He then brushed her bangs from her eyes.

"It's okay, Arianna. Go play," he told her gently. When the little one hesitated, he carefully sat up and took her hand. He stood and twirled her before lightly swatting her rear in way of sending her off. Arianna beamed as she scurried off to play with her ball. Tristan watched for a moment. He still felt so tired. The fight yesterday and healing the forest must have taken more out of him than he thought. He reached up and ran his hand through his hair as he sighed. Looking around the dwelling, he noticed Rose missing. Had she decided to leave? Once he was sure Arianna would be all right, Tristan ducked outside to see if the Drow was near the tree.

He'd left his weapons and jerkin near the fireplace to sleep. Now he stood in only his leggings and his dark green tunic, enjoying the lack of cumbrance despite how light his leather jerkin and adornments were. His boots made nary a sound as he stepped towards the river. Sunlight speckled the ground through the leafy canopy and sparkled along the gently flowing water. Tristan took a deep breath of air, soaking in the freshness of the morning. Rubbing some of the stiffness out of his shoulders, he tried not to focus on the pain still throbbing in his chest.

"Good morning."

Tristan spun around at the new voice, barely disguising a wince. His hand instantly reached for his dagger before he remembered it currently lay with his other weapons in the house. He adopted a flat look. Moving his hands into a neutral position instead, Tristan stayed in a ready stance, not threatening but ready to move all the same. His keen eyes studied the newest trespasser. The man currently leaned with his back against a tree close to the one housing Tristan and Arianna. He wore simple clothing —a tunic and pants with matching boots —all dyed black. A cowl hid his head while a black face mask covered the bottom half of his face. Ice blue eyes regarded Tristan with an intense yet calm gaze. The fair complexion around his eyes attested to his heritage as Nocium or somewhere similar, though it was paler than Tristan's, making the young man think the stranger hardly ever removed his coverings. For now, he kept his arms folded over his chest, his hands covered with fingerless gloves resting on his biceps. His choice of weapon hung in the form of a sickle and chain hooked to a sash he wore about his waist. As Tristan studied him a little more closely, the man's essence revealed him to be human. Well, at least he wasn't another dragon.

"Easy, lad," the man spoke in a smooth baritone. "I'm not here to cause trouble."

Tristan watched him suspiciously. "I suppose the legends

of the hostile, magic forest have begun to deplete," he remarked dryly. He must be exhausted not to have noticed this intruder traipsing through the forest. His dwelling wasn't exactly near the border. Even more perplexing, how did this stranger come across the protected grove?

"Magic, yes; hostile, not so much," the man replied easily. "I was actually enjoying a rather peaceful walk when I came through this little copse and noticed smoke coming from one of the tree branches. Imagine my surprise when I saw you emerge from said tree. Like I said, I'm not here to cause trouble. I just want to ask if you've seen a Drow maiden come through here?"

Tristan regarded him calmly. "She passed through yesterday," he answered warily. "She's left though. Why?" Was this man another tracker for Jeremiah? If he was, Tristan didn't know if he could help Rose at the moment. The pain in his chest had yet to subside.

"I've been trying to catch up with her," the man replied. "I have information for her. More than that, I cannot say." He straightened from the tree and lowered his arms in a show of meaning no harm. "I know she hasn't left. You're both good at covering your tracks, but I'm skilled at following obscure trails."

"She's not here," Tristan insisted firmly.

"Kid, don't play cat and mouse with me," the man spoke in minor resignation. "I currently don't have a problem with you. All I need is to speak with the Drow."

The lad contemplated what to do. However, the pain in his chest refused to subside this time. That coupled with his exhaustion made this situation even more difficult. The stranger watched him patiently. Tristan simply returned the look.

"What makes you think I've got anything to do with the Drow at all?"

"You're a terrible liar, for one thing," he told the younger man, a slight smile evident in the man's voice.

Between the pain and the persistent stranger, Tristan found himself surprised again when another stranger practically tumbled out of the trees. It was fairly obvious that he was not used to traversing forests. The newcomer was tall and broad, his chiseled torso bare aside from a leather vest. Loose leggings and thin sandals completed the look of an open-space dweller, though sea or sand had yet to be determined. Topaz eyes focused almost immediately on the two figures by the smoking tree, his brow reaching towards his clean-shaven golden brown head. The gold hoop in one of his ears swung slightly as he straightened, reaching to adjust the belt holding twin scimitars crossed on his back. "Well now," he commented in a low voice with a clipped accent. "Whatever have we here?" The soft creases lining his eyes spoke to many smiles; one currently painted his face with amusement.

Tristan stared at the newest person to enter his "protected" grove. What was going on today? Why had both these men managed to make their way inside here? Studying the larger man's attire, Tristan remembered Clo's words from the previous night. Their arrival was certainly a change, just like Rose's. A feeling of dread sunk like a rock in Tristan's stomach. He forgot it momentarily when he looked between the two men. While the bigger one seemed rather delighted, the first stranger looked a bit pensive. Tristan felt oddly like he now gazed upon a wayward child just caught by his parent. The afore calm, persistent stranger fidgeted. His eyes studied a patch of grass that suddenly seemed more interesting if not for the perplexed look in the stranger's eyes.

Tristan raised an eyebrow; however, he turned back to the newest trespasser. "I suppose you happen to be taking a leisurely stroll, as well?"

"I'm not this far inland for a simple woodland stroll." Another piece of jewelry slipped from hiding under the man's vest as he brushed off a few leaves and twigs. A leather strap held the medallion around his neck, the circle carved with a peculiar symbol: An intricate sun, with a large crescent moon and a multi-point star inlaid upon the circular area of the sun's face. He was grinning over at the pensive man now. "What's the matter, Jabez?" he addressed him jovially. "You look like you've gotten caught with a hand in the Captain's cookies."

"e be'er nae 'ave!" As if to add insult to Tristan's lack of awareness, yet another voice joined the two men. This one, however, was light and chipper, a young woman. Yet as her voice registered, so, too, did the fact that her essence was hidden from Tristan's gaze. The lithe figure leapfrogged onto the dark sailor's shoulders, grinning at the now-named Jabez and Tristan widely. The young woman— surely no older than her late teens —wore a flowing, layered skirt and a loose blouse, clothing typically worn by the nomadic Doran, complimented by hooped earrings. Her feet were bare, balanced easily on the large man's shoulders. Her russet hair hung down her back in waves, a large portion swooped over the left half of her cream-colored face. A spattering of freckles trailed across her cheeks and over her nose. A bright green eye sparkled at the men from the right half. "Mornin', Jabie. Fancy meetin' ye here, eh?" Judging by her tone, the girl wasn't surprised in the slightest.

Tristan was staring at the bald man's medallion; he'd seen that symbol before. This man was from an order of people devoted to serving the Will of Shaddai. His mother had shown him pictures and told him stories of them when he was a child. His reverie cut short when Jabez released a resigned sigh.

"Hello, Captain. I assume you came looking for the Drow, too?" The quieter stranger remarked. For as happy as the other two seemed to be to see Jabez, the man didn't seem particularly happy to see them. His countenance spoke more of guilt and embarrassment than anything. Tristan frowned. Why was everyone after Rose? He blinked when a small figure darted out from behind him.

"Arianna," he scolded quietly when the girl approached Jabez. At least she'd managed to throw on some clothes instead of running out in her nightgown. Her hair had been brushed, but the curls cascaded down her back since her brother hadn't put them up yet. She smiled brightly at a surprised Jabez, holding her ball up to him. Oddly enough, the man's gaze softened. He lowered into a squat before her and gently took the ball. Once he did, Arianna took a few steps back and motioned for him to toss it to her. Icy blue eyes actually brightened slightly, the only proof of a soft smile otherwise hidden. Gently, he tossed her the ball, praising her when she caught it. Captain laughed brightly. She planted her hands back on the darker man's shoulders, lifting herself up off of her feet and flipping onto the ground. A pair of cloth shorts flashed under her skirt, answering the unabashed acrobatics.

"Oi, now, Jabie, yer sleuthin' skills be lackin' today. Y'see, if'n ye hadnae run off, ye'd ken we were nae jus' followin' a Drow. We be lookin' fer a certain fores' dweller, too." She touched the side of her nose and winked at Tristan.

Tristan raised an eyebrow suspiciously. "What are you talking about?" he asked, wary. "What do you want with me?" Had they been sent to capture him? He wondered for a moment if the king sent them or if...Tristan suddenly caught Arianna's shoulder and pulled her behind him, leaving her ball with Jabez for now. The girl started to protest, but she stilled at the look on her brother's face.

"T'ere's more to t'is tale than mee's t'e eye, Tris'an," Captain noted softly, her expression slipping to an almost eerily calm as her gaze swept across the trees. "All of Aviyah be followin' along. T'e pieces be set." The green of her eye glinted slightly, reflecting the colors of the rainbow. "Sun, moon, an' star be alignin', just as Shaddai ordained."

"What do you mean?" Tristan asked cautiously. His mind kept going back to his conversation with Clo. Would these people be able to tell him the answer to the riddle behind his powers? Sun, moon, and star. He knew a lot of myths and prophecies tended to revolve around planetoid alignments. Was that what she meant?

"She often speaks in riddles," Jabez explained casually, seeming to get over his embarrassment. He regarded the girl a moment. "Captain, are you saying this boy and the Drow are the other two?" Tristan watched the group for a moment. He still wasn't sure he should trust them. He didn't know these people. This could all be some elaborate scheme to trap him, but then if their intentions were malicious Arianna wouldn't have approached them at all. He glanced at the ball in Jabez's hands. Could he really trust her judgment?

Captain nodded to Jabez, but she kept her eye on Tristan. "Ya ken t'ings are abou' to change, Tris'an. Ye can feel i' as strong as I do. Look at me fer a momen'. I ken ye donnae see me as ot'ers do." The girl reached up to her neck, pulling off a small jewel and handing it to the bronze pirate beside her. The boy paused, unsure how she knew his name. He didn't know her to his knowledge. There was only one reason he could think of why she would know his name, and it was one that made him very, very uneasy. Carefully he turned his eyes on her and sought out her essence. His eyes narrowed in a slight grimace as the dazzling display of rainbow-colored sparkles almost blinded him.

"What are you?" he asked softly. Now that he was used to the brilliance, he studied her essence a little more closely, his eyes full of fascination as well as confusion. "What… what are we?" It was the same. Rose, this girl, and his essence were all so different from normal beings. What did it mean?

"I be a 'umble pira'e cap'n," she responded cheerily, taking her amulet back from her friend so as to hide once more. "An' I be a wee bi' Psychic. Bu' t'e res' is best discussed in priva'e quar'ers."

Tristan stared at her thoughtfully for a moment. Then, sighing heavily, he ushered Arianna inside the tree dwelling before stepping aside. "We can speak inside. This grove is protected— or it's supposed to be," he offered quietly. He gave the forest a pointed look as though it understood he was blaming it for this current situation. Captain nodded, stepping towards the dwelling. She paused when thunder rolled overhead; she hadn't exposed herself that long. Surely it wasn't them? Even so, the grove was protected.

"We'll jus' 'ave to keep i' quick. Protected or nae, lingerin' gives others time to ge' 'ere." She paused near the door, turning to look back into the trees. "Ye may as well come, too, Rose," she called before slipping inside. The Drow hidden in the trees hesitated before dropping from the branches and cautiously following.

Tristan hesitated when he saw Rose. "I'd thought you'd left," he told her honestly. He felt strangely glad she hadn't. Perhaps he'd been lonelier than he realized. It had been nice to have someone to talk to who wasn't some immortal elf or his sister.

Rose smirked at Tristan, hefting up her string of hares. "I was hunting when I spied the visitors," she explained calmly.

"Thank you," Tristan told her sincerely. He took the kills and hung them near the fireplace to either cook or preserve later before moving to make tea for everyone. Arianna snatched her faerie carving and showed it excitedly to the new girl. She seemed rather happy to have strangers in her home, her smile lighting up the room. Jabez, for his part, hesitated at the door. He glanced at Captain and then back at the trees. Perhaps he should take the moment to leave. Captain grinned as she squatted down to Arianna's level.

"She's migh'y beau'iful, jus' like the li'l lass wha' owns her," she praised warmly.

Captain's escort was bringing up the rear of their little procession. He chuckled as he clapped Jabez's shoulder. "Come on. You know she'll just get more creatively persistent if you try to slip off before she's done." Jabez sighed but allowed himself to be led inside.

Once the tea finished, Tristan poured cups for everyone. Sitting with his own mug, he watched Arianna and Captain for a moment. The little girl beamed with the pirate's praise. She then scurried off to grab another carving. This one depicted a woman with long flowing hair and a regal but carefree demeanor. Her gown and hair had been carved in such a way that it looked as though the wind was blowing through them. She held a symbol for order in her hands. The likeness was from Tristan's own memory coupled with depictions he'd seen of her in books and had even sketched himself. Her figure and standing were well known in the world, but Tristan knew better than others what she really looked like. What she was like. His eyes grew sad when Arianna showed Captain and then Rose the carving. Jabez paused upon seeing it.

"That's a good likeness of Reina," he remarked. "Did you make it?" He turned his gaze on Tristan but grew quiet when he noticed the lad's expression.

"Yes," Tristan answered softly, not looking at the carving now. Instead, he sipped his tea.

"Yer brudda's go' a talen'. Sev'ral, realleh, but 'specially fer carvin'." Captain winked at Arianna before standing and letting the bald pirate hand over her mug of tea. "I suppose we'd bes' start with some official introductions, aye?" she asked cheerily, holding the mug in both hands as if her fingers were cold. "Tall, dark, an' handsome back 'ere be me guardian Solomon. 'e also 'appens to be a member o' t'e Order."

"Tasked with guarding the Moon Child," Solomon added.

"Oi, oi, steal me thunder, why don'cha?" Captain teased before sipping her tea. Tristan watched their interaction with half-hearted interest. His heart felt heavy with a decision he knew he would have to make soon. But seeing the carving of Reina only reminded him of what he would actually be leaving behind. Solomon's comment piqued his curiosity though.

"Moon Child?" he asked, unfamiliar with the term. He glanced over at Jabez when the man squatted down to play with Arianna so as to keep her entertained while the adults talked.

"Aye. Captain Isabella MoonChild at yer service, but if'n ye call me by me full name, I be slittin' yer throat," Captain announced with a laugh, giving a grandiose bow. "One o' three, I be. Sun, Moon, an' Star be wha' we are."

Rose frowned. "What we are?" she questioned curiously. "How so?"

Captain smirked. "What do ye ken o' the legen' of the Chosen Children?" She paused when lightning flashed beyond the windows, tilting her head slightly to count before a peal of thunder followed. They had time. A little more, yet. Tristan hesitated with her question. He'd heard of the legend, but not much of it. His father had been adamant that Tristan didn't need to learn it while his mother had told him stories.

"Their existence is an omen. They are born to combat great calamities and such, but their birth means that something dire will take place in their era," Tristan answered quietly. "Is that right?"

Captain nodded. "Pre'y much. As the legend goes, t'ese bein's exist wit' a power inside them— given them by Shaddai 'imself. T'ere always be three: t'e Sun Child, t'e Star Child, and t'e Moon Child." Captain gave a mischievous smirk as her words sunk in. One of three. The other two, Jabez had asked. While the words stirred in their minds, Solomon picked up the tale.

"What many do not realize is that this legend is not only true, it is current. The Three exist in a cycle. When one dies, another is born to replace them. In the northern deserts, there is a mountain oasis known as Ben-Gal. Home to what is known as 'the Order.' Order Members are charged with serving Shaddai and protecting the Children. I, myself, am an Order Member. Captain is the Moon Child. And, according to her abilities, she discovered that you are both Children as well."

"Aye, t'ough which 'as been kept from me," Captain admitted calmly, setting down the mug she had chugged while Solomon spoke. "All I be kennin' is tha' the pair o' ye are like me. Meanin' ye go' some special powers an' glowin' symbols to go wit' em."

"Like the star on my forehead when I call my barrier," Rose noted thoughtfully, sipping her own tea. "I suppose that would indicate I am the Star Child?" She glanced at Captain, who nodded in confirmation.

"Aye, which woul' leave Tris o'er t'ere t'e Sun Child."

The forest dweller grew quiet as he listened. He was one of these Chosen Children? He supposed that explained his powers, but it also made a few other things make sense now. Was this the reason his parents had been fighting? Did they even know? He realized absently that Clo must have known, recalling subtle hints the Drow had dropped. However, his mentor seemed to realize there was a time and place for Tristan to know, and now here he was sitting with the other two Chosen Children.

"What are we supposed to do?" he asked softly, staring into his mug. Captain opened her mouth to answer, but several flashes of lightning and a peal of thunder powerful enough to shake the entire tree dwelling stilled her. She met Solomon's gaze warily.

"Fer t'e momen', make it to me ship. We can figure t'e res' ou' from t'ere," Captain cautioned. Rose frowned at the sudden wariness in the girl's green gaze. "We nee' t' go." Tristan frowned at the storm beginning to rage outside. That was rather fast for a normal storm. However, he froze when Captain mentioned leaving. He knew what Clo had said, and that he couldn't stay here forever. That didn't make the idea of leaving his home any easier.

"Go. The forest will guide you out of here safely," he told them. He smiled apologetically at Rose. "I can't."

Jabez sighed as he straightened to stand. "No, lad. She means all of us. You and the little one included. So, pack your bags. There's no arguing with Captain, and I doubt you want her to order Solomon to toss you over his shoulder like a sack o' flour." He watched Tristan's eyes darken a little with the teasing threat. In a more solemn tone, Jabez asked, "Do you really think the Nocium king will leave you alone if he knows what we do? He'll raze this forest to the ground just to get you. And so will plenty others. Come on, lad. Where's your sense of adventure?"

"It died seven years ago," Tristan stated quietly.

Jabez stared at him. "Well, that was rather dark." He moved over to the lad and squatted down, so they were more eye level to speak. "We all have our fears, and we would all rather hide than face them. But eventually we have to confront them anyway."

Tristan sighed, his eyes straying towards Arianna. "I can't protect her outside the forest," he argued. "What's waiting beyond these trees is far worse than a dragon or a king and his army." His grip tightened on his mug as his countenance darkened. He didn't know what to do. He couldn't leave, but neither could he stay. Then again, what reason did he have to trust these people? None of his choices presented themselves as ideal. Still gripping the mug, Tristan lifted his head to look around at the treehouse he'd shared with his sister for the last seven years. "I have no reason to trust you," he intoned to the group softly.

"Do you really want to take the risk of not coming with us?" Jabez pressed gently. "From what I understand, it'd be far worse for you to be alone when they arrive than if you came with us. At least then we could help you protect the little one. She's your sister, right? I know you know you need to do what's best for her." When Tristan lowered his head again and lapsed into silence once more, Jabez carefully gripped the lad's arm and gave it a reassuring squeeze. "I know it's intimidating, stepping into the unknown with no guarantee everything will be alright. But a lad your age should be out on adventures. And your sister deserves a free life, not one cooped up in a forest."

"It's not that simple," Tristan murmured. He felt Jabez's gaze on him still, but Tristan didn't raise his face again.

"What else is keeping you here, lad?"

Tristan was struck with how sincere the man sounded. He hadn't expected this from a stranger. Hesitating for a bit more, Tristan finally answered very softly, "This is my mother's resting place."

Captain was silent, shifting her gaze slightly when Sol arched an eyebrow at her. The Order member could tell she must have known, but the far-away look in her eyes was for something else, as well.

"Aye, I ken I fel' an essence twined to t'e trees 'ere," Captain mused softly. She bit her cheek as she glanced outside at the now-pounding rain. "I'm afrai' yer mot'ers protection willnae protec' ye much longer," she noted cryptically. "Ol' fang-face willnae be leavin' ye alone— yes, Rose, I ken abou' 'im, too —an' there be worse folks on t'eir way. We can 'elp ye protect yer sis. In fact, we been plannin' on i'. Bu' if we donnae leave, we risk this place no longer bein' a place o' rest. An' we be t'rowin' the whole realm un'er t'eir feet."

Tristan ran his fingers through his hair. He knew he'd need to leave eventually, but he hadn't expected it to be so soon. Or so hard. His eyes shifted to watch the rain as he contemplated. Finally, he sighed heavily. "Is there time to pack a few things?"

Captain hesitated, glancing at Sol. "Aye. Bu' nae much." She stood, slipping out the door with a soft, "I'll watch fer 'em."

Solomon exchanged a glance with Jabez before slipping out after the pirate, catching the girl's intention to give Tristan and his sister some space to get their things. Jabez caught the hint as well, following the pair. Rose, however, remained inside.

"Would you like me to assist?" she asked softly, moving to claim the hares Tristan had set by the hearth. They may as well take the food with them. Tristan lingered by the fireplace once he doused the flames.

"I...I don't..." His voice threatened to break each time he tried to speak. He started shoving a few clothes and essentials into a pack. He made sure to get Arianna's two favorite carvings: the faerie and the depiction of Reina. He also grabbed his sketch book that held the initial pictures for the carvings and a journal. He even managed to pack her ball. "I think I've got it," he finally told her. He didn't look at Rose as he moved about the dwelling. Closing the shutters and doors, he made sure everything was good for a long vacancy. He quickly donned his jerkin, leather trappings, and weapons before making sure Arianna herself was good to go. Once finished with everything, he stood in the middle of the dwelling, staring at it sadly. Arianna held his hand, her expression sympathetic and uncertain. Rose stayed near the door while they worked, unmoving, watching. Was this how her mother felt when she left the Drow? Or how she would have felt were she older when she lost her family? She wasn't sure what to say, to do, to comfort the siblings. To encourage them. And yet, the uncertain look on that sweet little girl's face made her want to speak.

"Shaddai willing, this will not be the last you see of this place."

"I'm sure Clo will look after it while we're gone. He seemed to know we'd be leaving soon," Tristan spoke quietly, distractedly. Seven years of peace with his sister, of living with the elves and other denizens of the sanctuary forest, and now he had to leave everything again. He wished he had time to visit his mother's resting place before they left, but from what Captain had been saying, there was no time. Shouldering the pack, Tristan held Arianna's hand and led her outside, smiling bravely for her. "Thank you," he intoned to Rose as he passed her. He locked the dwelling once she followed him outside. He glanced up at the storm brewing above the canopy, his eyes scrutinizing. This didn't feel like a normal storm, though he couldn't place why. Rose's eyes had lifted to the skies as well.

"This seems rather unseasonal," she commented quietly.

"Aye. Righ' on t'e button, ye are," Captain answered. She sighed, lowering her own gaze from the clouds. The gray had quickly turned to black, lightning flashing between. "We be findin' ye shortly before some'un far less pleasant, i' seems. An' now we need to leave 'fore 'e gets 'ere."

Solomon had unsheathed his two scimitars, though his stance was still casual. "There is a cavern near here," he explained softly. "It leads to the seas and our ship, the *Effervescence*."

Captain gave a sheepish grin. "I' may also kin'a sorta act as a hideout for me boys, so t'ere may be a party when we ge' there. They ken be'er than to si' aroun' if I tell 'em to scoot, t'ough." Jabez shifted from where he'd been leaning against a tree. Tristan felt the man's gaze on him as he looked back again at his home. Would they come back? And if they did, how much time would pass before then? A crack of thunder snapped him out of his reverie. If what Captain said was true, then the storm harbored one who came for him. Was his pursuer from the king or from his own father? He didn't care to stay long enough to find out— not while he had his sister with him, at any rate.

"I know the paths through the forest, but I'll let you take the lead since you know which cave you need," Tristan told Captain. He crouched and let Arianna climb onto his back so they could move more swiftly. Despite the circumstance, the little girl grinned, excited to get a piggyback ride from her brother.

Captain nodded. "Sol." The large pirate nodded in turn, pivoting and taking off into the forest at a swift pace. Captain gestured the others to follow, taking up the rear of their little party. They wove through the trees along a practiced trail. It wasn't long before a cavern came into view, and raucous singing reached their ears.

Tristan moved with ease despite carrying his sister. He couldn't help feeling impressed by Solomon's speed, and Jabez moved like a shadow among the trees. Such a strange bunch, and from the sounds coming from the cavern, they were only going to get stranger. Outside the entrance, a woman stood guard. She looked to be no older than her twenties, her features beautiful yet fierce. Her silver gaze watched the storm closely as though trying to see something in it. Her ebony hair had been pulled back into a high ponytail with a couple of braids encircling the tied part. Her bangs just barely touched her brow line, staying out of her eyes. Small spiral shell earrings and a hairpin with a small bell served as her only jewelry. Unlike Captain, this woman wore dark colors for her clothes, contrasting with her slightly sun-tanned complexion. A sleeveless blouse with a corset-like bodice and a matching pair of trousers with the ends tucked into her boots complimented her toned frame while giving her freedom of movement. Twin daggers hung in their sheaths at her hip. As the group approached, the woman shifted her eyes to watch them.

"I see you found them," she called to Captain and Sol. Her gaze darted to where Jabez had stopped short of leaving the tree line. "And you found our prodigal. A rather successful venture, all around." Her face broke into a bright smile. "Oi, Jabie, I ken ye be there. Come on in or Sol'll throw you o'er his shoulder and carry ye in here." She continued watching as the young man emerged from the trees and gracefully moved to the entrance. Before he could duck inside, the woman gave his shoulder a welcoming squeeze. Tristan slowed as he approached, letting Arianna down for now. The little girl stared in awe at the woman, probably seeing something about her that escaped Tristan's eyes. He didn't bother peering at the woman's essence, not feeling it necessary for now. He had the strangest feeling that he knew her, yet he couldn't recall ever meeting her. As he pondered this, he waited for Rose to join him. Rose shifted from the trees as though his thoughts had summoned her, eyeing the new woman calmly.

"Aye, Aye, drinks be on me, bu' firs' we go'a get this sorry lo' movin'," Captain called as she brushed past all of them and into the cavern. Rose watched her with some amusement.

"She's certainly lively," she commented to Tristan as she stepped towards the cavern. She paused at the entrance. Tristan chuckled at Rose's comment, nearing the entrance behind her. His gaze strayed to the sky again to watch the storm warily. One hand slipped down to Arianna's head in a reassuring gesture when the girl gripped his pant leg.

While the entrance was small and like any other cave, the interior was immense. Men caroused about piles of treasure and tables they had brought along with them. Some of the men had instruments, others had large mugs of drinks, and almost all of them were dancing, laughing, or singing. Captain had woven her way through the dancing, swirling her skirt before hopping up on the table.

"'Ey! Cap'n! Give us a dance!" one of the men called, a few others cheering. Captain folded her arms and waited. The men hesitated at her expression, the dancing steadily dying down. Captain grinned.

"Aye, tha's be'er. I can 'ear meself think. Now then, ye idjits, 'aven't ye noticed the sky, eh? Pack it up! To the ship! Chop chop!" She clapped to emphasize the last two words.

A rough chorus of "Aye" greeted her words before the men instantly sprang into action. Tables were shoved aside, treasure tucked further in the cavern and hidden. The raucous men had suddenly become dutiful soldiers under their Captain's watchful gaze— even when her gaze wandered to the entrance again.

"Introductions can wait until later," the guard woman's voice pulled Tristan's gaze to her. She eyed him but smiled. "Captain's ordering everyone to move out, so out we move. Go on, git." She nodded towards the interior. "There's a back way out of the cavern. The men'll show ye the way." She didn't move into the cave herself yet, her keen eyes returning to the storm. Tristan nodded and headed inside with Arianna. He held his sister's hand to make it easier for them to navigate the bustle inside the cavern. He also wanted to avoid losing track of his sister in all the excitement. As he joined Rose, a hand touched his shoulder, causing Tristan to glance back at the source. One of the pirates motioned the trio to follow him to the back of the cave where the men were making their way to leave. Glancing at Rose to make sure she was following, Tristan followed the pirates.

Some of the men had grabbed up torches to light the way. For all their noise earlier, these burly men moved with surprising stealth now that things had grown serious. The thunder outside had gathered to such an intensity that it's rolling noise reached them even then. Arianna clung a little more to her brother as the thunder grew louder. Tristan didn't even flinch, too focused on keeping his sister safe to worry about the weather. He did wonder if Clo and the rest of the forest inhabitants would be okay. If the presence causing the storm was after him, would it leave the other residents alone or would it go after them for information? He silently prayed for the safety of his forest friends even as he held Arianna a little closer.

Fate's Tempest

Captain watched the retreating figures, a strange rainbow light shimmering from beneath the hair swept over half of her face. She stepped down from the table and moved to the entrance, watching the storm's ferocity increase.

"Reina's protection willnae 'old much longer," she noted calmly to the woman guarding the cave's entrance, Amaya. "Ye shoul' be gettin' to t'e ship."

The woman eyed Captain with a knowing look. "Aye. And wha' will ye be doin', Captain?" Despite being the first mate, the woman had raised Captain since the girl was small. She knew her surrogate daughter well. Captain snorted as she stared out into the storm.

"Countin' on ye to trus' me," she quipped smoothly, smirking up at Amaya. "An' trus'in' ye to keep tha' stubborn pair out'a too much trouble fer a bi'." She nodded back over her shoulder at the tunnel. "We go' a long way to go to earn t'eir trus'. Ye can prob'ly imagine; Fate 'as yet to be kind to either."

Amaya's eyes darkened slightly, but she nodded. "I be no stranger to those dealt a bad hand," she remarked. She watched the teenager again. "Ye thinking to take on our guest?" she asked, indicating the sky. "Sure ye can handle it alone?"

"Distraction, per'aps a bi' of a chat. I donnae plan on stayin' ou' too late, Mum." Captain grinned up at Amaya. Amaya rolled her eyes. She'd all but given up on getting Captain not to call her that. Though she'd never admit it, a part of her actually liked the sentiment. Sighing, the first mate shifted into the cave.

"Jus' be careful, eh? If I'm going to be babysitting, I'll be too busy to come help ye if things go south, ya?"

"When am I ever nae careful?" Captain jibed right back before stepping out into the rain. She was drenched in seconds, but that didn't douse the fire in her eye as she slipped a dagger from its hidden sheath and tested its sharpness. The trees at the edge of the clearing flashed in sharp contrast as lightning leapt across the sky. Captain's bright green gaze hardened. She slipped a purple bandanna from her pouch, tying back her russet hair. Her left eye remained tightly closed, a crescent-shaped scar etched into her skin and over the eyelid.

"Ye may as well come ou'. I ken ye're t'ere," she stated coldly. The bouncy Doran was gone— only cold-blooded pirate remained.

"I have no interest in a child such as yourself." The voice cut like steel through the darkness. Captain noticed the rain hitting an obstruction just past the tree line.

"If I be naugh' bu' a chil', t'en I be easy to deal wit', no?" Captain twirled the dagger casually. "So come on, t'en. I t'ink i's time to send ye down t' mee' t'e Sirens."

The figure paused a moment before stepping free of the trees. "You are in my way," he noted coldly. Despite walking closer, Captain could not make anything out about the man. The closer he walked, the more indistinguishable his features seemed to become.

"I willnae be movin' by choice," she responded. Then she snickered slightly. "I've seen ugly, brudda, bu' ne'er so ugly as to 'ide behind a spell."

"Was that meant to be a taunt? Physical appearance means nothing to me." She heard the sound of metal unsheathing as the man pulled out his sword, the only item she could make out clearly. His hands sparked blue, electricity racing along the blade. "I say again: you are in my way."

"And what is your quarry, StormShaper?" A familiar voice spoke up beside Captain. Jabez stood there, seeming to appear out of thin air. His ice blue eyes stared levelly at the advancing form. He stood with his shoulders square and his body relaxed but alert. Though he'd never interacted with this man, he had seen him, so to speak, and heard stories of him. A lackey from High Lord Tsukuyomi, the Head of House Shadow Veil, who served the king of Nocis. "Do you seek the Drow as the king does, or is your target someone else?"

"Oi! Wha' in t'e blazes are ye still doin' 'ere?" Captain hissed at Jabez, screwing her mouth to the side and squinting at him. The figure known as StormShaper paused.

"I give no further warning, Isabella MoonChild. You will lose this battle." The pair could all but sense his gaze shift to Jabez, yet the strange disfiguration of any noticeable features made it difficult to actually see where he was looking. "You will regret your interference, Jabez ShadowDancer. My mission is my own."

"Helping," Jabez answered Captain. "It's what brothers do." To StormShaper, he commented, "I wasn't aware I had a reputation outside of Shaedra. I'm flattered you seem to know me. From what I understand, you are loyal to High Lord Tsukuyomi, a famous noble under the king. Would this mission have something to do with his missing warrior?" He thought of the boy and the girl in the woods. Were they connected to Tsukuyomi? It seemed likely.

"Brudda's shoul' learn to trus' t'eir sis'ers a bi' more," Captain grumbled, unsheathing a second dagger. There went her excellent plan. Plan B, then. She just needed to come up with a Plan B. Blood and Daggers, the one time she wanted to ask for a vision, and she needed to focus on facing some high noble's bloodthirsty puppet.

"I do believe I already answered that my mission is my own," StormShaper responded calmly. He lifted his sword and aimed it at the pair, the brilliant blue energy still dancing along the blade. "Come. Either join the dance or move aside." The wind and rain seemed to swirl around him with the words.

"No need to worry about me, Captain," Jabez remarked to the girl. "I've been dodging the powers that be for the last few years. I know how to disappear when the time comes," he added the last part low enough only she would hear him. Reaching to his waist, Jabez retrieved his sickle and chain weapon, uncoiling it and taking a ready stance. Captain stopped fiddling with her daggers, grasping one firmly by the hilt in each hand— she had more, hidden but easily accessible. No sooner had her hands found their grips than StormShaper had seemingly blurred out of existence. Their only indication to his new location came with a stinging pain in their sides. He had somehow passed between them, wounding them both in the process. He hadn't so much as disturbed the rainfall in his path.

***

Tristan paused outside the tunnel as he eyed the ship anchored near the rocky bank. The boats awaiting them now would ferry the crew to the vessel. Tristan had noticed Captain's absence, but the woman who had been guarding the entrance didn't seem bothered by it. He wondered what the spritely girl was doing. Tristan glanced at the overcast sky. Something didn't feel right. A strange sensation tugged at him just beyond his own reach, giving him the oddest sense of incompletion. Perhaps the feeling was an effect of leaving the forest that had surrounded him for the last seven years. He gave Arianna's shoulders a reassuring squeeze when he felt the girl shiver. Rose paused alongside him, watching the smaller boats warily.

"Our safest path lies with that ship," she noted quietly, almost to herself. She glanced up at the darkening sky, the clouds almost black above as the pouring rain caught up with them. A soft shimmer of silver surrounded the trio to keep them dry. "Do you suppose she's fighting whatever she forced us to flee?"

"If that is the case, shouldn't we be up there helping?" Tristan wondered aloud. If the person was after him, shouldn't he stay and fight? However, he also needed to look after Arianna, and he didn't like the idea of leaving her with a bunch of strangers— no matter how sincere they seemed. He glanced up when Amaya touched his shoulder.

"She's not there for an all-out brawl," the woman told him. "Just distracting him long enough to buy us time to board the ship an' get ready to sail." She didn't seem to mind the rain, her dark hair and clothes beginning to look soaked. "The sooner we be on the ship, the sooner she'll join us. And from the look of it, Jabez stayed behind with her. He can take care of himself, same as she. Though, I hope she realizes that." The woman ruffled Arianna's hair and then nudged Tristan towards the next boat. "On with ye." Rose frowned at Amaya, but she followed Tristan to the boats, nonetheless. Solomon had stepped free of the tunnel by this point, staring back the way they had come.

"Let me guess: she stayed behind?" Rose heard him remark dryly to Amaya. The bronze pirate grimaced slightly, but he made no move to turn back.

"Aye," Amaya answered. She patted him on the shoulder. "She'll be fine. She's gotta strike out on her own at some point, or she'll never learn. Besides, Jabez is with her; he's plenty responsible for the both of them." She winked at the Order member. Solomon sighed softly, but he simply nodded and moved to board one of the smaller boats. The *Effervescence* stood tall above the waves, waiting for her returning crew. The ship flew no national flags, though an emblem of a stylized silver crescent moon with a geyser of rainbow splashed across its back lit up a black flag. Rose watched the pirates with curiosity as they scrambled about the ship, preparing it to sail.

"If you do not mind my asking, why do you all follow such a young girl?" Rose questioned Amaya. Amaya actually laughed.

"Solomon and I play along so as to let her learn. And the men know if they get too out of line, she's more than capable of handing their butts to them. Not to mention they'd have to get through her guardians, too. But the men like her— respect her despite her age —and Sol and I don't mind letting her lead," she answered cheerily. "She might as well get the practice."

While in the boats, Arianna peered at the rolling ocean from her seat beside Tristan, her eyes wide with wonder. There was a stretch of Nikko Mori that met with the sea, so Arianna had played in the shallows with her brother and some of their friends; but she had never been out on the waves. Seeing even more of it up close brought a smile to her face. When the boat reached the ship, Arianna eagerly started climbing the ladder to board, trusting her brother to be there if she slipped. They'd done this enough times when Tristan would climb the trees in the forest with Arianna, training his own body and letting the girl have a bit of adventure. Even now, the child stared with wide-eyed wonder at the large sea vessel. She'd never seen one this close. As soon as she swung over the bulwark and dropped nimbly to the deck, Arianna took off to explore, a big grin on her face. Following his sister onto the ship, Tristan simply moved out of the way and watched her to make sure she didn't get underfoot. He did smile when the girl found a spot clear of crew and began twirling around in the rain, seeming to dance with the storm rather than fear it now. Rose nodded to Amaya, turning to climb the ladder after Tristan. She hesitated on the deck before stepping to the side and reaching up to adjust the hood of her cloak. She knew she needn't bother, with the protections woven into the cloth, but it was a nervous habit. Drow were not especially liked outside of their own kind; they had earned themselves quite a grisly reputation.

Many of them deserved that reputation.

Once on the ship, Amaya took charge. She barked out orders with a resonant voice and kept the men in line simply with her tone. However, she stood atop the bulwarks and continued to watch the cliff, her demeanor casual but alert. Tristan hesitated before moving to stand with Rose. His hand started towards hers but then changed course and touched her shoulder reassuringly instead. He offered her a kind smile. Even so, his gaze shifted back to the shore and the forest beyond the sands and rocks. He still felt he should be helping Captain, but Arianna needed him, and if the assailant was after him, he'd simply be giving them what they wanted. His eyes followed the storm above where he guessed the battle to be. He startled a little when a horn blew, the sound carrying along the wind to the land. Glancing over, he saw Amaya pulling a horn from her lips.

"We'll set sail once Captain returns!" she called to the crew.

***

Jabez braced himself as soon as he felt the pain gripping him. He remained resolute, but his eyes narrowed slightly. Whipping around despite the pain, he aimed a counterstrike with his blade, the chain flashing through the air with his speed. Jabez never thought he'd be so grateful for the leather in his gloves. He had noted the electricity coming off the man, and he had no intention of getting electrocuted.

StormShaper said nothing, simply vanishing from the path of Jabez's sickle and the dagger that Captain had thrown alongside it. The pirate-girl cursed; their opponent had vanished yet again. She sighed, straightening and closing her other eye. *Alright ye scalawag, where the blazes—* her thoughts were cut off as she was slashed from behind.

She staggered forward, gasping in surprise. She hadn't even sensed him! She turned to retaliate, but he once again shifted out of view.

Jabez stood still, both his eyes closed. Focusing his mind, he used his senses aside from sight in an attempt to predict StormShaper's movements. In an instant, Jabez dodged behind Captain, his chain wrapping around StormShaper's blade to keep it locked in place. The force of the strike still caused Jabez to skid back a bit, but the young man managed to hold his ground. The sword's tip taunted dangerously close to the ninja's chest, his arms shaking slightly with the strain of holding his stronger opponent at bay. As StormShaper pressed his attack, Jabez dug his feet into the ground, but his back pushed into Captain's. Despite saving the girl from the initial attack, Jabez knew what the move cost him. He just hoped the leather in his outfit would be enough to thwart any electricity channeled at him. Jabez could almost sense the smirk from StormShaper as electricity raced along the blade and chain towards the ninja. As it reached his gloves, the current arced up into the air and dove straight for him. Before it could reach, Captain bent forward, allowing Jabez to flatten over her back. She winced with the pain from her wounds, but other than that she ignored them. She trusted the ninja to keep his arms locked so that StormShaper's blade would pass over them. She bent so that her nose almost touched her toes, allowing Jabez to kick off of the ground and against StormShaper's chest— successfully pulling the sword from his grip —before Jabez finished the flip to land on the other side of Captain. The pirate girl planted her hands and sprung forward, quickly spinning so that she also faced StormShaper. Her left eye was now open.

Unlike the glittering green gem of her right eye, her left iris was shimmering all the colors of the rainbow.

Jabez unwrapped the chain and gripped the sword in his own hand now, his sickle and chain in the other hand. He charged at StormShaper and attacked with both blades, showing his finesse with the weapons in the ease of transition in fighting styles. He knew he needed to be careful, especially now that he knew StormShaper could manipulate the electricity to such an extent. The leather would protect him, but he could still be shocked in certain areas. Perhaps he could use his chain as a grounding rod should StormShaper try to electrify the weapons. As Jabez charged him, StormShaper didn't move. The obscured figure held out his arm, catching the sword in his hand. When Jabez moved to strike with the sickle, he caught that as well. Electricity once more raced down the weapons, tearing through the ninja. Jabez knew the leather would only insulate so much against a pure current, and it seemed his opponent wasn't necessarily trying to fry him; more so attempting to force him to release the warrior's blade. StormShaper lifted his leg and kicked him in the abs. If the strain from holding the blade earlier hadn't driven the point home, then the fact that he actually went flying from the kick certainly should— his opponent was far more powerful than the rumors hinted.

The warrior shifted towards Captain when she appeared in Jabez's wake, daggers spinning in hand. Her eye glimmered as StormShaper shifted his grip from blade to hilt to block her daggers with his sword; she dodged around the blade with perfect anticipation, jabbing a dagger into StormShaper's shoulder. The cry that escaped him sounded more surprised than alarmed or hurt, but she gave a satisfied smirk, nonetheless.

"'uman or nae, donnae t'ink to be underestimatin' us in turn," she taunted, wrenching her dagger free and jumping back as he swung at her with an electrified fist. She was moving quicker now, more confidently. StormShaper softly cursed; her eye. He should have guessed. Well, he need only stab it out to eliminate the bother.

***

Captain skid back, dropping to a knee and panting slightly. She was losing track of how long they had been fighting, and she was running out of stamina from using her powers to such an extent.

"Oi, Jabie…" She coughed slightly, glancing away to spit some of the warm liquid trickling into her mouth from a soft graze against her scalp. "Ye shoulda run off when ye 'ad t'e chance. Ye look a righ' mess," she teased.

"I always have been the stubborn one," he teased tiredly. He breathed heavily and tried valiantly not to collapse where he stood. His clothes were tattered, and his shirt hung off his body in rags. Blood coated his flesh where his clothes no longer shielded him. His mask had miraculously remained intact, though, still guarding his face. He felt his body going numb with blood loss and his vision swam slightly. Pain lanced through him from his fractured ribs— one or two he was sure had actually broken during the fight. He refused just to give up and die, though. He glanced at Captain, willing his eyes to focus on her.

Captain shifted to a standing position, using an arm to wipe her mouth. She hesitated when first her eye seemed to shine brighter and then she heard a sharp horn blast. Amaya. So, they were ready. And if the vision dancing through her mind was anything to go by, they were also about to be rather upset with her. Jabez glanced up when he heard the horn blast. Time to retreat, if he could.

"I be thinkin' i's time to end t'is par'y," Captain announced to Jabez with a mischievous smirk.

"Aye, aye, Captain," he remarked to the girl, the teasing smirk evident in his voice.

Captain chuckled as she faced StormShaper once more. He was commanding streams of liquid to flow from the storm and around his arms, stopping his wounds from bleeding— though not healing them. He held out his hand, electricity flaring around it before turning to look at his two opponents once more.

"I tire of this," he noted calmly. "I have a ship to sink. I best deliver its captain." He shifted, blurring towards the pirate girl. Jabez growled, shifting back upright and dashing in an effort to intercept. Captain straightened.

"Hey, Jabie?" Her voice sounded strange, resonant. It seemed to echo in his mind as she spoke, ensuring that he heard every word. "Make sure t'ey move t'e friggin' ship, eh?" Rainbow light danced around her fingers as she lifted them and shifted as though to grip and weave something together. "'ave Maya give ye one o' my specialties. T'ere's a fresh batch on t'e ship." She gave a yank with her arms, and reality jerked around the trio. A sharp tug pulled at each before their vision erupted in a brilliant light. Jabez's feet met wood as he found himself struggling along the deck of the *Effervescence.*

Jabez barely managed to process this change before he found himself colliding with a pair of powerful arms that wrapped around him and stopped him short of the ship's bulwarks. He bit back a cry of pain even as agony forced the air from his lungs. The younger man allowed himself to relax in Solomon's hold as the pirate lowered him to the deck. While Solomon was helping the ninja, a member of the crew ran down into the ship's galley to retrieve a flask of what Captain liked to call "Concoction"— homemade healing brews. Jabez didn't even notice the other man holding the concoction out to him at first. Pain wracked his body, especially his ribs. Solomon grabbing him 'round the middle had only made them flare with renewed fire, making it difficult for Jabez to breathe. When he finally did see the flask held out to him, the ninja's eyes reflected the grimace hidden by his mask.

Tristan frowned when he didn't see Captain with the masked man. How had he even gotten to the ship? Then again, he'd seen similar teleportation abilities— just not usually among humans. As he contemplated the turn of events he tried to pinpoint Captain's essence. Rose frowned.

"I no longer sense her presence," she murmured to Tristan, following his gaze back to the now-distant shoreline.

"I will pour it down your throat if I must," Solomon commented to the ninja dryly, taking the flask from the pirate. "The taste has improved— somewhat." Jabez gave Solomon an unconvinced and slightly imploring look.

"If ye mean to kill me, you could have just let me fall in the water," he remarked. Tristan glanced up when Amaya sighed in exasperation before performing a back-flip off the bulwarks. She landed gracefully on her feet. Striding up to the two men, she snatched the flask, gripped the back of Jabez's cowl— catching some of his hair as well

—forced his head back, and jammed the flask neck into his mouth. Jabez choked as the liquid poured through the fabric of his mask. He tried to pull away to catch his breath. Arianna peered around Solomon as the man sat back on his haunches. She watched in fascination at the spectacle, almost smiling at the funny man and beautiful lady. Had the circumstances not been as serious, the sight would have made Solomon laugh, as well— however, Captain would have been the first to tease. When Amaya finally let up, Jabez fell back as he coughed for air once more.

"Oi, oi, I'm all right. I'm all right. Ye sure haven't changed, Amaya. Still keen on torturing the injured, eh?" he complained in quiet sarcasm.

"And you're still a baby about it," Amaya snorted in rebuttal. She glanced around at the crew. "What are you staring at? Get this bucket moving!"

Rose frowned as the pirates scattered under Amaya's orders. "What about your captain?" she questioned.

"We can find Captain better if we're alive to actually look," the first mate answered calmly. She glanced up at the fading remnants of the storm. "From the look o' things, I'd wager our pursuer be gone for now, but I'd rather not take chances." She looked over at Jabez. "What happened, Jabie?" Her tone became surprisingly gentle as she turned her attention to the ninja.

"Pain," Jabez answered readily. "A lot of pain. That warrior of Tsukuyomi's was pretty tough, and I doubt he was human. That or he's been magically enhanced. Perhaps both. When we heard the horn blow, Captain told me to make sure you moved the ship. Then there was a really bright, rainbow flash, and I was here. I honestly have no idea what she did or where she ended up." He sighed as he looked back at the cliff receding in the distance.

"Tsukuyomi?" Rose's gaze shifted to Jabez. "As in the Head of House Shadow Veil in Nocis?" Surely Jeremiah had not sent for the High Lord's champion. He couldn't be that desperate to reclaim her. But what if Captain's crew were not the only ones to know about the Chosen Children or their identities? Had Jeremiah known and never told her? Tristan tensed slightly at the name, but he continued to listen in silence.

"Aye. We fought his champion, StormShaper," Jabez answered. "He wouldn't tell us for sure who he had come for, though. I have heard that High Lord Tsukuyomi is looking for a certain warrior and has quite the bounty on his head to be brought back alive. Rumors place the warrior having last been seen in Nikko Mori." The ninja's gaze shifted from Rose to Tristan and back. "Tristan Nightshade is what I hear the warrior's name to be."

The boy sighed heavily. "So StormShaper came for me, then," he remarked. He hadn't really interacted with the warrior, but he knew of him. He looked to the side as he felt the group's gaze on him. "Arianna and I are the children of Tsukuyomi SoulMirror. I am Tristan Nightshade." When he glanced up, he just barely made out Jabez's eyebrows disappearing under his cowl when he raised them. Strangely enough, Amaya had little reaction to the revelation, though her gaze gained a subtle emotion Tristan didn't recognize.

Solomon crossed his arms. "It would seem the plot thickens, then. Who might you secretly be, miss? The Scarlet Swordsman?" he teased Rose, looking to lighten the suddenly somber air. The Drow didn't stir.

"That would be correct."

Solomon laughed. "And here I thought Captain was the psychic one."

"Well, since we're talking names, First Mate Amaya making your acquaintance," the feisty pirate remarked. Indicating Solomon and Jabez she added, "You've already gotten to know Solomon, and then this young one is Jabez ShadowDancer."

Jabez gave her a frown. "You make me sound like a child. I'm twenty-six," he protested lightly.

"Still a child by my reckoning," Amaya teased him, ruffling his cowl and thus his hair under the fabric.

"You most likely gathered from your captain that I prefer 'Rose,' so let's keep it to that," the named warrior noted calmly, watching Amaya and Jabez. Just how old was this woman? She spoke like a mentor, yet she appeared half the age of the weathered Solomon. Her ears weren't tipped like an elf, and yet Rose could almost sense the difference in the woman's blood. "I am surprised she did not warn you of our names; she quite obviously knew them."

"Captain reveals what she knows she should. Other times, she gets distracted by the more important factors, and the rest she keeps to herself for her own reasons," Solomon explained calmly. Arianna had been listening and watching the exchange in curiosity, but when Jabez's eyes found her she ducked behind Solomon playfully. After a moment she peeked at Jabez from behind the pirate's large leg. Jabez glanced at her and smirked.

"Oh, where could that little runt be?" he asked, feigning ignorance. He stiffly got on his hands and knees and made a show of looking around. "Not here. Nope, not there either." He suddenly reached around and tickled her side, making the girl jump and smile broadly. "There she is!" Solomon glanced down at their antics and smirked slightly. He reached down and ruffled Arianna's hair.

"Am I to be a shield?" he teased. "What happens if I step aside?" Arianna gripped his pant leg and tried her best to stay behind him. Still, Jabez refused to be deterred. He tickled her time and again, eliciting silent laughter from the girl. He laughed with her while her brother watched them with a soft, amused look. Sol chuckled.

"I do not make a good shield," he admitted. "How about a means of escape?" He reached down and carefully picked her up, lifting her high into the air before letting her sit on his shoulders. Arianna grinned as she did her best to keep her balance on the man's broad shoulders, her hands resting on his bald head. Jabez snorted.

"Alas my quarry has escaped me. For now," he remarked with a dry but teasing tone. He stood. Captain's concoction had already healed most of his severe injuries, so the man didn't have too much trouble moving. "So...how do we find Captain?"

Rose sighed as the conversation shifted, leaning back against the bulwarks and folding her arms. Everything had taken quite a surprising turn. She had gone from seeking freedom to wanting to warn a supposed enemy to boarding a ship with pirates. What would come next in this little adventure? And when would it end? From the sound of things, not for a while. Shaddai had chosen her, for some reason or other.

"From the 'rainbow flash' I would say Captain was keeping a secret," Solomon noted dryly. "Though why her little trick only landed one of you on this ship, I can only guess." He sighed, lifting Arianna up and spinning her as he set her down. "You should get some rest, Jabez. Even with a Concoction, StormShaper is not an opponent to be taken lightly." Jabez couldn't resist a smile at the man.

"Sending me to bed like a kid? Haven't I outgrown that?" However, he winced as his wounds throbbed slightly. Even though he could move a little easier, he knew the pirate was right. The Concoction hadn't healed the injuries completely. He paused when Tristan approached him, the lad watching him closely.

"I could heal you the rest of the way," the boy offered. "It's one of my abilities."

"Well, that's handy," Amaya remarked with a smirk. "Now we don't have to chug any more of Captain's Concoctions. Though, we might have to brave a few so as to avoid hurtin' her feelings." She winked at Solomon. Jabez chuckled softly at her comment. However, he kept his gaze on Tristan.

"I'll be all right. For now, it's probably best you save your strength on the off chance we meet with some unsavory characters. I appreciate the offer, though." He patted the boy's shoulder. Tristan nodded before stepping over to Rose and turning his gaze towards the receding shoreline.

"I've never actually sailed before," the Half-Drow confessed softly to Tristan, keeping her eyes on the deck. "It feels… strange." She did not watch as the shore steadily slipped from view. The pirates didn't necessarily have a destination, more a goal: don't get caught. So, for now, they picked a direction until otherwise notified.

"Nor have I," Tristan confided softly. He gave her a slight smirk. "Even before living in the forest I never ventured near the ocean. When Arianna and I started living in Nikko Mori, a friend took us to the shore. I've since taken my sister to the beach several times over the years, but I've never actually been out on the water in a boat. It's different. A bit soothing." With a sigh, he turned his gaze from the horizon and watched instead as Solomon helped Jabez to the sleeping quarters below deck. "What do you think of things as they've so far transpired?" he asked the Drow quietly. His eyes shifted to his sister. With both her playmates now gone, Arianna moved about the ship with Amaya. The woman didn't seem to mind, navigating the child with ease and even giving her small tasks to do here and there. Amaya's expertise with the child attested to her years of looking after Captain, a fond look filling the woman's gaze now and again. Even the crew humored the little girl, actually seeming happy to have her. Perhaps she helped ease the pain of not having their captain among them. Rose chuckled.

"It is quite a bit to take in, I confess. I never imagined a quest for freedom would lead to so much more."

"Someone once told me that life itself is an adventure; one gifted to us by Shaddai, and in thanks for the gift we should ever pursue to bring glory to His Name," Tristan told her. "I don't know what Shaddai has in store for us, but I do believe He's the One orchestrating all this."

"Wise words." Rose lifted her gaze to the horizon, watching the mysterious Mists in the distance. The soft white fog danced between the sea and sky, shimmering in the sunlight that had finally escaped the clouds. "Who knows? Perhaps we may finally learn what lies beyond," she murmured softly.

***

Jabez collapsed into a cot and stretched out to sleep as best he could despite his wounds. It felt strange being back on the ship after all these years, but he felt glad to be back—circumstance notwithstanding. "Thanks, Sol," Jabez told the Order member. "I appreciate the—"

Jabez. Captain's voice suddenly floated across the ninja's mind before the sleeping room faded. *A bright sky suddenly greeted his gaze before it lowered. He found himself looking at a pair of hands chained to the back of a wagon before the gaze moved again. A man rode beside on horseback, dressed in the armor of a Nocium knight. Another knight sat in the wagon's driver seat, though his armor looked strange from behind.*

Jabez stared. Despite the strange occurrence and images, he calmly watched, taking in what details he could. He recognized the wagon as a prison wagon, and the knights led him to believe the transport was headed for the Nocium capital. The knight riding alongside the wagon Jabez didn't recognize from this angle. However, when he caught sight of the armor of the knight driving the wagon, he wished he hadn't. The unique lighter armor with its more form-fitting adornment and lack of openings distinguished the man from the other knights. Lancelot. Oh boy. This looked fun. Then Jabez found himself back in the ship's quarters and

80

staring blankly at Solomon's concerned expression. The pirate had leaned over him when Jabez zoned, a big hand now touching the younger man's shoulder. Slowly lifting a hand to his head, Jabez fought to focus through the fatigue now plaguing him. At least Solomon's bulk provided some relief from the illumination of the light crystals in the lanterns hanging throughout the lower decks.

"I know where Captain is," he murmured as he regained his bearings.

Solomon frowned. "Your eyes were glowing, like hers do. She must have found a way to bind herself to you." Captain and her secrets. The girl wasn't a telepath as far as they had known. What other abilities might she be developing? "What did you see?"

"Lancelot has her. I think they were in Howsergale when I saw her. I'm betting Lancelot will take her back for judgment, though perhaps not all the way to the capital," Jabez explained.

"No, not the capital," Solomon confirmed as he straightened. "Captain had already informed us the king was moving to one of his smaller castles further inland, closer to Andor. Caer Talon, I believe." He smirked at Jabez. "I had best inform Amaya. We will need to plan on intercepting that caravan." Jabez started to get up to go with him, but the pirate's hand kept him from rising.

"I'm all right; I've handled worse than this," the younger man protested.

"Understanding what you can handle is different from the wisdom of discerning when you should," Solomon pointed out gently. "I know you are capable. But I also know the journey will only become more difficult from this point forward. Rest while you can, and better face the challenges ahead." The ninja sighed heavily but relaxed back onto the cot. For a moment he reached up and gripped Solomon's hand on his shoulder.

"I want to be useful. So far, I've not done much to help," he murmured. "I tried to help Captain, and now she's in the hands of Nocium officials."

"And yet she was able to use you as a connection to help us find her," Solomon pointed out softly. He touched a hand to Jabez's wrist. "Captain knows what she's up against. She understands the risks same as— if not better than —the rest of us. Shaddai will guide us where we are needed."

"I know He will," Jabez agreed softly. Finally, he released Solomon and allowed his body to relax fully. "I'm sure you'll wake me when we get there." With that, he closed his eyes to rest his mind and body.

Solomon walked briskly back up to the deck and flagged down Amaya. "Captain found a way to communicate with Jabez. She's currently in Howsergale as a prisoner of Lancelot. He says they are already on the move."
Rose frowned at the information, stepping over to them.

"It would be easy enough to reach Howsergale if we took the rivers inland, but I doubt they'll still be there by the time we arrive. If Lancelot is taking her for judgment, they'll most likely pass through Thorn-Drake— we could head them off there." Tristan listened from where he stood near the bulwark, his brow furrowing as he contemplated something. He had seen Thorn-Drake a few times in his younger years, but he had no true idea if the city's location remained unchanged from that time. If he had been certain of its whereabouts, he would have offered to run there himself. Amaya must have had an inkling of his thought process because she quickly doused any such plans.

"We'll stick together and take the channels. The last thing we need is for someone to go solo and wind up another prisoner," she noted even as she lifted Arianna to sit on her shoulders. Gesturing to Rose and Tristan, she added, "That goes double for you two, considering what you are and that both of you have bounties for your capture." At Tristan's confused look she added with a wink, "I be knowin' why Captain ventured into Nikko Mori and who she been seeking."

Solomon nodded. "Then it is settled. We had best change course; we wouldn't want to waste our daylight." As Amaya moved to relay new orders, Solomon returned below decks. He needed to make sure their cook had learned there would be a couple of extra mouths to feed. Tristan stood at a loss. He didn't know what to do. He had never sailed on a ship, so he wouldn't be much help; Amaya continued entertaining Arianna even as she gave orders to the men and helped with getting the ship underway. Tristan glanced at Rose for inspiration, though he didn't really find anything. He didn't want to stand around or get underfoot. Perhaps he could help in the galley— he did know how to cook and clean.

Rose moved for the stairwell, remembering the hares she had slain that morning. She had hung the strap over her shoulder, but with all the excitement had yet to take them to the kitchen. No, galley. She was on a ship now, she needed to use the proper terms. She nodded to Tristan as she passed him before carefully descending down the swaying stairwell she had seen Solomon use. She could smell dinner preparations almost as soon as she reached the bottom, so it wasn't hard to find the right room. Identifying the cook was even easier. He was a fairly large man, a testament to his love for partaking in his own craft. The pirate cook was unsurprisingly suntanned, with the weathering most mortals gained in their lifetime. The lines on his face drew a map of laughter and rough times, though they hadn't sunken so deep yet as to mark him an Old Salt. He paused in his peeling of potatoes to examine the cloaked figure in turn.

"Well, now. Ol' Sol be tellin' Ol' Nugget tha' we 'ad guests. Wha' can I do fer ye, lass?"

Rose unslung the strap, offering it to the man. "I caught these shortly before adventure caught us. I thought you might wish to make use of them." She did not bother to introduce herself; judging from the man's use of his name in the first sentence, "ol' Sol" had already handled that detail.

"Indeed, I woul'!" Nugget chuckled, gesturing to a small pantry with his knife. "Why don'cha string those up in' tha' cabinet, and I'll be usin' t'em fer yer upcomin' travels." Rose nodded, stepping quickly to the mentioned cabinet and stringing up the hares. She turned to watch him, folding her arms beneath her cloak and leaning against a counter space that was built into the wall.

"Is that difficult?"

"Wha'? Peelin' taters? Nah, miss, I coul' do i' wit' me eyes closed a' this point in me life. Haven't ye ever cooked before?"

"Not really," Rose confessed, watching the man's knife skin the plant. "I know basic meals. Fish over a fire, cleaning meat. Nothing complicated."

"Ah. Soldier cookin', tha' be what'cha know. Let the kitchens handle the regular stuff, s'long as ye ken 'ow to survive."

"Yes."

"Ainnae any shame in tha'. Teams accomplish t'ings much be'er than ye can on yer lonesome." Nugget nodded. "Look a' ol' me down 'ere. I ainnae much fer fightin' or explorin', bu' I ken 'ow to cook a mean stew." He grinned over at her, still peeling away. She did not doubt his statement of being able to peel with his eyes closed. "I coul' show ye, if ye like? From the soun' o' things, we go' a ways to go. Migh' make it a bi' less borin' fer ye."

Rose paused. Really, there was no harm. It could prove a useful skill. "I would like that." She straightened from the cabinet, retrieving a small stool Nugget directed her to before sitting across from him and taking an extra knife.

"You are all surprisingly kind for pirates."

That got a mighty laugh. "Aye. We ainnae wha' people expect. S'long as ye stay on our goo' side an' all." He winked. "Cap'n ainnae t'e bloodt'irsty sor', though she's go' a temper to match a storm. I reckon we only really carry t'e bran' o' pirate seein' as King Arden donnae like us much."

"I would not take it personally. There are many he does not like." She watched the way Nugget's hands worked, steadily mimicking his movement. Nugget chuckled again.

"Oh, aye. I be t'inkin' few realleh min' our relievin' 'im some of his finery. Specially since we donnae keep i' all ourselves."

"You give away your treasure?"

"I' be t'e Cap'n's orders. Anyone 'ho needs i', ge's some. Plenty o' people be willin' to hide pira'es if t'ey fin' t'em to be goo' people."

"Sounds a bit like the old tales of the hooded archer," Tristan commented as he entered the galley. He smiled at the sight of Rose peeling potatoes. "I— *umph*" he started when a small form plowed into his legs. Smirking he amended, "*We* came to offer our help, but it looks like Lady Rose beat us to it." He reached down and ruffled Arianna's hair when she poked her head around his legs. The girl smiled brightly at Rose and Nugget. Tristan had brought his sister with him since he still didn't feel very comfortable having her out of his sight, and he wanted to give Amaya a break despite the woman's assurance that she didn't mind the child. "I know nothing about sailing, but the past seven years gave me plenty of practice in cooking," Tristan commented. Nugget laughed.

"Well, I be gettin' downrigh' spoiled wit' all t'ese new 'elpers. C'mon, t'en, lad, ye can join t'e miss wit' t'e potatoes. An' ye, li'l lass, look like t'e perfect 'elper to wash up some dishes, eh?" He winked at Arianna. "Donnae you youngin's worry, Ol' Nugget's go' plenty to do roun' here. We'll be back ashore 'fore ye ken."

Of Damsels and Darkness

Captain stretched stiffly from her wonderfully comfortable bed of hard floor. Her body complained from having fought StormShaper, having used a difficult ability, and having been forced to walk several miles. It didn't help that bored guards meant extra beatings. Finnegan, the knight under Lancelot, could care less about her health and well-being so long as she was alive. There was something fishy about the man, but she didn't dare use her Sight around them— or while she was so worn out. It had been difficult enough to contact Jabez. *Jabez.* Her mind drifted again to the ninja. She glanced over when the door opened, her escort for the day coming to re-chain her to the wagon. The sun was barely peeking through the prison windows. Captain sighed, not bothering to get up. They'd just haul her around anyways, may as well give them more work to do. Sure enough, two guards entered the cell and hauled her upright. She blinked in slight surprise when Lancelot walked in.

"Oi, jus' wha' a girl needs t' see. A knigh' in shinin' armor. I doubt ye be 'ere to rescue me," she snarked.

"You seem rather lively today. Good, we won't have to spare any water or food to feed a criminal." Lancelot's replies were always smooth and cold, yet they sounded unnatural. His voice almost seemed to echo, but it wasn't the metallic sound that should have come from his helmet. The knight turned to the guards. "We have a long journey ahead of us. We're heading for Hawk Glen and then on to Thorn-Drake.

Best make sure we are stocked on supplies. Leave the prisoner with me." There was a chime of "yes, sir," before the guards left Captain to stand on her own. Lancelot was silent until they left. "You realize, I am sure, that piracy is a crime worthy of death."

Captain frowned, folding her arms. "Aye."

"I am here to offer you a chance to live. All I need in return is information. It would not do to see a child hanged."

Captain snorted. "Go choke on a codfish," she spat, her eyes narrowing. "I be no ta'le tale fer ye. I'd rather die a t'ousan' deaths."

Lancelot crossed the room, gripping the front of her shirt and lifting her up on her toes as she reflexively gripped his wrist. "When we're done with you," he growled, "You'll wish you could." He threw her so that she smacked into the stone wall, her vision spinning. "We'll speak on this again," he noted before walking out the door.

***

Lancelot held true to his word. Every night, he came with the offer, and when she refused, he would beat her before leaving. At one point during their journey, she had tripped from behind the wagon and fallen; the wagon had not been stopped, the men simply dragging her behind. She could feel Finnegan's eyes on her, hear him chuckling. Despite Lancelot being the senior knight, Captain felt as though Finnegan had more sway with the guards. The way he spoke to the others indicated a power of command— even Lancelot listened to the man from time to time, though Finnegan was careful to mask his comments as suggestions.

She wasn't sure how much time passed before they reached Hawk Glen. No one turned to look at her as they passed. No one noticed. No bread was brought, no one offered her any water. She winced as the guards hauled her upright and dragged her to a cell. They threw her in, locked the door, and left. Captain sighed, closing her eyes. It had been long enough, at least. She reached her mind out, desperate to contact Jabez. Images flashed through her mind, memories. The discussions that took place on the ship, Jabez and the others disembarking at the river...She could feel they were traveling, though she wasn't able to pinpoint them.

Hold on, Captain. We're coming. Jabez's thought brushed against Captain's mind, the ninja having sensed her presence. Captain couldn't help a tired smile. She was too weary to respond, but she left the channel open for a while just to have that presence, that reassurance. She paused, her green eye opening as the door to the guardhouse creaked open: Lancelot had come. He walked to the bars and knelt before them, his face still masked.

"My offer still stands."

"May t'e stars defecate on yer rottin' corpse."

Lancelot sighed, rubbing the back of his neck. "Why must you be so stubborn? Why are you protecting them?"

"Choke on a sardine an' die, live'sprout." Captain could sense the scowl beneath his helmet.

"My patience wears thin," he growled, standing. Captain just laughed softly, the laughter becoming violent coughing. She closed her eyes, wincing. She couldn't keep— The connection with Jabez dropped, and she coughed again.

Lancelot opened her cell, stepping in and gripping her neck before lifting her up onto her knees. He turned her face to stare at where his eyes would be under the helmet. "You make no sense." His gauntleted grip on her neck tightened, cutting off her air supply. "You claim to be a cut-throat scalawag, scourge of the seas, and yet all you are is a sad little girl with no future." He used his other hand to brush the hair from her face. "You are going to die. Whether before the king or on the journey. You have no hope. Why do you continue to protect them?" Captain slit her eye open and spit blood on his helmet with a smile. He hollered, slamming her into the floor. She gasped, her head swimming as fresh blood ran down the side of her face.

Lancelot laced his hand through her hair, picking her back up. He stopped when he noticed her crescent-scarred eye. There was a pause, as if he was considering it. He lifted up her chin, peering at it intently. Captain could sense his thoughts trailing to where he found her, sprawled alongside the road, alone. "How did you even get there...?" He lifted his other hand, forcing her eye open with his armored fingers. She screamed in pain as her Sight activated— images, memories, potential futures danced through her mind. Lancelot stared at the colors flashing across her eye. "Now *this* is an interesting development," he mused. The words echoed through Jabez's mind.

***

Jabez staggered dangerously as pain erupted through his skull. He lost all feeling in his arms for a moment, causing him to drop the kindling he'd been carrying. Clattering wood pieces hit the ground, though the sound seemed far off in the haze clouding the ninja's mind. The world blurred horribly and painfully out of focus. Forgetting the wood altogether, Jabez tried to focus through the pain and concentrate on just getting one foot in front of the other as he hobbled back to camp. He kept a hand pressed to his forehead as the pain lanced behind his eyes. Muffled voices reached him, but he couldn't make out the words through the agony. He staggered again, tripping on his own feet. A large hand on each of his shoulders steadied him. He winced when one of the hands left his shoulder to tilt his head up instead. Jabez's eyelids fluttered as he grimaced. He could have sworn he saw rainbows for a moment.

"Captain," he murmured.

Jabez found himself swept up in a strong pair of arms— Solomon had been the one to find him. The large pirate carried Jabez over by the fire before sitting down and laying Jabez in front of him. He touched a hand to the man's forehead, and a strange calm passed across Jabez's mind. Solomon calmly subdued the effects of Captain's powers, waiting for Jabez to be able to focus. One intense look from him sent the others back to setting up camp. They had been traveling the river for quite a while now. Amaya and the newcomers, as well as a few of the crew, now made the journey to rescue Captain. They had not left the ship abandoned, but Solomon knew they would need a few extra pairs of hands— and pirates were quite capable lads to have around when planning a jailbreak.

Amaya ignored Solomon's glare. She brought a water flask over and handed it to the pirate, figuring some hydration might help calm Jabez's nerves. The younger man shuddered as his mind allowed his muscles to relax. Slowly the pain subsided, but a dull ache remained. His eyes shimmered rainbow just like Captain's would.

"Someone's forcing Captain to keep the channel open. Lancelot, I think," he informed the two pirates. "Hawk Glen. They're in Hawk Glen now." Jabez hissed as the pain increased momentarily before subsiding again. He reached up and shakily gripped Solomon's wrist, not trying to push the man away but simply hanging on through the agony. Jabez felt wave after wave cascade over him. His muscles tensed as Lancelot forced Captain to maintain the connection. He tried to arch his back, pain searing through his head again. His grip on Solomon's wrist tightened slightly, though it remained rather weak still. From where he was currently playing with Arianna, Tristan watched the trio with curious concern. He didn't know what was going on, but it didn't look good.

***

Back in Hawk Glen, Lancelot's discovery was interrupted by a ruckus outside the cell. Two guards dragged a figure between them into the guardhouse. Despite their rough treatment, the prisoner walked with them calmly and coolly. He offered no fuss when the guards threw him into a cell, acting as if this was the norm for him.

"You get in there and stay quiet!" one guard demanded.

"Ha, ye donnae scare me, ol' bucke' 'ead," the young prisoner taunted, peering at them from under his wide-brimmed hat. "Wha's wrong wit' me recit'n' a few 'fairytales' as ta king calls 'em?"

The second guard growled, "Such stories are forbidden by the king's law. That means treason. Ye planning a rebellion, boy?"

The younger man laughed. "If t'ey be simple stories, then why does t'e king find 'em so offensive? No' as if I be smearin' 'is name in blood and callin' on some deity to strike 'im down."

"Tales of the heretic deity and His champions are blasphemy towards the Celestials," the first guard spat. "Now keep yer mouth shut, or I'll have you gagged!"

"Aye, sir pansy," the young man smarted. His hat kept his face mostly shrouded in shadow, but his coat lay open, revealing weather-worn and bloodied clothes. A simple beige tunic and brown breeches sported travel scars. While the outside of the trench coat looked like a simple dark leather fabric, the inside was dark blue with a decoration of embroidered stars. The young man moved to the wall and sat slumped leisurely against it, propping an arm up on his raised knee. As the guards left, the young man's head swung as he watched them go. Then he turned his gaze to Captain and Lancelot.

Lancelot had ignored the intrusion, studying Captain's eye intently. The girl's screams had faded, but exhaustion was apparent in every aspect of her expression. "Oi, Lance, wha' t'e bloo'y deuces are ye doin' to t'e poor girl?" the newcomer asked in casual incredulousness, noting Captain's look of pain. Alconai, the young man watching them, studied the knight in question. He had known Lancelot for years. He'd heard the rumors of his friend's knighthood, and as a traveling entertainer, Alconai had heard tales of the man's deeds and new armor. Not so long ago, they'd run into each other and caught up, Alconai getting the chance to see Lancelot in his armor firsthand. His friend had always been more compassionate with other people— firm but not unkind. One look at the way the man handled the girl told Alconai that something wasn't right with his friend.

Captain never used her abilities to this extent unless in dire circumstances; it wore on her too much. She could practically feel her mind fighting to slip away and fade into darkness. She grimaced as she thought of poor Jabez— no doubt that ability was being forced as well, and the ninja had far less practice than she with the effects.

Lancelot didn't respond to Alconai's inquiry, thoroughly ignoring his friend's presence and demand. He studied the girl's eye intently, wondering the extent and purpose of this ability.

Alconai's eyes narrowed. Discretely slipping his hand into a pocket, he pulled out a small round object. It didn't look like much, just a little wooden yo-yo. But he knew they could be rather annoying. The young man made his way to his cell's bars. With practiced accuracy, he let the yo-yo fly, having lengthened the string to use the little instrument in battle. Wood clunked against metal as the yo-yo slammed into Lancelot's helmet. "Donnae ignore me ye git," he demanded evenly. "Wha' happened to yer gen'lemanly spirit, eh?"

Alconai only got a couple of hits in before Lancelot's hand flashed up to catch the object. He turned his head to frown at it before standing and dropping Captain. The girl fell to her knees, shakily covering her scarred eye with a hand. *S-sorry, Jabie.* She shuddered weakly but forced the message before cutting off their connection. The knight had moved over to the cell dividers, now standing over the other prisoner.

"This is none of your concern." He didn't even remove his helmet or acknowledge that he knew the man, simply folding his arms as he glared through his helmet into the cell.

"I ge' tha' a lot. S'pose meddlin' be in me blood," the young man said easily, though there was an edge in his tone. He tilted his head back and to the side to peer from beneath his hat's brim. Thick, red auburn strands brushed the young man's shoulders and framed his rugged, handsome features. Golden hazel eyes met Lancelot's gaze levelly. "'Sides, it be me business when me friend isnae actin' like he normally does. No friendly greetin' or even a long-sufferin' sigh a' seein' me? An' since when do ye bully people, prisoner or no?" Despite the young man's intensity, he managed to keep a nonchalant appearance. "Wha' nanny goat kicked ye in t'e balls t'is mornin', Lance?"

Lancelot sighed, snapping the yo-yo's string. "I have neither time nor patience for your interruptions." He walked back to Captain, forcing her to look at him once more, though not forcing her other eye open. She didn't even bother resisting, just staring at him groggily. He finally released her, letting her fall to the floor as he left the guardhouse without another word.

When the knight had left, the young man turned to Captain. Reaching into a hidden pocket in his coat, he pulled out a red vial. He then very carefully rolled it between the bars so that it stopped by Captain. The red liquid shimmered in the dim lighting.

"T'ain't much but it'll 'elp. Jus' hang in there," the man encouraged her gently.

The Doran girl lay on the floor a moment, gathering the strength to just barely raise her head and look at the vial. Her arms didn't want to move.

Oi, willnae 'Maya t'ink this a righ' treat, she chided herself, *me all splayed on t'e floor like one'a me ol' dolls.* She focused her strength, reaching for the tube of crimson liquid. She could tell just by looking at the consistency that he was right— it wasn't very potent. But she would take anything to ease the pounding in her skull, let alone the rest of her.

"Aye, t'ere ye go, lass," the young man kept encouraging her. "I'd've gott'n i' closer, bu' I didnae want i' to break." He watched the girl with sympathy. She looked a right mess, but he figured he'd look about the same in no time. Captain grasped the bottle, her green eye sparking slightly as she forced herself onto her side for a better attempt at opening it. She chugged it.

"Ahhhh, tha's a righ' fix'n, no mistake." Her voice barely existed, yet she still managed to smile.

"Righ'cha are, love," the young man commented cheerily. "A friend o' the fam'ly taugh' me 'ow to make 'em; though, I be nae t'e exper' as she." He eyed her a bit as he leaned back once more. "Doran, are ye? Or so I gat'er from yer clothin'. Wha' ye done to ge' t'e bucke'eads all inna twis', eh?" From beneath his hat's rim, his golden-hazel eyes smiled at her. Captain chuckled, though it devolved into a bout of coughing. She managed to calm her lungs and catch her breath, slowly shifting herself over to the wall.

"Wha' can I say?" she joked lightly, reaching up and grabbing the stones to help haul herself into a sitting position. "Pira'es ainnae t'e mos' pop'lar wit' soldie's."

The man chuckled, a rich yet deep tenor. "Ye be a bi' far inlan' fer mos' pirates. Ge' tired o' t'e sea?" He moved back to his own wall and sat against it, watching her as they spoke. Captain snickered slightly.

"Oi, now tha' be a long story," she muttered, leaning her head back against the stones. "An' mayhap nae t'e bes' one to be tellin' a stranger. If I maybe 'ad a name…?" She peeked her eye open and glanced at him mischievously.

"Par'on me lapse in manners, mila'y. Alconai," the man supplied, tipping his hat to her. "An' wha' I be callin' ye?"

"Cap'n'll work a'ight," she responded with a smirk. "Donnae be mindin' a lack o' manners too much, ye're dealin' wit' a scalawag, remember." She paused, considering. His name tickled something in the back of her memory; names often did, but she rarely remembered the visions that taught them to her unless it was urgent. Many times, they were instances that might play out in her life, and she was more interested in the events than the people.

…Not to mention she was tired, but she really didn't want to think she was that exhausted.

"I be a bi' o' a vagabond meself, but me mum taugh' me ta be a gentleman, too," Alconai remarked teasingly. "'Ow long ye been a pira'e?"

"Oof, tha's a tough'un," Captain murmured, folding her arms and closing her eye once more. "I been a captain fer abou' four years now, bu' I practically grew up on t'e sea."

"Pre'y impressive all t'e same," Alconai said cheerfully. "I ne'er been ou' ta sea, but I ken wha' it looks like. Soun's freeing, sailing does. As fer me, I'm nothin' no'e-wort'y. Jus' a simple en'ertainer. Bu' I do ken 'ow ta work a crowd."

"I donnae doub' ye in t'e leas'. Bu' I ge' t'e feelin' there be more to yer story than tha'. I donnae ken many self-called vagabon's on firs' name basis wit' legendary knights."

"Lance an' me grew up in the same village. We been friends fer years, even after we went our separate paths— he a knight an' me a bard. We kept in touch, an' I been followin' the stories o' his feats. Heard rumors o' 'is spiffy new armor an' go' to see it no' long ago," Alconai explained easily. His expression grew concerned, though, as he continued, "But...I lost touch wit' him recently. Though' I'd see wha' was goin' on, bu' I couldnae raise 'im. Figured gettin' captured woul' be the next best thing. If'n I didnae want the guards to hear me spreading stories of the Sacreds, they'd ne'er ken it was me." He winked at her cheekily.

Captain snorted. "Fair 'nough." She opened her eyes to watch the door of the guardhouse. "T'ere defini'ly be somethin' up wit' yer frien'. He donnae soun' righ' when he speaks, and he's silent mos' o' the time we be movin'. T'e guards ten' to listen to t'e ot'er knight we be travelin' wit', a man named Finnegan."

Alconai listened, leaning back against the wall as though finding it rather comfortable. "I made t'e acquaintance of Sir Finnie las' I met up wit' Lance, but I didnae get much chance ta rightly ken 'im. Sounds a bi' shifty now." He'd have to keep an eye on Finnegan from here on. Perhaps the knight knew something about Lancelot's strange behavior— or was the instigator for it. For now, Alconai studied

Captain again. "Wha' was tha' po'er ye be spor'in earlier, if'n I migh' be so bold."

Captain was quiet as she leaned her head against the wall. Should she tell him? She had no reason to trust him, really. Yet something in her whispered that she could. Had she dared, she could peek into his past or future to better judge his character. However, she didn't feel like being dragged behind the wagon in a coma. She opened her mouth as if to answer, but the door opened, and she quickly shut it. Time to leave, it would seem.

Alconai tilted his head to regard their visitors. He wouldn't make any move to resist for now; though, he did think all of this was a bit much for stories the king declared were untrue. Still, he planned to bide his time while he figured out what was happening to his friend and how to snap some sense into the man. Shaddai willing, he'd manage to help both Captain and Lancelot. What kind of gentleman would he be if he left the young pirate to fend for herself, after all?

Lancelot nodded to the other two soldiers in the doorway. They moved to the side to fetch Alconai while the leader headed straight for Captain's cell. The man laced his fingers through her hair once more, dragging her upright and forcing her to walk in front of him. The girl didn't protest, though she gripped Lancelot's wrist in an effort to preserve her scalp. She let him force her to the wagon and chain her wrists behind it once more.

Alconai let the guards have him, and soon he was chained to the wagon alongside Captain. He didn't seem to mind, keeping up his cheery attitude. His hat shaded his face from the sun during the day and helped to keep the dust out of his eyes. He wouldn't let the guards take it, actually snapping at one's hand. Captain had actually giggled at that slightly. Having company behind the wagon was a morbid way to raise her spirits, but it certainly seemed to help. She laughed and joked with him, talking about her crew though being careful not to reveal anything too sensitive.

***

Jabez sighed with relief as the connection finally closed. He shuddered violently, quietly gulping down air. He felt sorry for Captain. If it hurt that much over the connection, he couldn't imagine how it must have felt for her. Jabez hoisted himself into a sitting position with Solomon's help. He kept a hand to his head, rubbing it slightly to ward off the lingering headache. Solomon carefully guided Jabez, making sure the man didn't overdo it.

Tristan watched the trio for a bit to make sure he didn't need to heal Jabez after whatever had come over the ninja. However, he could tell he wasn't needed. Silently, he strode to the edge of the channel. He searched for Rose's essence for a moment, but then his gaze followed his sister. Despite himself, he smiled. The little girl ran around the camp, jovially pestering the pirates and doing her own little tidbits to help them. Her pigtails bounced as she moved. He glanced then at Amaya, the woman returning to work once she knew Jabez would be all right. Tristan always knew whenever she moved due to the bell on her hairpin chiming a single note cheerfully with each shift of her body.

Rose stayed near the camp, but not quite in it. The pirates left her to her own devices, sensing her more isolationist tendencies. In the darkness of the woods around the camp, Rose knelt near the water's edge and gently splashed her face. She had finally lowered her hood and the scarf that covered the lower half of her face. She had released the braid in her hair, calmly brushing her fingers through the silver strands as she rinsed them in the water. She hummed softly as she worked with the strands, a soft song from her memories. She imagined her mother had sung it to her, but really, she couldn't remember. It may have been one of her original owners.

Tristan glanced Rose's way for a moment before turning his head in the direction of the running water. Closing his eyes, he listened to her song, the lullaby reminding him of days spent by the crackling fire with his mother. How he wished he and Arianna could live with their mother in such comfort again. His hopes of his father changing died long ago, but a part of him wished his father had changed. Would they all be enjoying an evening in the parlor, sitting by the fireplace? Sighing, Tristan quietly moved over to Rose.

"Would you care for some company?" he asked softly. Rose blinked over at him, slightly surprised yet smiling, nonetheless.

"Of course," she answered calmly, twisting her hair to wring out any excess water. "Tired of pirates after a peaceful forest?" she teased. Tristan smiled at her jest, but then his eyes grew sad.

"The song you were humming," he started quietly, "it reminded me of when my mother would sing to me. Her voice always filled me with warmth and peace. It reminded me I was loved. Watching Amaya and Arianna interact makes me wonder what would have been had my mother lived." He turned his gaze once more towards the water as he spoke.

"She does seem quite maternal for a bloodthirsty cutthroat," Rose commented as she stood, brushing her hair back and twisting it once more into a braid. Her eyes strayed to the camp, watching the first mate and Tristan's little sister through the trees. "From the sound of things, she helped to raise Captain. And yet she looks barely older than we. It's strange. All of it. This adventure, these people…" She paused, glancing back at Tristan. "I'm sorry. I don't mean to sound dismissive of what you have told me." Tristan shook his head.

"It's fine. I suppose this adventure is affecting each of us differently. The pirates seem comfortable with the whole thing aside from Captain being a prisoner. Arianna sees the whole thing as something new and exciting. For you, it's different from the life you've known. For me, no matter how much I want to enjoy the chance to see and do new things, doubt follows me. Doubt in my abilities as a Chosen Child, in my ability to protect my sister and be the brother she needs, and in my ability to one day face my father," he confessed softly.

"I would imagine this type of adventure happens on a regular basis for them," Rose noted with a chuckle, coiling her braid up around her scalp so it wouldn't hang free under her hood. "As for the rest…I've learned doubt is a part of life, but we mustn't let it control us. Only time will tell if anything will come of our positions and adventures. What will be will be, regardless."

Tristan nodded. "I suppose so. I know to trust Shaddai and His Will, but it's difficult at times. Still, that's part of having faith," he commented. "I hope that one day Arianna and I can return to the forest, but this time we'll have even more friends. And maybe one day we won't need to live in fear of our own father." His gaze drifted to Rose again. "If you ever wish to settle, feel free to live in Nikko Mori. Even if you decided against staying there, maybe you could visit."

Rose chuckled. "Let's see where this rainbow girl takes us before we start planning too far ahead into the future," she jibed, reaching down to replace her scarf. "For now, we should rest. From the earlier disruption, I'd wager Captain is not doing well."

Tristan moved to follow her back to the camp. Almost as soon as he stepped into the area, his sister dashed over and hugged him. The young man smiled and lifted her in his arms, tossing her up a little higher before holding her in a hug. Small arms encircled his shoulders as Arianna returned the embrace happily. Seeing his sister's smile always lifted Tristan's spirit. There was enough darkness in the world; he felt he owed it to her to bring a little light. Perhaps that was all being a Chosen Child was about: bringing light into the darkness— not just for his sister, but for all people.

Rainbows and Rampages

The next morning, Tristan sat with Arianna beside him in the boat with Jabez and Solomon as he and the two men rowed. Smirking, he watched as Arianna reached her hands into the water and splashed Solomon's back. At least she was entertained. Jabez eyed the little girl with amusement. She reminded him slightly of the captain: full of energy and smiling no matter how grave the circumstance. Everything was an adventure to those two. Well, almost everything. He wondered how the captain was. He hoped the guards hadn't been too rough. As Arianna continued dipping her hands in the cold water and then slapping them on Solomon's back, Jabez couldn't help a quiet chuckle. Solomon laughed as well, turning to look at the girl from his position at the front of the boat. He reached his own hand into the water before dumping a handful over her head, rubbing her hair. Tristan grimaced slightly when the water hit him as well, but his smile remained.

While the group had been quietly rowing down the river, Rose had been running alongside among the trees. She constantly scouted ahead before checking back with the group. Mostly she would speak with Amaya, as the woman was the closest they had to a leader. As she appeared along the boats once more, she found Jabez instead.

"Any contact since last night?" From what they had gathered before setting off in the rowboats, Captain hadn't reached for Jabez again— they weren't even sure the man was still connected to the eccentric girl.

Arianna shook herself happily, a bright smile adorning her features. Her silent laughter vibrated her whole body. Carefully rising from her seat, she threw her arms around Solomon's neck and held on to him as she stood. Her curious eyes stared at the passing landscape and the fish swimming in the channel. She waved at the fish as they passed. Jabez blinked in slight surprise when one of the fish twisted and waggled its fin above water as though waving back. He then slowly turned his attention to Rose.

"Not since last night," he confessed. "I get the feeling that means she's not doing well. We better hurry." Rose nodded, dashing ahead to Amaya's boat. Amaya actually stood lightly on the bow of her boat, perched with perfect balance.

"I don't think you will run into any trouble on the river. Perhaps I should journey ahead and see if I can detain them?" Her voice was calm and low, so that the others wouldn't overhear. The first mate glanced at Rose before turning her gaze to the horizon once more.

"Nah, stay with us. We'll have a better chance in a group, and I don't want to have to save two people if something goes wrong," the first mate told her. Rose bowed her head in reluctant acquiescence, but she paused and glanced over her shoulder when Jabez's eye suddenly sparkled rainbow. The Half-Drow managed to maneuver along the shore still, testament to her expertise in such an environment; she slowed her pace to come alongside Jabez once more, watching the ninja intently. Jabez grimaced as he instinctively touched a hand to his eye. He quickly tried to refocus so he could keep rowing and not throw their boat off course, but pain shot through his head like a jagged splinter. He managed to keep the connection open, though. Rose frowned at Jabez's reaction. Jabez wasn't a telepath, and he was human. She was beginning to worry that this connection could kill him if it continued.

Rather than chide the captain or cut them off, she gently intercepted the telepathic bond. She hadn't shared her own telepathic abilities with the group, but the situation called for her to act. She was careful not to invade Jabez's privacy in the process. She could empathize with the girl's loneliness and concern; she also realized the danger of letting the connection continue as it was. Tristan echoed her concern, reaching a hand to Jabez's temple and gently healing the man as he began rowing once again. Warmth soothed the ache away until Jabez was at ease. He nodded gratefully, and Tristan retracted his hand. Satisfied that the ninja was cared for, Rose turned her attention back to the Moon Child.

We're well on our way to you, Isabella.

I seem t' recall tellin' ye nae to call me tha'.

Rose smirked slightly. The stronger connection from her end meant less work for Captain to communicate, but it was obvious that the girl was weak. Still, she had spark, that much was certain. Rose sighed, increasing her pace to rejoin Amaya.

"She's not doing well," she noted softly. A part of her understood Amaya's reluctance to separate, but Captain wasn't faring well despite her new friend's attempts. More than likely, Lancelot had pushed her too far.

Amaya sighed. "She's a toughie, but even Captain has her limits," she remarked quietly. "Still, I think it be better if'n we stay in a group. Ye don't know what you're running into with these guards."

"Let Rose and I go ahead. We might be able to do something," Tristan quipped from his boat. He shook out his wet hair— Arianna had stopped splashing when she noticed the shift in mood. "It would be the two of us; we'd stand more of a chance," he persisted.

"So, you'd really be willing to leave your sister with us? And what happens if your father—"

"Rose and I aren't normal, or haven't you noticed?"

Amaya rolled her eyes. "And what happens when you two run into trouble while we're all the way back here?" she countered smoothly. "We're going together— that's an order." Tristan's lips set in a determined line. However, he dropped the subject for now. Really, he didn't want to leave Arianna with them, but he didn't want Captain to perish either. Rose wasn't as convinced.

She started to say something to Amaya about her experiences with Lancelot, but she suddenly stopped. Something ahead felt...wrong. She could sense the disturbance, a powerful presence, yet she couldn't focus on it or place it. Stranger still, it felt almost familiar. She met Amaya's gaze intently, signaling the boats to slow and pull in their oars for silence before dashing off into the trees.

Tristan had automatically stopped when he noticed Rose dart off. He wondered what had her on edge. He stared straight ahead again to see if he could determine anything.

His hand touched Arianna's shoulder to get her attention and then motioned her to be quiet. Arianna silently sat back down, her curious eyes watching the pirates stop at Amaya's signal.

The pirates were casting lines to each other in absolute silence. They rigged the boats together and let the current carry them, waiting. The moments seemed to pass sluggishly as the boats drifted. The group rounded a bend in the river and found themselves in a natural corridor. The banks rose steeply on either side, and bridges of dirt and tree roots stretched across in twisting paths to connect the two sides. The tree canopy diffused the sunlight, tendrils of green reaching down for the sparkling water. Amidst the greenery, sitting atop one of the large root-bridges, a dark figure seemed to wait calmly for the boats' approach. As they neared, however, he paid them no mind, staring intently at the water. Brown, rugged hair hung about his face and reached his shoulders. The stranger wore simple black leggings and a black traveler's shirt with a cloak, but an undershirt stretched up and over the lower half of his face as well as covering his arms. His skin was a sun-worn tan. Stuck in the root behind him was a rather large blade— tall and wide enough that he could lean against it rather comfortably; it was impossible to tell how far down the blade was stuck. The dark stranger glanced up as the boats drew nearer, piercing brown eyes locking gazes with Amaya before sliding to Solomon. The bronze pirate tensed as they locked gazes before steadily standing in his boat and folding his arms.

"Zatook ShadowBlade, Champion of Andor," he greeted calmly, yet every muscle spoke of tension to Jabez and Tristan. "Come you as friend or foe?" The man, Zatook, was silent. He met Solomon's gaze steadily before standing as well. He reached back to grab the hilt of his sword, hauling the blade from the tree root— displaying that it was, indeed, massive —before slinging the blade across his shoulders and turning to stare in the woods. Rose frowned as he watched her hiding place, wondering how he had known she was there. She gauged the way he handled his blade with ease. Now that Solomon had named him, she recognized the presence. She had felt him in Andor, but never seen him. Stories had swirled around the demon champion, the son of shadows and curses. Yet, for all his presence and reputation, Zatook did not attack. He turned to face Solomon again, reaching into a satchel and retrieving a small bit of metal. He tossed the medallion and chain to Amaya's boat, since the woman was closer and obviously in charge. The medallion was the same as the one Solomon wore, the mark of the Order. Easily catching the medallion, Amaya took a quick gander at it. She'd been watching the exchange between Solomon and this Zatook fellow, trying to gauge the tension between them. She'd heard of the warrior but had never seen him personally. Her silver gaze studied the medallion. Once she established it to be authentic, she actually laughed, the sound warm and full of mirth.

"Another of you lot, eh?"she remarked cheerily. "Should've just said so in the first place!" Despite her brighter attitude, when Amaya's gaze met Zatook's, it was like looking into deep starlight— full of mystery and understanding. "I suppose you're wanting to come with us then. Well, get aboard if ye can. We're not pulling to shore until we reach our destination. And don't capsize anyone or I'll hang you up by your hair!" She figured he might be like Arianna with the no speaking part, or perhaps he was just a quiet person. She tossed the medallion back to him. Zatook caught the medallion, slipping it in his pouch as he nodded to Amaya.

Solomon remained standing, watching him, his expression masked.

Zatook shifted his blade, stabbing it into the side of the root facing away from them. He waited until the boats were beneath before he lowered himself to hang by the hilt and dropped easily into one of the boats. He tugged the large blade free, slinging it across his shoulders as he sat so that it would not shift awkwardly in the small vessel. Jabez studied the man for a moment but said nothing. Instead, he resumed rowing when Amaya gave the sign for them to continue. Arianna for her part just smiled at the stranger. She resumed playing with the water and now had Tristan and herself thoroughly soaked. She noticed Solomon's serious demeanor and splashed him before her brother could stop her to see if he would laugh. Solomon paused with the splash, blinking back at the small girl. Something hid behind his eyes, yet for her sake he let a smile cross his features as he lowered back into the boat and playfully splashed her in turn. Tristan leaned back to avoid getting any wetter, but the water hit him as well, especially when Arianna shook the wetness from her hair. She laughed silently. He sighed, resigning himself to being uncomfortably drenched for this ride.

Something about the Andorian sets my nerves on edge, Rose confessed to Tristan, her mental voice sliding across his thoughts like silk. *There is a hidden darkness about him. Solomon's blood boils simply at the sight of him.*

I don't sense any malice from him, he remarked to Rose. His gaze shifted to Amaya, who didn't seem at all uneasy with the stranger's presence. *Amaya and Arianna seem fine with him.* He focused his gaze on the stranger all the same and tried to see his essence in an attempt at making out anything about the man. However, just like with Captain, he wasn't able to see anything of Zatook's essence. He shook his head. *I can't see his essence*, he informed Rose. *He must be hiding it somehow, like Captain does.*

Interesting, Rose mused across their new connection. *I suppose we'll have to let it be for now. But I would be wary.*

Water suddenly hit Tristan, causing the boy to sputter in surprise. He shook the water from his face. Beneath his wet bangs he sent a flat look in Solomon's direction. The next thing the pirate knew, a bigger splash than Arianna had managed so far crashed into his head. Tristan smirked as he pulled his arm back in the boat. Startling him again, water showered Tristan from the side and behind. The boy frowned when he heard Jabez's low laughter. The man continued laughing even as Tristan splashed him back.

"Oi, what are ye? Pirates or dolphins?" Amaya called back to them, her face set in a slight scowl. Tristan quirked an eyebrow at her. His hand once more dipped into the water, light racing through it toward the front of her boat. The light solidified before blasting water right into Amaya's face. He grinned in satisfaction when she shrieked in surprise. His smugness was short-lived, though, as the woman glowered at him. Racing along the boat edges with surprising ease, she leapt lightly from vessel to vessel before landing with a foot on either side of Tristan. She nudged Arianna to Solomon. Tristan released his own cry of alarm when slender fingers gripped his tunic and tossed him overboard, icy water engulfing him. Before he could even thrash around, the hands gripped him again and pulled him back above the surface. Laughter greeted his ears, Jabez and the other pirates showing no restraint in their amusement. The hands dropped the coughing, sputtering Chosen Child back into the boat.

"Take that, ye drowned rat," Amaya proclaimed cheekily. She then made her way back to her original perch. As she passed, Amaya paused beside Zatook. Without warning, she wrung her hair out over his head, sprinkling quite a bit of water onto him. "Lighten up. It'll help your complexion and make any gray day that much brighter," she teased before returning to her earlier position. Tristan for his part was ruffling the water from his own soaked strands, raining the liquid a little onto Arianna. The girl just smiled brightly.

Zatook blinked, reaching his hand up and running it through his hair. He gazed at the water on his hand before turning to stare at the pirate woman. He actually seemed a tad stunned.

***

Arianna bounced happily on Solomon's back as the group ran across the countryside. Tristan and Rose easily kept pace, but the Sun Child itched to go faster. He wanted to help Captain; he wanted to get Arianna somewhere safe again. The longer they were out and about, the greater the risk. Tristan sighed as he kept his focus on the group around him. Amaya kept everyone going at as fast and steady a pace as the pirates could handle. She herself seemed to run quite easily, the brisk pace not fazing her in the slightest.

Rose frowned beneath her cowl, eyes scanning the horizon. Though her day-vision was no match for an elf, it was still superior to humans. Therefore, she was the first to notice. The silent Order member was the second. His large blade was suddenly in his hand, his arm stretched to the side so

113

that the arrows ricocheted and clattered to the ground—instead of sinking into Tristan and Jabez. Rose dropped to her knees, sliding beneath the blade as her hands came together and she summoned her silver barrier. Solomon spun Arianna around to his front, turning his back so that the arrows did not reach the little girl or land anywhere that might obstruct his fighting. He barely winced as they found hold in his back, and he did not let the little girl see. He could deal with pain; he hardly even noticed it. He quickly set her next to Amaya, racing ahead to the Half-Drow's side and pulling out his scimitars.

Rose gave him a flat look, her eyes staining red as she touched a hand to the man's wounds and used his own blood to remove the arrows and stitch up his flesh. Jabez retrieved his sickle and chain. Swinging it around Tristan and himself, the chain blurred, creating a rotating shield as another volley fell. The chain deflected the arrows before Jabez expertly caught the sickle in his hand. Tristan's face set in determination as he pulled out his bow and took aim. Several shots soared through the air and felled the enemy yeomen. Twilight crystal erupted from the ground among the archers, piercing some of them.

Amaya whipped out her dagger and stood at the ready, her other hand resting on Arianna's head reassuringly. The girl held tightly to the first mate. Her eyes watched fearfully before searching for her brother. She caught his gaze at one point, and Tristan motioned for her to stay with Amaya for now. The child nodded even as tears glistened in her eyes. Once he felt more sure that his sister would stay, Tristan returned his focus to the group's assailants. A blinding flash exploded in the soldiers' midst. Suddenly, beams of light shot from the crystals Tristan had erected earlier and lanced through the enemies like thousands of javelins, the crystals amplifying the lights' intensity. Solomon lay a quick hand on Amaya's shoulder.

"There is a patch of trees just ahead; get everyone to safety there." He and Zatook did not even glance at each other as they both took off towards the enemy soldiers. They leapt just as Tristan's power collided with the archers a second time. Neither man faltered, each landing on the various boulders scattered in the river. With another large leap, they landed in the midst of the Nocium archers and soldiers that had gathered on the other bank. Rose frowned at the group; it was rather large for a simple tracking party. Were they sent by Jeremiah? Or by Lancelot? Did they know the group was following to rescue Captain?

Amaya nodded before scooping up the little girl and holding her securely with one arm. She then directed the rest of the group for the trees. At the edge, she paused to make sure all the crew made it. Jabez followed, but Tristan paused when he noticed Solomon and Zatook enter the fray on the other bank. He considered joining them; however, he decided to give Amaya a break. Ducking into the trees, he whisked Arianna into his arms. His sister hugged him tightly as the group moved farther into the woods. Rose stopped at the edge of the wood, peering over her shoulder and watching the two figures amidst the sea of faces. She looked back at Amaya.

"To a campsite, I presume?"

"Well, if you're wanting to be a pincushion, be my guest; otherwise, yes," Amaya replied jokingly. She then quickly followed the pirates into the thick of the trees. Rose glanced at the two on the far side of the bank once more and stopped. There were more enemy soldiers advancing towards the fight. She looked between the battle and the retreating group. *I'm going to help them*, she informed Tristan. *They are now outnumbered. Please stay and watch over your sister. I am concerned there may be two groups.*

Very well. Be safe. Tristan continued to follow Amaya and Jabez. When he felt his sister snuggle her face against his neck, Tristan glanced down at her. Feelings of fear and sadness washed over him from her. He hugged her comfortingly. "Everything's going to be fine, Arianna," he assured her.

As Rose ran, she let her power slowly awaken. A thin red light began to pulsate from her. It spread around her, forming into a crimson armor with black edges. Much like Lancelot's, her armor was more lightweight and thin, a solid-seeming piece of metal rather than shifting plates. She let her cloak fall to the ground as she leapt from the bank, not once landing on the river. When the Scarlet Swordsman landed in the midst of battle, fighting against them, panic spread through the Nocium force.

*****

Alconai shifted a bit as he struggled to keep up with the wagon. He now carried Captain on his back thanks to bloody stupid Lancelot. The knight had been taxing Captain's eye for the better part of the journey. Alconai stumbled slightly but just managed to stay upright. He imagined he now looked similar to Captain's condition, especially given the soldiers trying to make him fall.

Despite everything she had been through, Captain had yet to lose her smile when conscious around Alconai— it was tired, yes, but there. The girl's will was simply amazing. She even found the energy to insult Lancelot from time to time, her language growing more creative— the latest one was to call him the mutated spawn of a banana. Captain tightened her grip wearily as the guards attempted to trip Alconai, but she lifted her head when the wagon ahead of them slowed. A horseman was approaching them swiftly. Captain watched as the newcomer spoke with Lancelot up front.

"Ah, bugger i'," she muttered, "nae anothe' un..." She laughed slightly before burying her face in Alconai's back to hide her coughs. Warm liquid spattered the back of his neck.

"Hang in t'ere, lass. Don'cha be dyin' on me ye'," Alconai coaxed. He gave her a reassuring squeeze with his arms and kept forward. He watched the men for a bit. His eyes studied the horseman's lips intently, calculatingly. Nothing of interest. Just reporting on the goings on in the kingdom. How droll. He dropped his gaze to the back of the wagon, ignoring the blood drops sliding down his neck. He was already dirty, no need to fuss over it. The blood did cause him to feel concern for Captain's wellbeing, though. Captain nodded, laughing slightly.

"I mus' seem a mess. What'll 'Maya say?" she murmured, laying her head on Alconai's shoulder. The word 'intercept' drifted back from the two men. Alconai's head snapped up. He peered at the horseman's lips again.

"...Battalion o' soldiers and archers...intercept crew...make haste...or was tha' 'paste'?...no, haste..." Alconai muttered, concentrating. "Something about shrapnel...no, wait...oh, capital...how'd I get shrapnel? My eyes must be goin'. He talkin' 'bout your friends, love? Sounds like trouble. And I'm missin' all the action. What'll Jabie say?" Captain's head snapped up, and she winced.

"I ken yer name was familiar!" Her eye was wide in surprise. "J-jabie...tol' me...'bout ye..." She shuddered as all the energy left her body. That spark had been the last she was allowed for a little while. Her grip around his neck slipped, and she started to fall.

"Ye ken Jabie?" Alconai asked in surprise; however, he felt Captain falling. He braced himself for when Captain's bound hands applied pressure to his throat, choking him slightly. With some difficulty, he shifted her weight to ease the pull on his neck. He suddenly felt something snare against his leg, causing him to trip. A guard had apparently decided to take advantage of Alconai's distraction to finally make the minstrel fall. He gave it a valiant try, but in the end Alconai wound up falling forward into the dirt, the wagon now dragging him behind it. *I'm goin' ta feel t'is tomorrow*, he thought dryly.

The guard's laughter was interrupted by Finnegan's bark. "Oi, lad, are yer ears full o' wax? We was jus' sayin' we needed to get them up in the cage an' speed up!" The wagon stopped while Finnegan lectured the soldier, and armored feet soon appeared at Alconai's head. Alconai heard a clang of metal as Lancelot opened the cage on the back of the wagon before having both prisoners tossed in. Lancelot said not a word as he climbed back up front. The horses took off with a lurch, the wagon now moving at a faster pace. Captain lay on her side, curled in a ball. Her eyes twitched, and she clutched the side of her face with a groan. Alconai reached over and brushed back some of Captain's hair. "Donnae ken wha' more I can do to 'elp. Want me ta kiss it be'er or somethin'?" he asked, trying to take her mind off things a bit. He closed his eyes. *Wonder what Jabez is doing.*

***

The pirates at the front of the line stopped moving, quickly pulling their swords out of their sheaths.

"Welcome." A smooth voice drifted from the clearing ahead. A woman sat upon a boulder in the middle of the clearing with her ankles crossed. She was certainly not dressed for battle, wearing a rather alluring red dress with a long slit up the side. Ebony hair coiled intricately upon her head, and her pale skin was smooth and inviting. Painted red lips smiled at the men in the group. Moving to the front of the crew, Amaya eyed the woman disdainfully.

"And who the heck are you supposed to be?" she demanded. Tristan watched the woman. His eyes darkened with a dangerous look as he stared her down. There was something off about her. Beside him, Jabez raised an eyebrow. He kept his weapon ready, but he made no move to attack on the off chance she might be a potential ally. The woman stretched slowly, showcasing her form before sliding off the boulder. Most of the pirates had lowered their weapons, their eyes glazed.

"Now, now, what sort of greeting is this, hm?" she chided in a teasing manner. Tristan stared at the woman. His sword arm started to lower, but he didn't really know why. Arianna tugged questioningly on his shirt. As his senses clouded, Tristan carefully lowered his sister to stand on her own feet. He then nudged her behind him, still trying to protect her even as he felt his resolve weaken. He couldn't even see straight now. He tried to glare at the woman; however, he couldn't even pinpoint her location— *whoa.* Tristan's sight suddenly zeroed in on the woman, as if all his senses suddenly focused on her. He started when he heard Jabez cry out in pain. The older man fell to a knee, clutching the left side of his face. Tristan frowned, wondering briefly if the woman had possessed the ninja somehow. Amaya looked from the men to the woman. She tossed her dagger up and caught it by the tip of the blade.

"Either you stop, enchantress, or we'll see how pretty you are when I carve your face with scars," the pirate woman warned. The woman laughed coyly.

"Oh, what is the matter? Am I stealing your boy-toys? Hm?" The woman in red walked over to one of the pirates, running the back of her hand down his cheek; he shuddered under her touch. "So demanding..." She paused as Jabez cried out, blinking over at him in surprise. "Whatever is the matter with him?"

***

Captain felt as though her head was going to tear in two. The crescent mark on her eye shone with a rainbow shimmer as the channel opened *itself*. Her powers were going out of control. Suddenly, Jabez was connected. Not just by sight, as before: sound, touch, *everything* screamed in his mind. Alconai felt at a loss. He didn't know what to do. What could he do? As the wagon continued the bumpy journey to the capital, he just tried his best to comfort and support Captain.

Captain grit her teeth, every muscle in her body taut. She tried to protect Jabez's mind as much as possible. This had happened to her before, but Amaya had been there; that was the day Solomon had come, as if he had heard her crying out. He had— done *something*. Her mind had calmed. *Where is he? Where are the others? Are they coming?* These thoughts, memories of pain, and more skid through Jabez's mind, Captain completely unable to hide them.

***

We're trying, Captain. Bit delayed, I'm afraid, Jabez barely managed to get the thought across through all the pain wracking him. He continued gripping his head. He couldn't even concentrate enough to retort to the woman's comment. He felt warm blood trickle from his nose with the strain of the connection and the power flaring it. Attempting to tighten his grip on his sword, Tristan tried to pull his gaze from the woman.

"Stop," he ordered, his voice strained. Panic gripped his heart. He felt Arianna clutching his pant leg, her presence giving him a bit of an anchor. He had to protect her, but how could he if he couldn't clear his mind?

The woman in red gave an amused laugh. "Why should I stop?" she questioned, sliding her eyes towards Tristan. "This is all quite entertaining."

Tristan actually blushed when her gaze landed on him. "Who are you?" His voice sounded a mix of determined and awe-struck. Was she one of his father's followers? She didn't seem to be, and yet Tristan had been away long enough who knew what minions his father could have acquired? He had to admit she was rather beautiful. An image suddenly flashed through his mind: Rose by the water with her hair shining like starlight in the darkness of the forest. His gaze focused for a moment as the thought cleared his mind. Amaya came around behind the woman while her gaze was elsewhere and swung at her with her dagger.

Let me...help you... Captain's mental voice was strained, but Jabez could feel the strange power coursing through her. A power, he sensed, that had yet to come out around anyone besides Amaya and Solomon. Captain's biggest secret.

Sure thing, Jabez agreed wearily. The woman spun to the side almost like a dancer, avoiding the attack. She halted her spin by bracing and lifting her arm, a long metal armlet blocking Amaya's follow-up swing.

"That wasn't very nice," she chided. "Boys, restrain them please." Her voice turned into a silken purr as the other pirates moved to do her bidding, splitting up to capture Amaya and Tristan. The woman in red didn't notice the rainbow energy starting to spiral around Jabez's arms. She was, however, startlingly aware of Solomon and Zatook dashing through the trees in order to tackle Amaya and the others out of the way just as a blast of rainbow energy erupted from the ninja towards them; the power disintegrated everything in its path, leaving a trench and nothing else in its wake. Tristan was just barely able to sense the woman vanish into the trees; she didn't reappear. She knew better. Once his mind cleared of the woman's trance, Tristan glared after her even as he gathered a crying Arianna into his arms. He hugged his sister to comfort her. Amaya sighed in exasperation as she picked herself up.

Jabez collapsed to his knees, coughing up a little blood. The liquid soaked into the dark fabric of his mask, but he didn't remove the cloth. He felt like someone had just used him as a cannon— oh, wait, she did. Solomon was quickly beside Jabez, steadying the ninja. That strange, soothing feeling passed through him and on to Captain as well, calming both of them and allowing the power to ease. Solomon was still panting from their battle and latest sprint; it took a moment for the pirates to register that the two returned warriors were covered in muck, though it looked like more mud than blood. Jabez shuddered under Solomon's hands but breathed softly in relief as the feeling passed. His eyes wearily glanced over everyone, checking them to make sure everyone was all right. Shakily, he tried to stand.

Arianna continued to cry on Tristan's shoulder as her brother regained his feet. He sighed sadly, glancing down at her. Looking back in the direction of the channel, for a brief second, he considered turning back. Arianna didn't need to get involved in this, and, as much as he wanted to help Captain, Arianna's safety came first. Despite what Captain and the others said, he couldn't help feeling he'd have an easier time keeping his sister safe if they stayed in the forest. Or perhaps he could find them someplace else for now. Either way, his sister didn't need to be in or to see all this violence. Amaya barked orders to get farther in the woods. She smacked a couple of the pirates and ordered scouts to find a place to camp. It was getting too dark to continue their trek, but she didn't want to camp here now that they'd been discovered. That's all she needed. Wake up with a blade in her face. As the others started moving, Tristan remained rooted. Indecision dominated his demeanor. He absent-mindedly rubbed Arianna's back as he thought.

Rose came up behind Tristan, her reclaimed cloak draped over her arm. A few of the pirates hesitated as they caught sight of her. Like the two men that had come before, the blood of her enemies trailed across her skin, though without the mud; however, even as they watched, the Half-Drow's eyes stained pure red— the blood lifted away and vanished. Her eyes returned to normal as she placed a hand on Tristan's shoulder.

"Are you injured?" She shot a glare at the pirates, and they quickly retreated. She knew they could catch up to the camp, so she made no move to follow.

"No," Tristan answered her quietly. Meeting her gaze, he asked in turn, "You?" His mind recalled envisioning her while in the enchantress' grasp, but he wasn't entirely sure why he had. Even as he watched Rose, he continued to rub Arianna's back as the child slowly calmed.

"Nothing serious. I've already healed it," she assured him calmly. She lifted a hand to gently rub Arianna's back, concern flashing across her gaze. "Those two fought well," she added, nodding after the others. "For seeming to dislike his presence, Solomon knew how to complement Zatook's fighting style."

Tristan followed her line of sight. "They seem to have some kind of history," he agreed quietly. After a moment he sighed. "I don't know what to do. If things keep going like this, I'm afraid Arianna will be in more danger than if we stayed in Nikko Mori." His gaze lowered in uncertainty. "But I don't want to just leave Captain either," he confessed. "It's by protecting us that she was captured, so I feel it only right that I help her."

Rose gently wrapped her arms around the pair, pulling Tristan into a hug. "I am sorry. Had I not come through your forest, you would have remained undiscovered." She shook her head. "But that has passed, and you are known. Whether with us or no, Jeremiah will hunt you. As will your father, from the sound of things. The best way to end this is to defeat them. I don't want either of them to find you or Arianna. Even more than that..." She hesitated. After a moment of silence, a single thought floated across his mind: *I don't want you to leave.*

Tristan startled when Rose hugged him. Slowly, his free arm slipped around her back and pulled her close to him. It felt strange to hold someone other than his sister. She didn't want him to leave? Her words caught him off guard as much as her hug. And yet, they sent an emotion through him he didn't quite understand. He did know that he didn't want to leave, either. As much as he missed the forest and worried for his sister's safety, he liked traveling with the pirates. He enjoyed spending time with Rose—something about her drew him to her and it seemed her to him.

I...I don't want to leave you, he confessed.

Then it's agreed. Come what may, we'll face it together, Rose promised, leaning against his shoulder and smiling at Arianna encouragingly. Arianna tried to give her a brave smile. She had finally calmed down, but Tristan still felt her tears trickling down his neck. In a quiet voice, he sang to her— the lullaby his mother used to sing to him before she died. Arianna sniffled a bit, but her grip on Tristan started loosening. Soon she snuggled her head on Tristan's shoulder and fell asleep. As he continued rocking her, Tristan considered what Rose had suggested earlier in the trip.

Should we act on your plan? I'm not sure how I feel about leaving Arianna, but Amaya and Solomon seem like they would keep her safe. And the sooner we get Captain back, the sooner we can find a safer place for her, he noted over their connection.

Rose hesitated. *I am uncertain. I have little doubt our abilities would suffice, but Amaya seems adamant that we stay together. Yet I fear under Lancelot's watch, Captain may not make it to trial.*

Is he really that bad? Tristan asked. He had only known his father's followers, and some of those he knew could be cruel. But he didn't know of King Arden's men.

Rose sighed. *On his own? No. But with his prisoners, he becomes a whole different person. I have…often wondered if he acted under his own power, but I was not allowed to use my abilities to discern such things outside of orders.*

Do you think he's under someone's power? Like a mage or some such? His mind recalled the woman he'd faced just moments ago. Or would the one in charge be far worse?

It is a possibility, Rose confirmed, lifting her head to meet his gaze. *And from what I have seen of Captain, she is faring poorly as it is.*

Shifting Arianna in his arms, Tristan began leading their trio to where the pirates had set up camp. *Then we best not wait. I can lay Arianna in the camp, and then we can make an excuse to go search for something.* Plans in place, they moved to catch up with the others.

Trust

"Solomon, Zatook, you two are a mess! Wash up when you get the chance or no supper for you!" Amaya yelled at the two Order members. Tristan watched the first mate moving throughout the camp, juggling several tasks as she had on the ship. Rose couldn't help a soft snicker as Zatook and Solomon ducked away to find the river. She moved as though to find her own camping space just under the trees. She always camped near but not within the pirate camp. She nodded to Solomon as the man returned and moved to check on Jabez. The older man knelt beside the ninja.

"How are you feeling?" he asked softly. He knew all too well the power behind that blast— he had seen what it could do to Captain. The ninja was sitting on the ground and leaning against a tree. His breathing sounded labored as he attempted to catch his breath after the ordeal earlier.

"Just…glad I could help," he rasped. "A little rest, and I'll be fine, I'm sure." The back and forth channeling had sapped his energy clean out of him. Then Captain used him as a human cannon. So now, he was beyond tired and felt like a rag-doll. Jabez's eyes slowly drifted shut, his body slumping slightly. He sighed heavily, forcing his eyes open again. "What I feel like the most right now is a failure," he intoned softly. His hands shook subtly. His gaze was distant, lost in memories.

Solomon touched a hand to Jabez's shoulder. "You are

doing very well. Not many can withstand Captain's power without some form of protective enchantment. You have not failed; you only fail if you abandon hope." Silently, Jabez nodded. He glanced around at the group. What a strange band they made. Then again, he, Solomon, Amaya, and Captain made quite the team once upon a time.

"We had all three of the Chosen Children. Now one of them— the one we've protected for so long —is a prisoner of the king's guards," he murmured. "Irony much?"

Solomon chuckled. "At least King Arden does not have her yet," he noted. "And if we have anything to say about it, he will not get her." He shifted to a sitting position. "The presence of the soldiers concerns me. It seems they know we are coming, but I am unsure how they knew where to find us. It is possible they have someone who has the Sight or a scrying spell." He glanced up when Tristan exited his and Arianna's tent.

Jabez shrugged. "Probably," he commented. His gaze shifted to Tristan, watching the boy move to talk to Amaya. The ninja shifted, his eyes looking suddenly alert as Tristan motioned to the woods. Amaya eyed the boy for a moment but reluctantly nodded, and the lad headed back into the forest. As Jabez watched, he noticed Amaya's gaze lingering on the boy before she moved to continue looking after the crew. The ninja huffed a soft chuckle. She knew. And she let him go anyway. "And there go the other two Chosen Children. I think they're enacting Rose's earlier suggestion, and Amaya seems on board with it this time. Though, she's letting the kids think she doesn't know what they're doing."

Solomon sighed. "Our enemy has changed tactics; we must do the same. Perhaps this is Shaddai's way of helping us learn to trust them. Still, I do not like the pair of them going alone. There are few among us who could keep up with a Half-Drow at full speed, and I believe there is more to Tristan than he lets on." He paused when Zatook returned from the river, the silent warrior shaking out his wet hair. A look of conflict crossed behind the pirate's expression before he stood and moved towards Amaya. Amaya glanced at Zatook, noting his wet hair. She smirked, but then she turned her attention to the approaching pirate. Her smirk didn't fade.

"Yes, I'm aware the other two Chosen Children just took off. No, I'm not too keen on the idea, and yes, I was planning to send someone to tail them," she remarked coolly but cheekily.

Solomon quirked an eyebrow. "I had assumed as much. I came to offer the suggestion of Zatook. He can travel very quickly, faster even than Elven-kin."

"Fair," the first mate acquiesced. "He shouldn't have trouble finding them, and he's so quiet they might never know he was there. Then again, they might welcome the help." Waving to Zatook, Amaya called him over. "Gotta job for ye. Tristan and Rose went off ahead of us to find Captain. Go on after them and just make sure they don't get killed. Think ye can handle that?" She winked at him. Zatook nodded. He touched a hand to his forehead, his heart, and then his mouth in the Order's formal salute before disappearing beneath the trees. The next the pirates knew of him, a large burst of air gusted through the camp before all was still once more.

***

129

Captain had been sleeping deeply against Alconai's shoulder. Though he didn't know about her exchange with Jabez, she had grown considerably calmer and more comfortable. Lancelot had kept the wagon moving through the night, though he had fallen rather quiet. The rest of their escort were currently taking their orders from Finnegan. Alconai lay back in the wagon. His hat covered his face as though he were asleep; however, he was as awake as ever. He didn't know what had happened, but he felt glad Captain no longer seemed to be in pain. Judging by the fast pace and the landscape he had spied, they were on their way to the city of Thorn-Drake.

Finnegan made a noise, the horses responding and slowing to a halt. He glanced between Lancelot and the two prisoners.

"Well, now, here be a slight conundrum, eh?" It took a moment to translate what he was saying, the knight's accent thicker than Alconai and Captain's combined. "Me chum's go' some business here, an I cannae have him bein' all cold an' grumpy wit' t'e nobles, can I?" He glanced over at Alconai, amusement on his features. Alconai peeked at him from beneath his hat, narrowing his eyes at the knight. "A' the same time, I cannae have you interfering or getting help, can I?" He pointed a finger at Alconai and made an odd motion. "So, a curse of silence I place on ye. Enjoy." With a click from his teeth, the horses lurched forward once more. Lancelot made no move, no reaction, during the entire exchange.

Alconai glared at Finnegan. *Curse ye, ya slimy git. May yer eyeballs mel' ou' o' t'eir socke's!* Alconai settled down again. He had other ways of being heard without a voice. Not the first time he'd been cursed. Sighing, he shifted to get comfortable again as he contemplated this discovery. Finnegan was a mage at least to be able to cast curses. It would explain a few things if the man was using magic to control Lancelot. The question now was what kind.

Finnegan chuckled deep in his throat before clicking at his horse so that it quickened its step to come alongside Lancelot. He then reached up, taking off his glove and biting his finger. A small trickle of blood appeared, and he flung it over at the senior knight. It vanished into Lancelot's armor. Finnegan then replaced the glove and reached over to shake the knight. "Lancelot, we be here." The knight stirred, raising his head.

"Hm?" He blinked, looking up and glancing around. He reached up, taking off his helmet as he stared at Thorn-Drake. A look of confusion and then recognition passed behind his clear blue eyes, and suddenly he smiled. He turned to the horseman. "Many thanks, comrade. I trust I can leave my charges in your care?" His voice sounded completely different. Rather than cold and devoid of emotion, he seemed energetic and lighthearted. The face beneath the helmet was oddly soft and gentle, with pure golden mussed hair. The horseman merely nodded as they passed through the gate, directing the wagon towards the guardhouse. Lancelot stood, dropping down from the still-moving wagon and heading for the guardhouse to polish his armor— and himself —before heading to his meetings.

Alconai glared after Lancelot. Well, that explained a lot. So, the horseman was a blood mage. *'ow perfect*, he thought derisively. From the look of it, his friend didn't seem to know he was being controlled. Alconai wasn't sure if it'd make a difference for him to try and get Lancelot's attention, but at least the man might realize something weird was happening and be able to start resisting it. After carefully shifting Captain, Alconai fished a tiny, metal spike from his boot and started using it to tap out a message on the cage bars. It was a code Lancelot and he had developed in their childhood.

Lance paused when he just caught the tapping, turning to look around where the cart had parked. Generally, if Nai was tapping at him these days, he wanted to get him away from the other soldiers. Probably picked a fight with the town guard about his stories or something. But he didn't see his friend's well-worn cloak or ready grin. As he turned to look back towards the wagon, his blue eyes seemed to pass right over the cage without taking it in.

"Oi, ye lug, quit yer lollygagging," Finnegan jibed as he handed off the reins of his horse to another guard. "They'll have seen us coming and be waiting for you."

Lance frowned, a slight knit to his brow, but he let out a soft 'yeah', and turned to head off. Nai would have to wait. Besides, if he was near enough for Lance to hear, he no doubt heard Finnegan in turn and realized Lance had something he had to do before they could really talk. He shook his head, moving down the street.

Alconai considered for a moment. While he didn't really want to give Finnegan another chance to take over Lancelot, he knew there wasn't a whole lot either of them could do at the moment. There was a good chance if he pushed it, the blood mage would take over Lancelot to thwart Alconai's efforts. He just had to trust that his friend would come find him. Silently, he prayed to the Sacreds for guidance. Alconai shifted back into a seated position and leaned against the side of the wagon. First his brother had been taken and now a blood mage was controlling his best friend. What an adventure this was turning out to be. Alconai pondered these thoughts as he was dragged from the wagon and into the guardhouse.

***

Arianna woke with a start. She couldn't feel Tristan anywhere. Quickly scrambling off the bedroll and out of the tent, the child spun a small circle in search of her brother. Her eyes darted around the camp, but still she saw no sign of Tristan. Hurrying over to Solomon, she grabbed the big man's hand and started tugging it urgently. Waves of confusion and fear slammed into him. Tears started in Arianna's eyes as she desperately tried to send her feelings to her brother but with no success. Tristan was long gone. Solomon quickly took to a knee, pulling the little girl into his arms.

"Easy, Arianna, easy," he soothed, gently smoothing her hair. "It is all right. Your brother is well." Arianna continued to cry as she wrapped her arms around his neck and hugged Solomon tightly. Her tears trickled down his skin as she cried against his shoulder. From where she'd been watching, Amaya gave the little girl a sympathetic look. She moved to her friend currently holding the child and knelt to their level. Rubbing the girl's back soothingly, Amaya tried to comfort her.

"Oh, dear child. What be these tears, eh?" she questioned gently. "Your brother will be back soon enough, won't he? Yes. Don't ye worry, Anna."

Solomon rocked the young girl. "Aye, he'll be back," he echoed. "Maybe they'll even have Captain with them by the time we catch up." Slowly, Arianna calmed, but Solomon could still feel her heartache. She had never been away from her brother, and even when he did leave to hunt and such, he was never far. Now, he had gone without a trace. Amaya sighed but left the little girl in Solomon's capable hands. For now, the woman attended the rest of the camp.

*****

Rose sat at the edge of the circle of light the fire provided. She and Tristan had covered a lot of ground, even picking up a trail for the wagon in one of the villages they passed. They had finally paused to rest and eat. Rose felt a small sense of unease— almost as though instead of the hunters, they were the hunted. She glanced around in all directions, her dark vision seeing far more than most humans would see even during the day. Despite her keen vision, she didn't see Zatook until he landed just outside the light of the fire with a soft whoosh of air. From where he'd been surveying the land, Tristan spun around, his hand instantly going to his sword. However, he slowly lowered his arm when he saw it was only Zatook. He did wonder how the man found them so quickly. Then again, the man didn't seem like a normal human already. Tristan decided not to pursue answers at this time, simply releasing his blade and relaxing.

"I guess Amaya sent you," he murmured. "Well, we're not going back without Captain." Zatook only nodded, sitting beside the fire with his legs crossed. Rose stared at him a moment, but it was clear he had no plans of dragging them back.

I... think he's here to help us, she noted hesitantly to Tristan.

Tristan watched Zatook. *Well, we'll have a better chance if he does.* "You're going to help us? We're almost there anyway." Zatook merely nodded again in response. Tristan's eyes strayed to the stars.

He thought of nights similar to this, when he would watch the night sky with his sister and sing his mother's lullaby to her. Guilt gripped him at the thought. He hoped Arianna was all right with Solomon and Amaya. He also hoped she'd forgive him for leaving her with people they barely knew. His thoughts halted abruptly when a sudden chill shimmied down his spine. He knew that feeling all too well. Tristan forced himself not to look around; he knew he wouldn't see anything anyway.

Rose settled back down by their fire, offering the silent warrior some of the meat she had been cooking. Zatook eyed the piece in his hands for a moment, then glanced at them. With a sigh, he lowered his face mask. Rose wasn't surprised by the scars covering the areas he kept hidden; she was surprised by their shapes. While a few scars may have been from various battles, all the rest were Xs. Large ones, small ones, smooth and rough. Some lined neatly, others crammed in the gaps where they could fit. A few even stretched across his lips.

Tristan glanced at Zatook, noting the man's scars. However, he made sure not to stare. Perhaps he could heal them later when things had calmed down a little. For now, he kept watch. He gripped his sword hilt a little tighter and tucked his emotions further down, but he felt the chill again. Part of him wanted to push the feeling away, but he knew that would only make things worse. His father was looking for him.

Rose watched him quietly. She could practically feel the tension in the air, but she didn't pry into his thoughts. "Tristan. Eat. We will need our energy when we catch up to them." Tristan hesitated but then moved to the fire. Slowly he chewed the meat Rose gave him, nodding his appreciation. He sat near Rose as he watched the horizon, thinking of things to come.

"My father's trying to find me," he murmured. "We should move as soon as possible."

Rose nodded. "When we've finished eating, then. I can go for longer than a human without sleep, but food only lasts so long." She hesitated, glancing at Zatook, but he made no move to protest. She took that as agreement. Tristan nodded his own agreement.

"I'll be fine for traveling longer," he said. He wanted to get Captain and get back to Amaya before his father sent an army after them. He also wanted to return to his sister as soon as possible; no doubt she was worried about him and possibly scared. Once more, Tristan felt guilt weigh on his heart. He hated leaving her— all the more reason for them to finish this and return.

Broken Bonds

Alconai shifted to sit against the wall. Finnegan had confiscated his metal rod after he attempted to get Lance's attention, but the cocky git hadn't thought to see if he had more. Once he knew he was alone, he dug a new tiny rod from his boot and began work on his shackles. Alconai figured this was as good a place as any to escape. He needed to get Captain away from here before they both ended up on the gallows. With Finnegan being a blood mage and controlling Lancelot, things were likely to go bad fast. At least Finnegan had dropped the curse. Captain slept deeply in the next cell over. She hadn't stirred since curling against him in the wagon. As much as Alconai wanted to help his friend, he needed to get Captain to safety first.

He paused in his digging when he heard a commotion beyond the door to the guard room. Lance was back, though from the sound of things he was controlled once more. Most likely Finnegan wasn't going to give him a chance to investigate the tapping. What caught Nai's attention, however, were the orders his friend was giving. It sounded like they expected trouble, and soon. They were upping the guard around the station— great —and expecting...reinforcements? Why would a town guard need reinforcements? He shook his head, getting back to the lock. No matter; it may just be the perfect distraction for him to slip out with Captain— or this could nip his plans in the bud. Time would tell; either way, they didn't have much.

***

Eventually Tristan, Rose, and Zatook made it to the edge of Thorn-Drake. The group stopped to survey the area as they planned their attack. Rose watched the city carefully, her eyes staining red as she looked beyond the walls and homes.

"If I remember correctly, that's the guardhouse," she mused. She shifted, drawing a rough map of the city in the dirt and marking where she remembered the prisoners being kept. "Don't let the walls worry you. Thorn-Drake is one of the more defensive cities, but they aren't heavily armed. Mostly guardsmen, occasionally some soldiers. We know with Lancelot and company present, there are two knights."

"Can you pinpoint Lancelot? I can keep him distracted at least if need be," Tristan told them. He hoped he could do this without using his powers. They didn't need more trouble. "Zatook, you should probably get Captain. You seem like you're the stealthy type, and the guardhouse will have several soldiers in it." Zatook nodded in affirmation, glancing towards the town.

"He's just outside of the guardhouse. And he's not alone. I sense blood magic." Rose frowned deeply. "Unnatural at that. There's a mage in there, and he's not a Drow." Her voice was a soft growl at the revelation. "I'll take that one, then." Tristan sighed and focused on the essences, his eyes sharpening and seeming to glow slightly in the darkness. With her amulet that she'd shown him, Tristan couldn't make out Captain's essence, but— from Rose's description —he managed to find Lancelot. Motioning the other two to move, Tristan silently made his way into town with them.

He sensed the wards as they approached. Clo had taught him about wards and even how to cast a few. These he could tell were meant as alarms for attacks and escaped prisoners. They wouldn't react to the newcomers. Well, not yet anyway.

As they drew closer to the guardhouse, Tristan split off from Rose and Zatook, slipping through the shadows as silently as if he was back in the forest. When he drew close enough, Tristan stopped. He debated using his bow, but being in town didn't provide a lot of advantage for a long-range weapon. As he studied Lancelot's armor, he realized it was designed like the Scarlet Swordswoman's: no seams. Just one solid piece, and Tristan had no way of knowing if his arrows could pierce it. Sighing, he drew his sword. His father had Tristan trained in a few different weapons and styles when Tristan was younger, but he didn't know if his skills would be enough to keep up with an experienced knight. Still, he only needed to distract, not defeat. Stepping from the shadows, Tristan stood before the knight, watching him calmly. It was possible the guards would know his face if his father had a bounty for his capture.

"Might I convince you to release my friend so as to avoid senseless battle?" he asked calmly. There was a lull. A pause between the conversation of the guards ending. A breath that ended in the sigh of Lancelot's own blade leaving its sheath.

"Secure the prisoners. I doubt he came alone." Lancelot stepped away from the guardhouse towards Tristan, blade at the ready. "Nightshade. So, you've come out of hiding at last."

So much for stealth, Tristan thought. However, he trusted

Zatook and Rose to handle the others. For now, he needed to focus on his own battle.

"I take that as a 'no', then," he remarked calmly. He decided to let Lancelot strike first to get a glimpse of his opponent's style. Despite having lived in a forest for the last seven years, Tristan poised himself in the appropriate stance, attesting to his knowledge and practice of the fighting style. Lancelot and Tristan circled each other a moment, both having the same thought— let the opponent come first. But he knew there were more because of the message they had received; he couldn't stay idle for long. Finally, Lancelot darted forward and swung his blade towards Tristan.

Tristan parried the blow and lunged in his own counterstrike. He kept his eyes on his opponent as they danced, their blades ringing with the strikes and blocks. Though Lancelot possessed more experience, Tristan showed his own finesse by keeping up with the knight and not giving an inch. As they broke apart to circle again, a low rumble of thunder broke the silence.

"I must admit, I can see why Lord Shadow Veil wants you brought in alive," Lancelot confessed amidst the ringing of blades, pivoting slightly to parry a blow. "You are quite skilled."

"My skills have little to do with it," Tristan retorted lowly. When another rumble of thunder resounded overhead, his gaze darted up at the clouds, trying to determine if the storm was a natural one or the work of his previous pursuer. He dodged away when Lancelot attempted to rush him while his attention was focused elsewhere. He couldn't keep this up, not if his father's warrior approached in the storm.

Locking blades once more with Lancelot, Tristan suddenly shoved against him with far greater strength than even the strongest of humans. He pinned the knight against a wall. Tristan glared into where he knew his opponent's eyes should be. He needed to buy a little more time, just until Zatook got Captain to safety. Lancelot growled as he struggled against the grip, trying to find some way to break it. Where had this power come from? What was the High Lord hiding about his favored prodigal?

While he kept Lancelot pinned, Tristan's eyes sharpened and glowed as he checked the essences in the guardhouse. What were they waiting for? Even as the thought crossed his mind a sharp pain tore through his chest. Gasping, Tristan grimaced and faltered in his hold. Lancelot took his chance, slipping free and darting around in an effort to turn the grapple against him. He barely noticed the droplets that started to fall from the sky, and yet…they fell heavier than rain. Thicker. Red.

***

Captain grimaced as her eyelids fluttered. Alconai had made it into her cell at this point and was working on her shackles when he saw the now-familiar rainbow shimmer beneath the lids before her eyes opened. "Tell 'im 'e's la'e," she muttered groggily. Alconai arched an eyebrow, but just who Captain meant was answered when the shadows around them suddenly shifted, slithering to life as they surrounded the stones of the wall and then crushed them. Tristan had already alerted the guards after all, the need for silence was slight. Zatook quickly strode in, glaring as the guards Lancelot had sent entered the room. They stopped, staring. They recognized him. It was time to put their fears to reality. Shadows swirled around him before dashing out and disarming the men. They screamed, letting go with a bit more ease than he had anticipated, and fled. Initially, Alconai moved in front of Captain when the shadows began gathering. Now he blinked at Zatook, glancing between the warrior and the fleeing guards.

"I like yer style," he praised cheekily. To Captain he asked, "Friend o' yers?"

"Oh, aye, t'ough we've ye' to meet," Captain murmured. "Oi, 'elp a girl up, would ye luv? T'ey go' more potions a' me camp." Zatook stepped around Alconai, gently lifting Captain to cradle her in his arms. "Ye may as well be comin' wit' us," she noted as cheerily as she could muster. "Jabie'll be righ' glad to see ye, even if he's as expressive as a tur'le some days."

"Ye betcha. I been searchin' for me brudda for thirteen years; there be no way I be wastin' ta opportun'ty to see 'im," Alconai agreed with a bright smile. "'Sides, ta Nocium king donnae fancy me righ' now. Migh' be safer in numbers." He winked at Captain as he adjusted his hat. His thoughts shifted to Lancelot for a moment, but from what he'd seen, Finnegan didn't mean his friend any real harm. And Lancelot wouldn't be killed over a couple of escaped prisoners. To himself, Alconai vowed to return and help Lancelot the first chance he got. For now though, he had a brother to see.

"We shoul' leave while we go' t'e chance. T'e ot'er two are on t'eir way, an' we ainnae in any shape fer an all ou' figh' righ' now." Zatook hesitated as thunder rolled overhead. "Oi, yosh." Captain sighed. "Alrigh', we bes' ge' movin'. Can ye carry both of us?" She glanced up at Zatook, who nodded. A gust of air blew about him as his cloak shifted, rising up and changing shape until two large, ink-black wings extended from his back. The sounds of fighting outside were growing louder. Rose had found her opponent as well, though they fought with more than blades.

Alconai raised an eyebrow at Zatook. Oh, he knew this man. From the display of powers to the guards fleeing, Alconai recognized him from the stories of the Demon of Andor. Captain certainly had some rather fearsome friends, but how had she made such an ally? Questions for later. "Oi, big fella, ye may be strong an' all bu' ye still only 'ave two arms, and Captain needs ye more. I can slip ou' jus' fine if'n ye take Cap'n," he told the warrior. "Soun's like ye go' more friends keepin' ta guards busy." His gaze shifted to the doorway. Was Jabez one of the ones fighting outside? A part of him wanted to go check. Maybe he could help his brother for once. Zatook gave Alconai a flat look. Shadows wrapped around Captain, transporting her to his back and then securing her. He held out a hand towards Alconai. The entertainer quirked an eyebrow at the display.

"I be thinkin' he ainnae takin' 'no' fer an answer," Captain chuckled.

"All righ', all righ'," Alconai surrendered, holding his hands up in a placating manner. He stepped up to the man and took Zatook's hand, but he hesitated when the blood drops fell.

Captain winced. "T'is is bad. Le's go." Zatook nodded, stepping out into the alley with his charges before getting airborne. They could see Tristan and Lancelot locking blades, and a few streets away Rose battled with Finnegan and what guards had not fled. She, too, had hesitated with the blood rain, but Finnegan would not allow her enough respite to grow concerned.

***

Bracing his foot against the wall, Tristan ran up the wall a little, arcing and twisting out of the grip. He staggered back as the pain persisted. He hesitated when the droplets registered. Holding his hand up, he studied the red substance now coating it. As tempted as he was to look up at the sky, he refrained to avoid getting the blood in his eyes. Instead, he focused through the pain and concentrated on Lancelot, taking his stance once more. His gaze flicked upward when he noticed Zatook flying away from the guardhouse with not only Captain but another person as well.

Rose, Zatook is away with Captain. We need to retreat, he called across his connection with the Drow, masking his pain so as not to worry her.

Go. Her voice was a whisper in his mind, her focus on her battle. Finnegan alone would not have presented much challenge, nor the soldiers as a group. Together, however, they were proving rather formidable. She would down a pair of soldiers only for Finnegan to heal them or wound the mage only to be interrupted by the soldiers while he healed himself. And now the rain. She could sense it didn't come from the one across from her, so who?

Tristan frowned at the sound of Rose's voice. As he continued his battle with Lancelot, he broadened his awareness of the essences around him, searching for his comrade. There, amidst a group of soldiers he found her facing the blood mage. *Are you in need of assistance?* he asked, concerned. He didn't want to leave her behind if she couldn't escape on her own. Kicking Lancelot away from him, Tristan dodged down an alley before dashing at speed able to match an Elf-kin.

An opening would be appreciated. I can get away aside from that. Rose growled as she blocked the soldiers' blades, spinning with both of hers to knock them away before pivoting and lunging towards the blood mage. Finnegan hadn't bothered fighting with traditional weapons, whips of crimson extending from his hands.

Tristan considered his options as he closed in on Rose's location. Sheathing his sword, he slowed, ducking into the shadows as he retrieved his bow. These soldiers wore only chainmail under leather armor—plenty of places to penetrate. Using his inhuman abilities once more, he let several arrows loose, the points slamming home in the soldiers. He didn't aim to kill, not this time. They were simply doing their duty. However, he hoped to at least give Rose enough time to escape.

Several more arrows found their targets, incapacitating the soldiers. He pulled an arrow with a point made from his twilight crystal and fired it into the air above the group. *Shield your eyes,* he warned Rose. Calling on his other power, Tristan imbued the crystal with light, the faceted surface of the gem magnifying the brilliance to blind their foes. *Go,* he told her. Eyes closed, Rose used her blood senses to dodge around the soldiers before opening her eyes again and darting towards Tristan.

***

Alconai gave a low whistle as he used his other hand to keep his hat on his head. "T'is is like somethin' straigh' ou' o' one o' me tales," he commented. "Blood magic, dashin' knights ba'ling. T'e works." His grip on Zatook's hand remained tight, but the entertainer seemed otherwise unfazed by the goings on around them.

"Welcome to me life, lad," Captain called cheerily; she frowned when something flickered through the clouds, a shadow. She started to holler to Zatook, to warn him, but the shadow dove faster than her voice could travel. A force drove into them harshly, slamming them down towards the ground. Zatook pulled in his wings, arcing into the dive before righting himself and alighting on the ground. His shadows shifted Captain back to Alconai's grasp, and he gestured them towards the nearby trees. His other hand went out to the side, shadows shifting in a long shape before depositing the hilt of his blade into his hand. He caught it, flaring his wings once more to meet the shadow in the skies where it waited for him. Alconai held Captain to him as he ran for the cover of the trees.

"Donnae suppose ye ken where we be goin'," he commented to the girl in his arms. He ducked under a tree to get out of the blood rain. "Why blood? Tha's jus' disgustin'."

"Fer now? Shelter. So he donnae 'ave to worry abou' protectin' us. Then we'll le' me ot'er friends catch up. Zatook can ge' us to t'e ot'ers from t'ere." She chuckled about the blood. "Some'un be showin' off. And it ainnae tha' son of a frog from t'e wagon." She closed her eyes, reaching to see where the others may be. *Oi, Jabie, 'ave the boys start makin' camp. I wan' somet'ing warm to eat when we ge' t'ere.* She chuckled slightly. What a way to let them know she was safe, right?

Alconai glanced at her. "Wha's wit' all ta blood mages in

t'is town, eh?" he asked incredulously. However, he headed farther into the trees. He didn't see any caves, but he figured the canopy would be enough to protect them for now.

***

I can get us past the wards that've probably been activated, Tristan told Rose as they momentarily paused in an alley. His eyes glanced over her. *Are you all right? Any grievous wounds?* His hand brushed hers lightly a moment as he put away his bow for now.

Nothing I can't handle. We should focus on escape. Rose promised softly. *I sense two presences in the storm. One is fighting Zatook, but the other...Tristan, StormShaper is coming.*

Follow me, Tristan told her before dashing through the alleyways. As they approached the wards, he sent some of his power through them, using Clo's teachings to temporarily dispel the barrier. As they raced toward the edge of the forest, Tristan kept his eyes open for his pursuer. He didn't want to get in a fight with the man, but he realized he might not have a choice.

Rose had nodded, racing after him. She barely noticed something blur ahead of them before StormShaper was there, sword drawn as he pivoted and lunged back towards Tristan. Tristan dodged to the side, narrowly missing him. *Go on ahead. I'll handle him and then join you,* he told Rose. The pain in his chest had subsided for now, thankfully. Dark crystal spikes sprang from the ground in an effort to slow his assailant down. Rose hesitated, glancing up into the sky where Zatook fought, as well, and towards the forest where Captain and her new friend were retreating. With a growl, she turned back towards the woods and ran.

If you get captured, I'll kill you, she threatened in his mind.

StormShaper had pivoted around the crystals, the Obscure fogging his features seeming like a shattered mirror on a carousel. He arced out to the side before leaping up and crashing towards Tristan with the speed of a lightning bolt. Tristan slowed enough to plant his feet and meet the charge. The dark crystal formed a shield in front of his hands to protect him. The impact rent the air with a deafening sound of thunder. Tristan felt his shield strain as his feet skidded back in the crimson mud, but he held firm. Glaring at his opponent, he stepped to the side, guiding the momentum with his shield to send StormShaper around him.

"What do you want?" he growled. "Have you come for me or is your target another?"

StormShaper skidded in the bloodied mud, one hand down to maintain his balance and the other holding his outstretched blade. "I have many missions," he replied cryptically. "You would know this were you to return to our Master." He kicked off from the mud, leaping up and spinning to add momentum to his next strike against the shield. Electricity danced along his blade, testing the crystal as well. The shield held against the blade and the electricity, but Tristan quickly disengaged so the electrical charge wouldn't reach him through the substance. Disintegrating the shield, Tristan pulled his sword once more. He doubted he could hit an opponent this fast with an arrow, so for now he planned to use his blade.

"I will not return to that murderer," he snarled. "He has never been and never will be my master."

"Mere words cannot untie your bond," StormShaper growled, blurring forward again. The wind swirled around them, keeping the droplets of blood away from their battle.

"What *bond?*" Tristan demanded. He met his opponent's blows with vehemence, his eyes flashing with anger. "He has no means to control me any longer. My mother made sure of that. He is nothing to me now."

"His bond as your master. There need not be a physical tie, merely the knowledge of such," the man countered. Surprisingly, or perhaps not, he was meeting Tristan blow for blow.

"*I* don't acknowledge him as my master," Tristan growled. He shoved against StormShaper, frowning when the swordsman barely budged. Calling on his powers, dark crystal spikes sprung from beneath the man's feet to catch him off guard and wound him.

"Your opinion does not change the fact," StormShaper spat. He tensed when he felt the ground shift, springing into a roll away from the spikes. His feet braced in the mud before he leapt back at Tristan, swinging in a wide horizontal arc. Tristan slid on his knees under the blade, the sword whooshing past him. His own blade sliced towards his opponent's legs. He needed to get away and get back to the others, but how? The swordsman was skilled, no question, and he seemed rather persistent.

StormShaper leapt over the blade, letting the wind whisk him a few paces back before throwing himself back towards Tristan. He let loose a flurry of attacks, testing the young man's speed and reflex. The forest dweller met the attack with his own show of finesse. Keeping pace with StormShaper, he dodged and parried the blows, sneaking in a few attacks of his own. Sparks danced between them as their blades continued their deadly dance. Mud caked Tristan's legs and made maneuvering difficult; however, he managed to match his opponent move for move.

StormShaper kept up his assault, waiting. He knew. He knew the other warrior had been running through the night, fleeing their master. He knew the group had been assaulting Thorn-Drake to rescue the Moon Child and that Nightshade had faced off against Lancelot. They were matching blow for blow, now. He just needed to wear him down. Just enough. Mud and blood rain made Tristan's clothes feel heavier, the fabric sticking to him under the leather. He tried to step away from StormShaper to assess his situation, but the warrior gave him no room to disengage. His limbs started to feel heavy, fatigue creeping into his body. Even with his inhuman strength and speed, Tristan couldn't keep going forever. As though to emphasize such a point, he barely dodged a strike from StormShaper, the tip of the blade whistling just shy of his collarbone. However, the strike proved just enough to unbalance Tristan, the lad staggering slightly. StormShaper took his opening. He increased the pace of his attacks, shifting his footwork to fall into a more fluid style. He almost seemed to meld with the wind as he danced around his opponent quickly, working to strike. Anywhere would do. A wound would wear his opponent down faster.

Tristan did his best to keep up, but his own movements began to grow sluggish. At one point he failed to dodge fast enough, and StormShaper's blade sliced across

Tristan's arm. Wincing, Tristan thrust a few dark crystal spikes up from the ground to separate them. He needed to leave. StormShaper leapt back, holding his sword in an odd position as he dodged the spikes. Tristan could only imagine the smirk on StormShaper's face as he eyed the blood trickling down his blade. Holding his hand up, Tristan prepared to use his Child powers to create a blinding light like he did with the soldiers. A sudden coldness engulfing his body halted his attack. Silently, Tristan cursed; he knew this power.

Tristan... the young warrior winced. It felt as though ice ran through his veins, freezing his blood. *Tristan...insolent, disobedient boy. Did you really think I wouldn't find you? You flashed your powers about carelessly upon leaving your mother's protection.*

Tristan glared as he mentally snarled, *Leave me in peace.* However, the icy feeling only grew stronger, stealing his breath. StormShaper had hesitated when he first felt his master's spell. Tristan's blood had run the length of his blade; he had yet to wipe it off. He took the momentary distraction to do so before spinning his blade and readying himself.

Never, the voice of his father stated calmly. Tsukuyomi was no telepath, but Tristan knew there were spells that would allow his father to communicate with him and affect him. They weren't strong enough for Tsukuyomi to control him outright, but he could incapacitate him for a subordinate to take him. He swung his sword in warning when StormShaper approached. *You belong with me, Tristan. My son should stand by my side,* the man coaxed. *Come home.* Tristan backed farther away from StormShaper, trying to concentrate on his opponent rather than his father's influence.

I won't go back to you. Not after what you've done, not when I know what you plan to do. The coldness intensified into a sharp pain.

You understand nothing, child. If you will not come willingly, then my champion will bring you to me. As Tristan started backing away, StormShaper stepped after him. He planted one of his feet in the mud and shifted it before lunging towards the renegade warrior.

Grimacing, Tristan thrust his hand forward, creating a shield of his crystal. Light filled the substance and intensified into a brilliance rivaling the sun. Tristan let the power flow over and through him as well. He felt his father's spell recede in the wake of the holy light. Tristan took his chance and sheathed his blade before racing away and into the forest. Even if it was different from Nikko Mori, Tristan still knew how to disappear among the trees. He left his pursuer behind as he made his way deeper. A dizzy spell forced him to stagger to a stop, leaning against a tree as he waited for the world to still. He knew it would pass soon enough. Between his father's influence and the pain he'd endured during his fight with Lancelot, he wasn't surprised to feel so fatigued. Once he felt sure no one followed him, Tristan allowed himself to slowly slide down the tree trunk to sit at its base, leaning against the bark as he caught his breath.

***

Tristan. Rose's mental voice called back for him, the Half-Drow growing concerned. *Were you able to escape? Do you need my aid?*

I escaped as far as I'm aware. I can make it if I know where to go. Just a little winded, he answered. His eyes scanned the trees with a watchful gaze.

Zatook is still in battle to cover our trail. Captain is guiding me to where she has found shelter. Can you find me?

Perhaps, Tristan answered. He forced himself to his feet and peered into the forest, searching tiredly for Rose's essence. He tried to let their connection guide him as well. Slowly, he began making his way toward where he sensed Rose and the others. Rose had paused to wait for him, leaning against a tree and closing her eyes. Tristan joined her against the tree, closing his own eyes as he rested a moment. "Should someone help Zatook?" he asked quietly. He felt his energy replenishing slowly, but he was still tired.

"They seem evenly matched." She opened her eyes slightly to gaze at the grass. "If the stories of Andor's champion are anything to judge by, he should be fine." She lifted her head, turning to watch him. "You are bleeding," she noted softly, reaching a hand towards the scratch on his shoulder.

Tristan glanced at the wound. "StormShaper. We were evenly matched, but I had already fought Lancelot. I started to tire, and he took the chance to wound me," he explained quietly. "I knew it would be difficult to go up against more seasoned fighters. They've both seen real combat, I'm sure. I trained when I was still with my father, but then I lived in the forest for seven years. Clo taught me what he could, and I continued my own training. But that doesn't compare to actual experience in combat. Life or death. Rain or shine. Being in the forest my fighting style changed to suit my surroundings. Now it needs to change again if I'm to protect my sister and anyone else out here."

Rose slid her finger along the cut, mending it as her eyes stained red. "Once things have calmed down, I can spar with you," she offered softly. "I am sure a few of the others might offer to join in, but you would not need to hold back against me like you might one of the pirates." As her finger reached the edge of the cut, Tristan's hand caught hers.

"I'd like that," he told her softly. His gemstone blue eyes met her stained ones for a moment. "Thank you," he said before slowly releasing her hand. Sighing, he straightened from the tree. "Where's the camp?"

Rose had blinked when he caught her hand, and she blinked again when he met her gaze. Her cheeks felt warm. Why? It took her a moment to process his question, the red receding from her eyes to return her blue and red irises. "Not much farther. Captain has fallen asleep, but she let me see their path before doing so. She also noted that Zatook has a way to transport multiple people long distances, so we can return to the main camp quicker once we're all together. I'm sure Arianna will be glad to see you."

A look of guilt flashed across Tristan's gaze as he looked out into the forest. "She's probably worried. I've never left her with strangers before that she remembers. I just figured the sooner we got Captain back, the sooner we could get Arianna someplace safe." He gestured for Rose to lead the way.

"I can say I agree with the sentiment. And knowing who we faced, it was wise to leave her," she assured him calmly, leading him through the woods to where Alconai had made a small camp.

It was dark, now, the clouds remaining despite the

lightning's retreat. Alconai and Captain hadn't lit a fire, not wanting to be easily found by their enemy— especially with her now asleep. Rose walked easily through the pitch forest, the vision of her people a welcome boon. As they approached the camp, however, she paused long enough to return her hood and scarf. She knew nothing of this 'Alconai' Captain had befriended, and she was wary enough around the pirates. She doubted he could see her, but she wasn't taking chances. She touched a hand to Tristan's wrist to signal they were there.

Tristan returned the gesture as thanks before lifting his head wearily. He focused just enough to see the man's essence and determine his location. "Seems Captain's made a new friend," he commented, partially to alert the man to their presence, though he kept his voice low just in case. Almost without realizing it, Tristan rested his head against Rose's shoulder as exhaustion began to set in his body. He didn't know why he felt comfortable around Rose. He'd begun to see them as kindred spirits, so perhaps that was why he trusted her so readily. Or perhaps he was more tired than he realized. Still, if he got the sense Rose didn't want him leaning on her, he would move.

A warm chuckle acknowledged his comment. "And ye mus' be t'e ones wha' helped wit' t'e jailbreak. Much obliged to ye both for keepin' t'e guards chasin' t'eir tails," Alconai's rich voice greeted them. "Name's Alconai FoxFeet, at yer service." Tristan could just barely see the man's silhouette take a sweeping bow.

"I'm Tristan Nightshade," the younger man introduced. The newcomer seemed nice enough, but Tristan found himself feeling not as wary of Alconai. Perhaps his time with the pirate crew was making him more trusting. "Beside me is our companion Rose."

"'Tis a pleasure," Alconai told Rose cheerily. "Donnae suppose ye ken me brother Jabez, eh? Cap'n mentioned he be travelin' wit' ye."

Tristan blinked slowly, his mind sluggishly processing that bit of information. "You're Jabez's brother?" Really, Tristan shouldn't be surprised. He knew next to nothing about the quiet man. "Aye. He's been traveling with us. Quite the coincidence for Captain to run into his brother as a prisoner."

"Coincidence or Shaddai's Will. T'e king donnae like me spreadin' tales of Shaddai an' t'e Sacreds. So t'e soldiers locked me up to shut me up, and that's where I met yer Cap'n. Spritely one, she is." He grew quiet for a moment. "I been earnin' my way telling t'e stories. S'much as I love singin' and storytellin', me main goal was findin' me brother," he added solemnly. "How is 'e?"

"Being his brother, you'd be better to judge his behavior. He's quiet, reserved, but he seems a good sort. He comes across troubled but companionable all the same," Tristan answered. He heard Alconai sigh softly.

"Thank ye. I wasnae sure wha' to expect." He grew quiet once more for a moment before adding, "I suppose we jus' be waitin' on t'e shadow user, aye?"

"Yes," Rose nodded from where she now sat across from the man. "I have informed him of our current refuge." She had been content to let Tristan handle conversing with the new man; he seemed more comfortable around others than she. Though she couldn't help a soft chuckle; who would have thought the Scarlet Swordsman and the Demon of Andor would work together to break a pirate captain out of jail? Had someone suggested such a thing even a month ago, she would have had them sent to the healers. "Zatook." She lifted her head towards where she sensed the warrior, and he quietly slipped from the trees. He had to make a point to rustle some leaves so the others would know where he was. She brushed against his mind, but he wouldn't let her in. She shook her head, but asked aloud nonetheless: "Do we leave now? Or do you need to rest?"

They both paused when a low peal of thunder rumbled in the distance. For answer, Zatook offered a hand to help her up. "Alconai, you had best retrieve Captain. It seems we are leaving." Rose took the hand before checking to see if Tristan was good to haul himself up. The lad was exhausted— she could tell without her blood magic. They all needed a good night's sleep.

Tristan had moved with Rose when she sat down since she didn't seem to mind him leaning against her. Now, he accepted her help to stand. He allowed his hand to linger in her grip. While he found he enjoyed the warmth of her touch, he also figured this would make it easier for her to guide him in the dark if need be. With as tired as he seemed to be, he didn't trust himself not to trip and fall flat on his face.

"Oi, oi, ye make me soun' like a sack o' produce," Captain murmured from where she had been sleeping, but she didn't turn down Alconai's aid. "Ye donnae 'ave to take us righ' to camp, Zatie," she added with a yawn. "Jabie be ou' scoutin', he can ge' us t'e rest o' t'e way."

With Captain's permission, Alconai swept her up into his arms. The thought of seeing his brother filled him both with excitement as well as anxiety. "Come on, ye lo'. Le's not keep Jabie waitin'."

A soft woosh accompanied a darkness even Rose could not see past surrounding the group. There was no sensation of movement, no breeze, yet when the darkness fell away the group was entirely elsewhere. All save Zatook himself, though Captain didn't seem concerned.

"'efore ye ask, 'e's makin' sure ol' sparky cannae follow us," the Moon Child piped up groggily. "Jabie shoul' be nearby…" She snuggled into Alconai's grip slightly, yawning. Now that they were no longer in the same forest, Rose held out her hand. She could only call the stardust to surround things, but she allowed a soft layer to cover her hand and provide a gentle light for the rest of the group.

Soon enough, Jabez emerged from the shadows, seemingly drawn towards them by the light. As he recognized Alconai though, Jabez hesitated. When the entertainer turned to look at him, the ninja took an involuntary step back. His icy blue gaze held the look of a startled animal as he stared. Alconai for his part raised an eyebrow in question at first, not recognizing Jabez due to his mask. However, considering the previous conversations and the demeanor of the ninja, the pieces quickly clicked into place.

"Oi yosh," the minstrel murmured, squinting at the man. "Is tha'…Jabie? Is tha' ye?" He remembered his brother being taken by ninjas, so the outfit wasn't much of a surprise. But was this really Jabez? And if so, was he dressed for the part because he followed the people who took him?

"Hello...Alconai," Jabez finally responded, his voice uncertain. "It's...it's been thirteen years. You've grown a lot— I hardly recognize you."

"Jabie," the younger brother breathed. Then he set his mouth in a firm line as he gathered his thoughts. "I donnae ken whet'er to deck ye or hug ye. Are ye still wit' t'em sons o' wombats tha' took ye?"

"No, no. I got out a few years ago," Jabez answered.

"T'en why t'e blazes didn' ye come home!" Alconai demanded, his eyes full of desperation and remorse. "Do ye ken 'ow long I been lookin' for ye? I never stopped." The ninja averted his gaze as sadness and shame filled his eyes. Instead of answering, he glanced at Captain and took in the state of the group.

"I promise we'll talk, but for right now we need to get to camp," he told them. Alconai looked as though he might protest, but then he sighed heavily and shifted Captain in his arms.

"Lead t'e way," he murmured.

Jabez nodded. His eyes held a guilty expression. Tristan and Rose shared a glance, but at this point they were more focused on reaching camp before sleep found them first. Captain touched a hand to Alconai's shoulder.

"Oi, oi, I didnae bring ye to jus' deck 'im," she mumbled semi-teasingly. "Give 'im a chance, Nai. 'e's doin' much be'er than 'e was when Sol me' 'im. An' he missed ye to pieces." Alconai watched after Jabez as the latter guided them through the trees. He knew his brother must have suffered at the hands of the people who took him, but Alconai wasn't certain how to feel. He supposed he would just have to talk to him about it later. For now, they needed to reach safety.

Captain's eyes slid to half-mast in his arms as they walked before steadily closing once more.

Fireside Shadows

After a bit of a walk, Jabez arrived with the rescue group to the pirate camp. The men had already pitched tents and gathered supplies to tend any injuries the group may have obtained. He caught Amaya's eye and gestured to Captain. The first mate gave a relieved sigh when she spotted the girl. Approaching Alconai, Amaya reached up and brushed aside some of Captain's bangs.

"Hey, Captain," she greeted gently. "You look like you could use a scrubbing and some clean clothes." Holding out her arms she gestured for Alconai to hand the Moon Child to her. "I've got her, lad. Thank you for your help." Alconai nodded and then gently transitioned Captain from his hold to Amaya's. The first mate held her like the girl weighed little more than a toddler. Captain mumbled something when Amaya took her, curling into the woman's grasp as if it were the most natural place for her to be. She almost looked like a child with her mother if Amaya had looked older. As Amaya moved to a tent to tend Captain, Rose caught Tristan and Alconai's shoulders and pulled them off to the side. Though her hood was back up, Tristan had a fair idea of what she was doing even before she slid her fingers through the blood coating them. She made a small motion, and all of the sanguine droplets gathered together. She let them form an orb before solidifying them and grabbing the crystal-like material to slide in a pouch. With a nod to both, she moved to find a place to sit; one of the pirates brought her a steaming bowl of stew, which she took with a soft thanks. Alconai made his way over to Jabez.

"Quite t'e group ye go'," he remarked as he looked around. "And Captain is t'eir...Captain?" He grinned a little at that. Jabez simply nodded. The brothers' eyes met for a moment as Alconai's smile faded. "All righ'. Damsel's in good care." He adjusted his hat before asking, "How long've ye been free?"

Jabez grimaced, his eyes full of guilt. "Nine years," he answered, averting his gaze. Alconai's eyebrows disappeared into his hat when he raised them, his golden gaze flashing in disbelief and anger.

"T'en why didnae ye come home, Jabie? We've been worried sick o'er ye for *thirteen* years. We 'ad no idea whet'er ye be alive or dead or worse."

"Worse," Jabez interjected. "Much worse. Nai, when I escaped I wasn't in my right mind. The things they'd done...I broke. I broke so badly I had completely lost my mind." Icy blue eyes lifted to meet molten gold. "I didn't escape thanks to cunning or skill or even luck. I snapped and turned on the ninjas who were with me at the time, slaughtering them. I had fallen into a fit of insanity that I didn't know how to wake from."

Jabez shifted his gaze away as he thought back to those dark days. He hooked his fingers into his belt, unsure what to do with his hands but feeling fidgety. "Do you remember Hoshiko? The healer who lived across the river from us when we were kids?"

"Aye, I 'member Miss Hoshiko," Alconai confirmed,

nodding.

"I don't know how, but she found me and managed to get me calm. She started looking after me," Jabez explained. "Those days are hazy at best in my mind, but I remember her presence. Patient and soothing like a light guiding me out of the darkness of my mind." His voice grew fonder with the recounting.

After a moment of silence, he lifted his gaze to watch Solomon across the camp. "I don't remember much of the journey, but Hoshiko took me to the headquarters for the Order. They worked with me, got me healthy again. But it wasn't just my body that needed healing. My mind…I don't remember much of it, but I do know I spent most of the time in fear of anything and everything around me." He caught his brother's gaze once more. "I attacked people, Nai— people who were trying to help me. It took a year just to get me to where I could interact with people more normally. Even then, I wasn't right."

He watched Alconai as his brother watched him, but his younger brother didn't say anything yet, simply listening. Alconai's eyes had lost some of their anger; the emotion now replaced with concern. Jabez sighed, rubbing the top of his head but careful not to remove the cowl. "As better as I was getting, I still had relapses. Solomon," here he gestured to the pirate entertaining Arianna, "he helped me, looked after me all that time. After I'd been there a year and had improved enough, he decided to take me with him on a mission. I never would have thought it would lead to us joining up with Captain and Amaya and eventually joining a pirate crew, but here we are.

I stayed with them for about five years. I still wasn't

comfortable around people, and Solomon had to watch to make sure I didn't relapse and do something harmful— to myself more than others at that point." He chuckled at the memories. "Being around Captain, I couldn't stay in my shell for long. When I felt ready and Solomon was sure I would be alright on my own, I made my way home."

Jabez turned his eyes towards the fire, his gaze distant. "No one was there." He knew the look Alconai gave him without needing to see it: heartbroken realization. "I thought the worst might have happened. But then I started asking around. I learned you had left as soon as you were old enough to search for me, and Da had gone off somewhere— no one knew where or why. They assumed he was looking for me, too.

During my travels, I realized the ninjas that took me were still looking for me. They've never known about me having siblings or living parents. So, to protect you, I stayed away. I didn't try to send correspondence for fear of them finding you. I divided my time between working as an informant for the Order and helping them on occasion. I even tracked you down, Nai, a few times. Got you out of more than one scrape, too." Jabez eyed his brother from the side with a slight twinkle in his gaze. However, he grew somber again as he straightened and turned to fully face Alconai. "I'm sorry. I was trying to protect you, but I should have found a way to get word to you that I was at least alive and well." He fell silent, letting Alconai process everything he'd said. However, to his surprise, Alconai pulled him into a tight hug. Stunned, Jabez slowly put his hands on his brother's back to return the embrace.

"I jus' be glad yer alive, Jabie. We coul' 'ave worked somet'in' ou', figured all t'is ou' toget'er. Bu' t'at's t'at and t'is be now," Alconai told him softly. "I won' pretend ta no' be hurt or angry t'at ye stayed away, bu' I forgive ye. I'm sorry I didnae find ye sooner. Yer me big brother. Ye've always been t'e protector o' our fam'ly. Tha's jus' ye bein' ye. I be tryin' to do be'er, bu' ye beat me to i'." He chuckled as he pulled back to meet his brother's gaze. He reached up with a hand. It wasn't until Alconai's thumb lightly caressed the exposed skin above his mask and came away wet that Jabez registered the tears slipping from his eyes.

He'd dreaded hearing what his family would say to what happened— afraid they'd reject him. He felt so much shame and guilt for what he'd done during his captivity and even after he'd obtained freedom, he hadn't known how to face them. So, he'd protected them from a distance, thinking it was better that way. But his brother forgave him. Jabez felt his heart break even as relief flooded him. Alconai pulled Jabez into another hug as the ninja's shoulders shook with silent sobs. He held Alconai tightly this time and pressed his eyes against his brother's shoulder as he cried.

"Thank you," Jabez whispered. "Thank you for forgiving me."

Alconai rubbed his back. "Always." The brothers pulled away, Jabez wiping at his eyes to dry them. Alconai watched him a moment. "Da went to find his past," he explained softly. "Mum…had left 'im a le'er before she died. She'd given strict instructions tha' he only open it when we be grown. He ne'er told me wha' it said, but he star'ed preparin' to leave soon after. He was goin' to the Temple of Mythril. Tha' was t'e last I heard from him." Alconai shrugged. "I remember 'im always ge'in' headaches. Somet'in' to do wit' 'is lost memories an' tryin' to remember t'em," the redhead remarked.

"He couldn't remember anything from before he met Mum. Maybe she knew something— a clue to where he could start looking for answers," Jabez agreed. He'd been five when his surrogate father, Kouta, had met his mother, Ziv. Alconai had only been a toddler at the time, so the younger brother didn't remember their real father. However, Kouta had taken to the family rather well, and the boys soon enough considered him as their father. Still, Jabez always wondered about the man's life before he came to be with them, and he was sure his father wondered as well. He recalled the headaches Alconai mentioned and how they often went to Hoshiko for medicine and counsel— the same healer who had helped him when he escaped. What would be at a temple of Mythril though? The family were avid believers in Shaddai, but had his father been a follower of Mythril before?

"I donnae ken," Alconai confessed. Then, he laughed. "We always been a family o' misfits an' troublemakers," he teased with a smile. "I suppose it be only fair tha' Da gets a turn." Alconai shook his head. As they lapsed into a bit of awkward silence, he studied his brother's getup, arching an eyebrow curiously. "Go'a admit, bit strange seein' ye in ta garb o' yer captors. When I firs' saw ye, I though' ye were one o' t'em," he teased gently. Even with the mask, Alconai could see his brother's soft smile in the man's eyes. He tilted his head slightly to get Jabez to meet his gaze. "Ye ken ye donnae need to 'ide your face from me, righ'?"

"It's good for stealth and easy to move in. I've also got pieces of light armor that blend with my clothes for some added protection," Jabez answered about the outfit. He hesitated for a moment. "The mask," he sighed before continuing, "it's more for my sake. It helps to keep people from the ninjas from recognizing me. I also have a hard time facing my own reflection. Some scars run farther than skin deep, and I've got both. You've forgiven me, but I have yet to forgive myself."

"Jabie," Alconai started but then seemed to think better of it. Instead he squeezed his brother's arm. "Whene'er ye be ready, we love ye no ma'er wha' ye've done or 'ow ye look. Always have, an' always will."

"Thanks, Nai."

When Solomon saw the group, he gently tapped Arianna's shoulder and pointed Tristan out.

"See there, lass? We told you he would return, right as rain." The lass had been refusing to sleep again; perhaps this would calm her. He had been walking around with her in his arms in an attempt to lull her, but to no avail. Now, he set her on her feet.

Tristan smiled apologetically when his sister whirled around and stared wide-eyed at him. The next instant she ran to him and threw her arms around his neck when he knelt to catch her. The child snuggled her face against the crook of his neck as Tristan stood with her, tucking an arm under her to hold her.

"I'm sorry, Anna," he told her softly. "I'm here now; I'm okay." He glanced at Rose before moving over to Solomon. He'd seen Amaya head into a tent to tend to Captain. "I hope Captain's all right. I didn't have a chance to get a good look at her, and unfortunately I'm a bit tapped out to be much help," the younger man commented. His eyes landed on Jabez speaking with Alconai, but he quickly shifted his gaze away to give them some privacy.

"Tired, but well enough," Solomon assured him. "Amaya is tending her now." He nodded towards the two brothers. "Alconai over there was imprisoned with her. Turns out our knight friend is controlled by a blood mage. And Alconai is apparently related to Jabez." He smirked over at Tristan. "Captain's been filling me in," he added, tapping his temple. "Even dead-dog tired, she's trying to get everything and everyone taken care of." He glanced up at the sky; they could just see the sky lightening above the trees. "It seems our storm friend has left. Captain says Zatook should return shortly. He's making sure they actually leave and do not follow him."

The young forest-dweller nodded, unable to help glancing at the brothers again. "Alconai introduced himself to us before we returned. I didn't realize Jabez had family outside his association with Captain's crew," he commented quietly. He blinked when Jabez caught his gaze and frowned at him. The ninja excused himself from his brother and approached the young warrior.

"Tristan," he greeted warmly, though his gaze seemed concerned. With everything happening with Alconai and Captain, the ninja hadn't said anything to the Sun Child or the Star Child. "Glad to have you back, but are you hurt? You look a bit pale."

"I'm...I'm okay," he remarked softly. He still felt rather tired, but he figured some sleep would do him wonders. He felt his sister's gaze shift to his face even before her hand touched his cheek in concern. And then it hit. Like a tree slamming into his chest, the pain he'd felt when he fought Lancelot tore through him with a vengeance. His arms tightened around Arianna both in reaction to the agony and to keep from dropping her. He ground his teeth together to keep from screaming and made Arianna turn her head away so she wouldn't see his face contort in pain. He felt hands catching his sides as his legs buckled, his body leaning against a solid form. While Jabez held him, Tristan barely registered through the haze Solomon taking Arianna from his weakening arms.

"Easy, lad. I've got you," Jabez's voice sounded muffled in his ears as the ninja gently lowered him to the ground. He watched in a pained haze as Jabez slipped the ninja's belt free. Tristan felt the man's hand on his jaw next, working his mouth open just enough to slip the leather between his teeth. A part of him briefly felt grateful. He didn't want to scream; he didn't want to scare Arianna. She had seen him have attacks before, but he'd never let himself scream. Jabez's hands gripped his own when Tristan instinctively tried to claw at his chest. Feeling his arms pinned over his head, Tristan tensed as the pain persisted. Why? Was it from using his powers so much or had something else triggered it? Solomon shifted away to distract Arianna while Rose moved to help Jabez restrain Tristan. She watched him in concern, remembering the time in his forest. The price he spoke of.

"We should get him into a tent, but I don't know that we should move him," she noted softly. She lay a hand on his chest, closing her eyes and checking to see if there was any way to ease the pain. It wasn't an illness, so she doubted there was anything she could do. As she searched, Rose sensed something warring inside Tristan, causing strain on his body. The boy grimaced, his teeth leaving marks in the leather in his mouth. He barely registered the feel of Rose's hands on him through the pain wracking his body.

"I think I can move him all right," he heard Jabez tell her.

Tristan groaned softly even as the ninja gently gathered him into the man's arms. In an attempt to refrain from clawing at himself, Tristan clenched his hands into fists. Soon, a cool shadow fell over him as they entered a tent. A bedroll offered some protection for his back when Jabez lay him on it. However, Tristan groaned softly in pain as the man eased him to stretch out in an attempt to better see him. Carefully, he removed Tristan's upper garments and jerkin. The cool air chilled his sweat-dampened skin, but at the same time it brought some relief. Jabez uncurled Tristan's hands and pressed them together as though in prayer before wrapping the fabric of the tunic around them and tying it to keep him from hurting himself. As he looked down at himself, Tristan saw the markings along his body glow, the light bright without his clothes covering it. He barely made out Jabez's frown at the sight.

"Ah." Rose's voice was soft as she moved to his other side, sliding a hand along the markings. So, his power was at war with the thing he protected? Or the price he paid for protecting it? The phenomenon was strange. "It is not an illness or a wound which plagues him, though I do not fully understand it. I do not think there is anything I can do to ease it." She slid a hand up to where she sensed the pain resonating. Tristan breathed heavily as the pain persisted, wishing it would cease. He didn't want them to ask questions, but he knew they would want to know. Why was this happening more lately? As he stared up at Rose and Jabez's concerned, thoughtful gazes, a new sensation slowly spread through him. Warmth and peace gently eased his inner being as the pain steadily subsided. The markings along his torso faded back to their normal, lighter hue. The boy's eyes gradually closed until his breathing steadied in sleep. Jabez frowned at the lad, curious as to what happened.

"He seems all right now," the ninja remarked quietly. "Whatever it was has passed. At least for now."

Rose nodded. "This is, apparently, normal for him," she murmured softly. "All he has told me is that it is the price for guarding something dangerous." She paused when she sensed Zatook returning, standing and stepping out of the tent. A moment later, Zatook stepped out of the darkness. His cloak was draped over his shoulders, but slightly tattered. Blood ran down his form in tiny streams, though Rose wondered just how much was from his opponent versus the crimson rain. She frowned when she noticed a strange black liquid mingling with the crimson. His outer clothes were fairly tattered from the battle, but the black undershirt had fared surprisingly well.

Once he made sure the young man was all set, Jabez left Tristan's tent and rejoined his brother. He then studied Alconai and noticed the rebel didn't look any better than Jabez currently felt.

"I think you need a bath," he joked. Despite his teasing, his eyes held weariness, his body still recovering from his connection with Captain and having her powers transfer through him.

Alconai gave him a withering look. "Ah, geez. Ye 'avenae seen me in 'ow long? An' yer already chidin' me for bein' filthy? After I've been in jail, dragged behin' a wagon, an'..." Alconai rolled his eyes. "I missed ye, too, ye frog-faced baffoon." He smiled softly when Jabez chuckled.

"You know I'm not wrong," he teased Alconai, smirking at him. "Though I feel like I could use a nap. What a pair we make, eh?"

Alconai rolled his eyes. "All righ', all righ'. Poin' made. I be goin' now to wash," he conceded playfully. He headed to the area where Zatook had just returned and disappeared into the woods. Jabez watched him with a fond gaze.

Amaya emerged from Captain's tent and quirked an eyebrow at Zatook's state. Grabbing a spare rag, she approached him and took his hand, leading him to a clear patch of grass where he could sit. She then started cleaning off the blood. She'd done this for the crew often enough that it just felt natural for her.

"You bleed black, huh?" she remarked low enough only he would hear. "Definitely not human. But I won't tell them what you are." Zatook's eyes snapped to Amaya in alarm, and he almost pulled his arm away. She met his gaze and winked at him with a smirk. "Your secret is safe with me." At her assurance, he allowed her to clean him and just eyed her warily. He really wasn't used to letting others patch him up, only certain people on rare occasions. Amaya didn't seem to mind his wariness, nor did she make any comment to him flinching from her. When she finished cleaning and wrapping what wounds he would let her see, she carefully pat his shoulder and moved back to the fire. "You're welcome to join us," she called back to Zatook as she joined Solomon by the fire. He'd managed to calm Arianna, but the child still looked rather worried for her brother. Even as she pouted slightly with her head resting against Solomon's shoulder, her eyes fought to stay open.

"What's this then, little one?" Amaya asked, smiling softly at the girl. "No need to fret; Big Brother's going to be just fine." Reaching up, she gently brushed some of the child's brunette bangs from her face. Amaya then slipped Arianna from Solomon's arms, standing and gently cradling her. As she wandered around the fire, Amaya lightly rocked the little girl, letting the flickering flames calm her with their warmth and light. As Arianna closed her eyes Amaya softly sang in another language. The lullaby floated soothingly through the camp and seemed to help put the pirates at ease. She then sang it in the common tongue, "Sleep, little child. Dream of sun and moon in a garden of stars. Watch midnight and twilight dance in jet and violet. Then, child, fly home with the morning and return safely into my arms." Solomon couldn't help a smirk when the child curled up to Amaya, but he held his tongue for now. Zatook's attention riveted on the pirate when she started singing in Andorian— Andor was, after all, his homeland and the enemy of Nocis.

Tha's cheatin', tha' is. Captain's thought floated snarkily across Rose's mind. *Makin' e'erybo'y sleepy when we go' t'ings on our min's...*

Then why complain to me? the Half-Drow responded incredulously.

Why nae?

Rose snorted at that, pausing when Zatook turned down a mug of something from one of the pirates.

What do you know of our silent warrior?

Qui'e a bi'.

And how much will you tell?

... He's a frien'. T'e res' be 'is to tell.

Rose sighed. She figured as much, but it would have been nice to know a little more than the fact that he couldn't speak, used shadows, and wasn't human.

Once the child breathed softly in sleep, Amaya took her to Tristan's tent and tucked the girl in on a bedroll beside the boy. Jabez had already untied the young man's hands, removed the belt from his mouth, and covered him with a blanket once Tristan had fallen asleep. After a slight hesitation, Amaya reached up and brushed some of the brown hair from the younger man's face, watching him. She then tucked the blankets around both siblings a bit more to make sure they would stay warm enough before leaving the tent.

By the fire, Arianna wasn't the only one affected by Amaya's song. Jabez now sat near the flames, elbow propped on his knee and his head balanced in his palm. He had moved there after leaving Tristan to sleep, intending to wait up for his brother to return from washing. However, his eyes were closed now, somehow the man deep in sleep despite his position.

Solomon snorted slightly, smirking at the ninja and shaking his head. He shifted, not moving subtly but still quiet. He had years of practice not waking those who might otherwise be easily woken when moved in their sleep— this fellow in particular. With a nod to the others, Solomon moved Jabez to a different tent so the man could rest. When he returned, he reached for a stick to shift the logs on the fire. Most of the crew had been dwindling to their own resting areas; soon it was only he, Zatook, and Rose. The shadow warrior nodded to him before standing and moving to take watch at the edge of camp. Rose sighed, moving towards the trees.

"You could always come sit with the rest of us. You do not need to stay on the edge," Solomon offered warmly. Rose watched him for a moment.

"I mean no offense. Firelight and night-vision seldom go hand in hand. I do not like having my sight limited to a small circle."

Solomon nodded.

"A fair reason. No offense is taken." He nodded after the woman as Rose slipped into the shadows of the trees. Solomon, for his part, was not yet ready to sleep. His mind was on many things, his charge and the Andorian warrior among them. Amaya emerged from the tent at the same time Alconai returned. While the latter joined the pirate by the fire, Amaya slipped into Captain's tent once more.

"Ye ken, I ge' t'e feelin' Cap'n and 'Maya's relationship be more like mot'er and daugh'er, bu' t'ey look to be sis'ers age-wise," the entertainer commented.

Solomon chuckled. "Amaya is a motherly soul, though she'll deck you for suggesting such a soft thing." He nodded towards Tristan's tent. "You saw her with the little one." He paused to shift the embers once more, working to keep the warmth alive. "She did practically raise the girl, though. From the time Captain was a wee one smaller even than Miss Arianna."

Alconai smiled at the mental image of Amaya raising a younger version of Captain. "'Maya donnae look a day o'er twenty, bu' t'en looks cannae always be trusted. Speakin' of caring for people, I ken ye be ta one wha' looked after me brother. Thank ye." He shifted his hat as he got more comfortable by the fire. "I ken 'e looks up to ye, an' I be glad 'e had someone lookin' out for 'im."

"Your mother would have done no less in my stead," he noted softly. Before Alconai could pipe up, he continued. "Yes, I knew Ziv. She was a fine healer for the Order before she decided to settle down with her family. I would have known the rest of your family more had not my duty been in other lands at the time."

Alconai watched him in surprise. When Jabez had first mentioned the Order, he'd wondered if his brother had met anyone there that had known their mother. What luck— or rather, a blessing —that a friend of hers had been there to look after her son. "Sounds like Shaddai led 'im to ye. I be glad," Alconai commented quietly. His gaze grew uncertain for a moment as he contemplated his next words. "Jabie said tha' 'e was nae in 'is righ' mind when 'e was wit' ye. I cannae imagine t'e horrors me brother endured."

"More than any man should be forced to bear," Solomon answered, his gaze on the young flame between what remained of their logs. "But bear them he has, and surprisingly well at that. Though, I must say, Captain did far more to draw him out of his quiet shell than I." He chuckled. "I keep trying to convince your brother to join the Order officially, but as of yet he has refrained. He is determined to do things his own way for now."

"Sounds like 'im," Alconai remarked with a fond smirk. "Though, 'e sounds like 'e's already startin' to follow Mum's path. Said 'e's been given' t'e Order information an' whatnot." He grew somber once more as he watched the flames. "I wish I'd been t'ere for 'im like 'e's always been t'ere for me. Apparently sometimes withou' me kennin'."

He sighed as his thoughts drifted from Jabez to Lancelot. There was another one under someone's evil thumb. "Bi' of'a change o' topic, but wha' ye ken of blood magic?"

Solomon grew quiet, contemplative as he debated his answer. "Much and yet not nearly enough. None of what I know is pleasant, yet it is not nearly enough to see the horrid practice end. I can tell you the magic is natural to Drow and their kin, but them alone. Others found practicing the art gained their power through far more gruesome means."

The young minstrel nodded. "Do ye ken how to break a blood magic hold o'er someone? Back in Thorn-Drake...a friend o' mine be one of t'e knigh's. 'E was the one seemed migh'y interested in tha' power Captain 'as. But I donnae think 'e be the one what really 'as an interest. Finnegan, a blood mage, was controllin' 'im. While I been ridin' in t'a' wagon I rarely saw me friend act in 'is own mind. Wha' 'e did to Cap'n I ken 'e woul' 'ave ne'er done to her, regardless of lawlessness on 'er par'."

Solomon reached up to rub his chin. "I know of two ways. One is far more likely than the other. The risky measure is to try and help him break free himself. A single moment of clear thinking can be all that is needed. But it is difficult to break through a spell if it has been cast for a long time or if the caster's will is stronger than the one controlled." He stood a moment, grabbing a couple of logs to toss onto the growing flame. "The second is to find the blood stone. When a blood mage controls someone, they start with a physical item. A gemstone made from the victim's blood. When they grasp the stone with intent fed into the magic, it becomes nigh-impossible to break free. But if the stone is crushed, the spell within is lost." He paused, shifting the logs into a better position. "From the sound of your friend's predicament, finding the stone is by far the more sure path. It is most likely on the mage's person."

Alconai nodded once more. "I 'ad 'eard stories, but I like gettin' me facts before I go tryin' ta mess wit' anything, especially anything magic. One wrong move an' I coul' easily hur' someone rather than 'elp 'em," he noted gravely. "I owe t'e cod a fist in t'e face any'ow." He lifted his hat a moment and ran his fingers through his hair before settling it back on his head. "Wha' be t'e deal with Cap'n's rainbow eye?"

Solomon hesitated. Captain seemed to trust the lad, and he was Ziv's son. Jabez's brother. If he was to travel with them, he needed to know what he was in for. "Captain is the Moon Child. The glow accompanies her powers, many of which we are still learning. She has the three Sights: past, present, and potential futures. She also carries a destructive capability. A few of her powers I would wager are the magic of her people as opposed to her magic as the Moon Child." He sighed, leaning back and letting the stick rest at his feet. "I imagine you noticed her discomfort when your friend forced her abilities. Captain is young, and she has immense power. To help her gain control until she could practice and grow, I suppressed her abilities with a seal. Opening her eye grants her unfettered access, but she rarely risks it."

As Solomon finished, Alconai let out a low whistle of awe. "She be one o' t'e three, eh? Hindsight, i' makes sense, 'specially with someone from t'e Order takin' an interest in 'er well-bein'. Tha's an awful 'eavy load o' responsibility for someone so young to be carryin'." He rubbed his chin thoughtfully for a moment. "Ye mentioned ta power o' 'er people. I suspected 'er to be o' t'e Doran. Tha' be righ'?"

Solomon nodded. "She is Doran," he confirmed. "Though she has no clan among them. Most Doran prefer to wander the land as opposed to the sea, but she has met a clan or two in her time. I suspect we will need to find more who have their particular magic; they are protective of their ways, as welcoming as they are to outsiders."

"Aye. I've traveled wit' a few o' t'e clans, tradin' stories wit' 'em an' sharin' music," Alconai commented. "Do ye ken wha' happened to Cap'n's clan? One o' 'em disappearin' be something they wouldnae discuss wit' anyone, friend or no."

Solomon was quiet. "I know, but it is not my place to share. That decision rests with Isabella herself."

Alconai inclined his head in understanding. He could respect that response, and he'd rather hear the tale from Captain herself if she ever felt up to telling him. For now, he flashed Solomon a cheeky grin. "So, 'er name be Isabella. I's a pre'y name, though I take i' she donnae prefer i'."

Solomon snorted. "She'll accept Izzy once she gets to know you a little more," he offered with his own grin. He shook his head, using the stick he had adjusted the logs with to stand. "For now, methinks this old pirate should see himself to bed. Our silent friend has taken first watch." He looked down at Alconai, handing off the stick. "I would say don't sit up too late, but if you're anything like your brother, you'll do as you please until you fall asleep where you sit," he teased.

"Oi, I prefer me sleep, thank ye," Alconai joked back. However, he turned back to the flames for a bit longer, his mind full of discoveries, questions, and concerns. One thing he knew for certain: all of this would make quite a story some day.

Joy in the Midst

The next morning, Tristan and Jabez both remained asleep, but Arianna skipped around the camp merrily. Amaya had been kind enough to brush the girl's curls and pull them into her signature pigtails, so the hair stayed out of her face while the child romped. Now, the woman watched her as Arianna played with the wooden faerie Tristan had carved for her. She danced around the crewmates here and there, curls bouncing cutely, but mostly stayed out of their way. At one point, she hugged Amaya rather tightly. Amaya smirked and ruffled the girl's hair before shooing her off to play. The child beamed with delight.

Zatook returned as the camp woke, settling himself under a tree near the cookfire. He still kept an eye on things, but it wasn't as strict of a watch since the others were up and about now. Solomon snickered at the little girl's antics, catching her as she darted by and lifting her in a spin before returning her to her feet. Zatook watched in his typical silence, but an odd fondness was in his gaze as he watched the little girl.

Arianna laughed silently with Solomon's antics, dodging away from the man with a bright smile on her face. Despite her energy and happiness, she paused in her play at one point and simply stared at her brother's tent. Her face grew a tad perplexed as if she'd been waiting for him to come out and join her. When Tristan didn't emerge, Arianna released a small sigh. She clutched the faerie to her as her vibrant eyes scanned the camp. Despite all the people, she looked lost and alone. She spotted Rose, and the Half-Drow saw the crystalline orbs glisten slightly. Arianna blinked and looked around again. Suddenly her face lit up once more, and she scampered into the trees. Rose straightened, quickly moving after the little girl. As much as she was glad to see Arianna enjoying herself, she knew darting off into the woods alone was dangerous. With Tristan unconscious, she had silently taken it upon herself to watch the little girl in his stead.

Arianna hurried to a patch of flowers. Maneuvering around the carving in her hand, she started picking certain ones. When she finished, she glanced back at Rose, noticing the Half-Drow for the first time. Arianna hurried over to the woman and urged her to take the faerie carving. The child then surveyed the area once more, and her face lit up again. She gripped Rose's free hand before scurrying to another patch of flowers. Rose took the doll hesitantly, not sure what Arianna wanted her to do with it. She let the little girl pull her around, and even managed a slight smile. Arianna's joy was infectious. Releasing Rose's hand, Arianna started picking the flowers, weeding through them with surprising carefulness and knowledge. In her excitement, the girl showed the flowers to Rose, the child's eyes sparkling. Rose knelt, touching a hand to their petals.

"Very pretty," she told the young girl. She paused when she noticed a few of the more specific ones. "These are medicinal. Aren't you the little healer?" She winked.

Arianna beamed with the praise. She cradled the flowers for a moment to free her hands.

"Brother taught me," she signed. "He and the faeries played

games with me to help me learn. Some of the elves from the village taught us, too, and so did Clo."

Rose smiled. "Very wise of them. I'm sure these will help Tristan feel better." She reached a hand out and gently touched Arianna's head, though she didn't ruffle it lest she mess up the girl's pigtails. Arianna nodded her agreement, smiling brightly with the touch. Once she finished picking the flowers she wanted, she took Rose's hand again and led the Drow back to camp. Arianna found a spot out of the way and sat down with her flowers. She then started dividing them up: one pile for the medicinal and one for the pretties. When she finished, she took the medicinal pile to Solomon and pointed to Tristan's tent. The bronze pirate smiled warmly at the tyke as he accepted the flowers. He placed his free hand on his chest and bowed at the waist.

"I'll see to it personally," he promised her.

The girl smiled brightly before stretching her arms out and twirling happily. She then waved gratefully to Solomon as she returned to Rose's side. Arianna tugged on the woman's hand until Rose sat down. Then she motioned for Rose to push back her hood. Rose hesitated, casting a glance at the pirates. She had removed her cloak before, but she was still wary when revealing herself. She sighed, reaching up to push the cloth off of her head and lower the scarf around her face. Her different-colored eyes glanced warily around the camp again, half expecting someone to raise a fuss. A gentle touch on her cheek brought a strange warmth to Rose's face. Arianna smiled reassuringly at her, the child's blue eyes aglow with soft understanding. The little girl then moved behind Rose and undid the woman's braid before she gently started combing her fingers through her silver hair.

Arianna's hands moved with gentleness and caution, careful not to pull too hard or hurt the Drow. Once the hair was brushed, the girl began taking strands from the front and braiding them back like a crown. She wove the flowers in with the hair until Rose had a beautiful circlet of blossoms. Rose relaxed under the little girl's touch, letting her hair be braided. It had an almost surprisingly relaxing effect on the Half-Drow, evidenced by the closing of her eyes and the hint of a smile on her lips. Arianna left the rest of Rose's hair down. She used the flowers to tie off the braids when she finished and then nimbly moved in front of Rose to survey her work. The little girl smiled brightly, satisfied. Amaya glanced at them from where she came from helping Captain. The older woman smirked at the child's enthusiasm. It seemed making friends and brightening peoples' lives was one of the girl's gifts.

"Well, doesn't she look all prettied up," the first mate called to the two girls. "What's the occasion, Anna?"

Arianna's smile remained as bright as ever as she simply pointed at her brother's tent. Amaya glanced in that direction. Then she burst out laughing. She gave Arianna a wry, knowing smirk. "You wouldn't happen to be trying to play matchmaker, eh, Anna?" Amaya teased the child. She laughed again when the girl shamelessly gave a single nod. Rose blinked at the pair, a hint of surprise flashing behind her eyes. She frowned, glancing away and pulling her hood and scarf back over her face before standing. Amaya's laughter had caught a few other gazes, including Zatook's. Rose very purposefully did not look at anyone. The pirates shook their heads and got back to work, but the dark warrior was curious about the conversation— and the Half-Drow's reaction.

Amaya's smirk widened. "A bit shy, huh, Rose?" she teased. She then glanced down at Arianna when the girl started tugging on Rose's hand again. "I think she wants you to keep your hood off." Arianna nodded before signing to Rose that she looked pretty and should let Tristan see it when he woke.

Rose didn't pull her hand away, but she didn't lower her hood either. "I'd rather not." Zatook frowned at the little girl waving her arms and hands about, and it deepened when Rose actually answered her. "I'm a warrior," she noted quietly. "Not some...fairytale damsel." There was hesitation in her tone as she folded her arms and shifted her weight to her other foot.

"Warriors can be pretty, too," Arianna protested.

Amaya chuckled at the exchange but didn't say anything. She noticed Zatook's look of confusion and nudged the little girl in his direction.

"Hey, Anna, leave Rose be for now. Not everyone likes to show off their looks. You see the man over there? That's Zatook. He's like you; he can't talk. Why don't you go teach him how to do the signing so he can communicate with people better and understand you, too," the first mate encouraged. Arianna sighed, but left Rose in peace. Instead she moved over to Zatook, pointing first at her throat and then his inquisitively.

Zatook blinked at the little girl. He didn't miss Solomon glance at them warily. The dark warrior sighed, subtly nodding at the silent inquiry. They shared their silence. Arianna smiled with surprising gentleness for a child. Reaching out, she took Zatook's hands and started guiding him in making signs. She pointed at things around the camp, beginning small until he got the hang of it. Tristan had done the same with her when they learned from the elves in Nikko Mori.

Amaya had noticed the exchange between Solomon and Zatook. Approaching the pirate, she crossed her arms and watched Arianna interacting with the silent warrior.

"So, what's the history between you two?" she asked casually. Solomon paused in his task of crushing the herbs Arianna had brought to them. He didn't glance at Amaya, eyes on the mortar and pestle in his hands.

"Long and complicated," he answered softly. "Even with the medallion's blessing, I find it difficult to trust him." He shook his head. Order medallions were symbolic in more ways than one. They were heavily enchanted. His medallion could tell him if one of the Children was in peril, if the Order's base in Ben-Gal required assistance, or if it had been wrongfully taken. Zatook's had not professed any danger. "I called him a champion, but that is not his title. The world knows him as the Demon of Andor."

Amaya arched an eyebrow, but her gaze shifted to the silent warrior. "'Demon of Andor', huh? How came he by that name, do you know?" she asked as she finally looked down at the pirate. "Sol, I ken ye ken something more about this warrior than his title. No demon could be part of the Order, so what's the full story? Or are you going to make me go play the signing game with him to get answers?"

"Would you believe me were I to tell you the lad is over five centuries old?" Solomon asked softly, lifting his gaze to watch as Arianna gingerly corrected one of the signs the warrior was mimicking. "Not a demon, no. But the son of something similar. He is old, powerful, and not free. It is not the supposed demon I do not trust— it is the one who typically holds his leash." He was silent for a moment. "I lived in Andor for a time. With my wife and daughter. I saw many things."

The first mate watched him closely, letting out a low whistle when he mentioned the fighter's age. "I've heard stories of the likes, but never thought I'd see one for myself," she admitted, impressed. "I didnae ken ye had a family. What happened, if ye don't mind my asking?" Solomon had never mentioned having a wife and daughter before now, so Amaya assumed something had transpired. Was Zatook involved?

"My wife, I lost to illness. My daughter, I lost to tragedy born from love." He paused in his summations as his gaze finally left the Andorian, shifting instead to stare emptily at the forest. "His master ordered that she die, and so she did. By his hand." He tilted his head towards Zatook. "I would have killed him myself then and there had not I heard his own sorrow quite clearly. Pity stayed my hand then; I suppose it continues to do so."

Amaya touched a hand to Solomon's shoulder and gave it a reassuring squeeze. "Sometimes it takes more strength to spare a life than to take one," she remarked quietly. "I am sorry for your loss." Her eyes drifted to the Andorian once more. "I take it the king of Andor holds his leash."

Solomon nodded. "Mm. And yet, the king holds little respect for the Order— despite the Queen being a well-respected member in the past. We have had little contact with her in quite some time. Trying to find her was part of my reason for living in Andor as long as I did. Another has taken my place, now. I left after Aditi was killed." Amaya listened calmly even as she watched said warrior. She knew loss, but nothing like Solomon's.

"Perhaps the king has lost his leash," she commented. "Or do you fear him being a spy?"

Solomon nodded to the second option. "That is my gravest concern. And yet, the medallion was not marked as one stolen; perhaps the queen sent him. I suppose time will tell."

The first mate patted Solomon's shoulder encouragingly before moving over to Arianna and Zatook. "Having fun, you two?" she asked, smiling. Arianna beamed up at her and started signing in excitement. "Whoa, easy there. Slow down," Amaya teased. "I'm glad you're happy teaching dark and gloomy here how to communicate." She ruffled the girl's pigtails. Turning her gaze to Zatook she asked, "Your medallion…did the queen of Andor give it to you?" Zatook nodded, his hand slipping to the pouch where the medallion hid. He glanced back the way she had come, locking gazes with Solomon for a moment before the pirate stood and moved away. Zatook returned his gaze to Amaya. The woman didn't seem fazed by the men's interaction. Instead she met Zatook's gaze levelly. "Does the king still have sway over you? Will you obey if he orders you to betray us?" Zatook stared at her a moment, frowning. The girl was teaching him things like 'butterfly' and 'hello,' hardly communicative with so serious a question. He started to lift his palm, as if to show her something, when Captain suddenly pounced on Amaya's back and wrapped her arms around the woman's neck.

"Oi, oi, 'Maya," the girl grumbled in her first mate's ear, sounding half asleep despite the fresh, colorful skirt now falling about in strips that managed to stay modest and a clean white blouse. "Give me a bi' o' credit, aye?" She winked from Amaya's shoulder, grinning with mischief. "'e nae t'e psychic 'ere, af'er all." She glanced down at Zatook, who was now watching her with the same intense gaze he seemed to give everyone and everything. Amaya easily wrapped her arms under the girl's legs to hold her properly in a piggyback position— a testament to her familiarity to Captain's antics.

"I thought it a rather straight-forward question that needed only a nod or shake of the head," the first mate remarked. Her gaze turned back to Zatook. "So long as ye donnae try to stab us in the back, we should be good," she told him, smiling brightly once more.

Captain snorted. "Zatie doesnae fin' anyt'ing simple, do ye?" she teased, winking down at the warrior. She paused as his gaze shifted slightly, then smirked. "Ye coul' always le' me in t'ere, ye ken," she teased, reaching up to tap her temple. Zatook's gaze flattened, and he looked away. "Sui' yerself."

"Not everyone likes ye rattling around in their heads, Captain," Amaya chided good-naturedly. "Besides, should you even be up yet? Ye've been through a lot." Her gaze turned back to Arianna when the little girl tugged inquisitively on Zatook's sleeve to see if he wanted to continue with their lesson. Zatook hesitated at first, but a flippant wave of the hand from Captain let him know he didn't need to ignore the little girl.

"Aye, aye, I ken. Bu' mis'er doom'n'gloom o'er t'ere isnae

goin' to ge' any cheerier if we go abou' actin' like 'e's some kin'a spook," Captain noted. She didn't answer the bit about her being through a lot; she did lean her chin on Amaya's shoulder. "Sol doesnae nee' to worry. Leas' nae fer a while, long as I can See," she added softly. "Bu' if 'e were ordered, 'e cannae resis'. Nae all chains be made o' me'al." Unseen by Captain, something dark flashed across Amaya's gaze before retreating. Instead of commenting on the girl's remark, she bounced Captain playfully.

"All in all, ye might want to go see to your new boyfriend. He's been worried about ye," the first mate teased.

Captain snorted. "Oi, oi, wha's t'is abou' a boyfrien', eh? Like I go' time for tha'." She laughed softly, sliding from Amaya's back, nonetheless. "'sides, figured 'e'd be all o'er Jabie fer a bi'."

"Aye, they had their spat while you were sleeping," Amaya told her, smirking. "Just when we get one of you back on your feet, another one falls over. Tristan's under due to something plaguing him. Jabez and the Drow seem to think it's not an illness though."

"S'nae gonna ge' any be'er fer us, ye ken," Captain pointed out softly, staring towards Tristan's tent. She didn't seem surprised to learn he was down for the count. Her gaze was far away, through the tent and beyond. "T'e nigh' always be darkest before t'e ligh' o' t'e star's be comin' ou'."

***

Tristan felt himself floating in mid-air. Slowly opening his eyes, he glanced around, and yet he saw nothing but darkness. Darkness...and cold. He felt so cold. Tristan...my

190

son...*the voice sounded louder and seemed to surround him. Tristan bolted upright as much as he could. No...he tried to get a foothold on something—anything.*

No, Tristan. You'll be joining me again. Whether by your own free will or by force, you will come back to me.

"Never," *Tristan snarled, even as he uttered the word outside the vision. The darkness thickened. It wrapped around his limbs, immobilizing him. He struggled to reach his weapons, but the darkness tightened its hold. The boy's own power formed in front of him. A black hand burst through the frail shield and gripped Tristan's throat.*

You will not escape me. Not even the farthest reaches of the realm can hide you from me. *Tristan struggled to breathe.* I will take that which your mother sought to hide...and you will help me.

"No!" Tristan cried out suddenly, blood spurting from his mouth as the markings reappeared along his flesh. He coughed violently but didn't regain consciousness fully yet. Outside, Alconai and Arianna both snapped their attention to Tristan's tent. Arianna watched as the man ducked into her brother's tent, but when she tried to follow, Amaya held her back. The woman glanced at Solomon and indicated the child. Once he had the little girl, Amaya also disappeared inside the enclosure. Alconai held the boy down, but Tristan continued to thrash. His eyes snapped open, their vibrant hue glowing with power as the forces within him warred once more.

"Oi, lad, easy!" Alconai called to the younger man. Despite trying to restrain Tristan, he had no idea what to do. Amaya's gaze watched the struggling boy with surprising calm even as she helped Alconai hold him down. Rose was not long in joining them, moving to kneel by the young man's head. She let the other two focus on restraining him, instead attempting to find the source of his struggles. She touched her hand to his temple, delving into his mind.

Tristan!

The lad's mind cowered from Rose's and curled in on itself at first. A dark presence battled with Tristan's own power for a moment longer before dissipating. Now the boy's mind seemed utterly blank though wracked with pain. Slowly his power receded even while another lingered. However, even that influence gradually ebbed into a dull echo deep within him. Tristan shuddered violently before finally stilling. He breathed heavily now, barely noticing when Amaya left and returned with one of Captain's tonics. Gently, she and Alconai helped Tristan drink the healing liquid. The younger man didn't care about the taste as the soothing drink wet his parched throat, easing his pain and healing his strained body. Rose closed her eyes as she concentrated. The dark power and the odd echo were concerning, but for now her task focused on the pained yet blank feeling.

Tristan. She called for him again even as a silver light spread around her presence, working to soothe him. Outside of their mental connection, the circlet of a star and filigree shone upon her forehead once again. Tristan's consciousness flinched when she brushed it, but he didn't flee this time. For all his toughness when he was awake, his mind seemed rather timid at present— like he remained gripped in the throes of a nightmare. His body trembled from the mental and physical stress he'd just endured. In the wake of the dark presence lingered great emotional anguish. Images of a beautiful, regal woman flashed through his mind: memories of his mother. Her gentle, warm smile gave way to a resolute expression, the images fading into each other. Guilt for failing to protect his mother from his father haunted Tristan's consciousness. And yet, other emotions grew from pain. Resignation gave way to a strong determination. Images of raising Arianna pervaded, hardening the resolve more and more. Steadily, Tristan regained his usual consciousness, his mind full of warm light and strength once more. Still, he didn't pull away from Rose. Instead, he allowed her near.

I'm sorry. I didn't mean to be a burden, he told her quietly.

You have yet to become one, Rose assured him. *Still, you have everyone worried.* Her mind thought back to the presence and the echo. The first she could guess: the warrior had worried about his father, after all, and the images of his mother and sister surfacing would make sense after a paternal visit. The echo, however, concerned her. It reminded her of the mysterious glow in his chest. *We could better help you if we knew what we were tending,* she noted, striving to keep her typical briskness at bay.

There is nothing you can do to help, Tristan told her. *I willingly endure in order to protect my sister and keep this power from my father.* In reality, Tristan's eyes slowly focused as he relaxed on the bedroll. His gaze fell on Rose. *Thank you for trying to help me.*

"He's fine, for now," Rose announced out loud for the benefit of the entertainer and the first mate nearby. "I can watch him." *Even the darkest of curses has a treatment, if not a cure,* she pointed out calmly. He obviously wanted to protect this secret as it was, so she wasn't sure how far to press. Especially surrounded by pirates, friends of the Moon

Child or no. Amaya nodded and released Tristan. Looking between the two, she smirked before leaving the tent. Alconai gave them a cheeky grin.

"I ken when I no longer be needed," he teased, winking at them. "I be leavin' ye two alone now." With that, he followed Amaya outside. Tristan frowned after them a moment but then returned his attention to Rose.

I appreciate your concern, but I'll be fine. How is Arianna?

Rose twitched an eyebrow at the remark. *Teaching Zatook the Language of the Silent,* she answered with some amusement. *And picking flowers both medicinal and not.* She sighed as she remembered the crown, reaching up to lower her hood even as she grimaced. *She insisted.* Perhaps seeing his sister's amusements would bring him some form of comfort. He studied her hair a moment as a fond smile spread across his lips.

"You look beautiful," he told her quietly. "Arianna has a good heart. She always wants to help others and be friends. I imagine she'd make a good herbalist or healer someday." Tristan sighed softly as his body recovered from his ordeals.

Rose chuckled. "If the pirates don't enchant her, first. She seems to rather like them all."

"I suppose that wouldn't be so bad. Captain seems to get along just fine," he joked. "But I think Arianna may be too gentle for the swashbuckling life. It's part of why I never had her help me with hunting or taught her to fight. If she wants to learn when she's older that's fine, but I'd like to preserve her kind innocence for as long as possible."

Rose glanced away, staring out the tent flaps. Even if she couldn't hear the little girl, she could sense her with Zatook. She reached as if to tuck a strand of hair back, not used to it being loose, but hesitated and lowered her hand.

"Life has a way of taking that innocence too soon. It's refreshing to see it linger," she noted softly.

"All I want is to protect her. I'm glad she's had the chance to grow outside our father's influence," he commented softly. "I've been trying to protect her from the darkness haunting us, but I fear outside the forest she'll be swallowed; and I'll be powerless to stop it."

"Is it not within the darkness that sun and star shine the brightest?" Rose glanced down at him, the rare glimmer of mirth in her gaze.

Tristan scoffed softly. "Darkness awaits me both in sleep and wakefulness," he murmured. Then a weary smile tugged at his mouth. "Are you the star come to brighten my darkened world?"

"I doubt I hold quite that much importance in these events, but I would like to at least assist."

"Shaddai created you. In that fact you hold more importance than the rest of the world," Tristan whispered. "And He gifted you the powers of the Chosen Children; therefore, you possess a very important role in the things to come." Rose was quiet, turning to look once more out the tent. A soft "perhaps" floated back towards Tristan before she shifted to lift her hood once more.

"Speaking of the Children, I should see if Captain has any

ideas for what our next move should be." She started to stand. "I doubt we can stay here much longer, with Arden and your father's men both hunting for us."

Tristan tried to ease himself up, wincing as he moved. He didn't want to lie around; they needed to plan what to do next. What would they do? Where would they go? He sat still for a moment to let his body adjust. Grunting softly, he tensed when pain flared once more through his entire being. His breaths came in ragged gasps as his hands clutched the blanket draped over his legs. Agony contorted his face. A dull throbbing filled his ears like a heartbeat.

"I'm all right," he murmured through gritted teeth. "It'll pass." Why was this happening again so soon? Was it getting worse?

Rose had already knelt again, a hand on his shoulder to steady him. "Are these...spasms usually this severe?" She shook her head, gently pressuring his shoulder. "You should lie back down." His body trembled where he sat hunched over his legs. He shuddered in short spasms, his breath hitching every time he stilled and then releasing jaggedly. He couldn't answer her. Sweat dotted his face and body, making his clothes stick to his dampening skin. The pain intensified, causing him to go rigid and stop breathing altogether as he bit back a cry. Finally, after an agonizingly long moment, he shakily released the tension in his body and exhaled. As horrible as it felt, he knew no amount of remedies could cure it or help it subside. But still he bore it. He would always choose to bear it. Tristan shuddered but finally managed to shake his head.

"It's never been like this. We need...to get somewhere safe..." he insisted. "Arianna needs..." He tried to push himself to his feet. Being hunted, they needed to find somewhere more secure to recuperate. As he struggled, a soft glow started emanating through his chest, seeming to take the shape of a spherical object hidden beneath the bare skin of his chest. Rose kept her grip, not letting him rise. She frowned at the glow; this wasn't like his powers. It must be the source that combated them, this secret Tristan guarded. And yet, even as she could see it glowing, she could not sense it. Her blood magic could not reach it or ease Tristan's suffering. Her brow furrowed, her lips pursing.

Before she could question him further, a strange presence seemed to saturate the tent. Outside, a soft golden light cascaded through the camp as a strange song whispered through the breeze. A calming power spread through the inhabitants, a vaguely familiar warmth passing through Tristan and easing his pain. Tristan tried to physically shrink from the power, afraid it might be a trap. However, the pain left him even more exhausted, though it was lessened now. The strange glow in his chest started to fade but didn't disappear. He frowned in discomfort. The power wrapped around Tristan, easing him and fighting back the pain. It granted him energy, almost as if pure life flowed from the light and into his body. Tristan shuddered but slowly he eased into the warmth. The glow faded as the pain began to recede, but something darker throbbed through the glow, the gold turning to black outlined in burgundy. Tristan shivered. Whatever the item was, it seemed to be corruptive in nature, trying to spread its influence through the young man like a poison. However, his Child powers were keeping it at bay for now.

Rose watched in fascination as the golden power swirled around them, holding a hand into the light and watching as streams of it seemed to dance around her fingers.

"What is this?" she asked quietly.

Slowly, Tristan eased. He remembered this presence. He recalled the warmth seeping into and around him on cold, lonely nights and during extremely difficult days. He'd only been eleven when he was charged with caring for Arianna, and this presence had comforted him often in that time. The pain finally faded, as did the light in his chest. Shakily, Tristan lifted his hand to let the golden light swirl around him.

Who are you? he asked softly.

The light danced around his fingertips, a swirling golden essence that filled the air. *A friend,* came the gentle whisper of a reply, the voice of a woman. Steadily, Tristan eased back into a restful sleep.

Outside, the pirates stared at the dancing lights in awe, blinking as a swirl circled around Arianna— it even seemed to ruffle her hair. Arianna twirled and danced in the light, stretching her arms up into it. More than once she made the hand sign for mother. Amaya tensed at that, but she said nothing. Instead, she simply lifted her own hand into the light, watching it swirl. Alconai gazed at the display in awe. He had heard stories of beings with unique powers, but it was said that they were rare to see. Tentatively, he reached out and gently stuck his hand into it. It wrapped around the entertainer, comforting and easing his worry for Lancelot and Jabez.

Tristan wasn't the only one to feel the light's healing effects. The same power swirled around Jabez, easing his tiredness and rebuilding his strength. Captain smiled at the light as it played around her fingers, and even Zatook eased despite receiving no healing of his own. As gently as it had come, the light faded away. Arianna pranced and smiled brightly, thoroughly happy. She ran over to Solomon and tugged the man's hand as she pointed excitedly at where the light had been. She then made the sign for mother again. Solomon gently scooped up Arianna, twirling her in a circle before holding her.

"Mother?" he asked, tilting his head. Did the girl think that light was her mom? Arianna's silent laughs wracked her small body. She nodded at the man's question. She then made another couple of signs: "All Mother."

Amaya glanced over when Jabez slowly emerged from his tent. He seemed a bit dazed but otherwise no worse for wear now. He stared around at the camp, blinking a few times. Captain practically danced over to Jabez, slinging her arms around him in a hug.

"Oi, ol' man, bou' time ye woke up!" she teased brightly.

Jabez rolled his eyes. "I'm only twenty-six, I'll have you know," he commented quietly. However, he wrapped an arm around her and gave her a reassuring squeeze. "What did I miss?"

"Aye, aye, an' tha's pre'y ol' when pu' up against li'l ol' me," she quipped, loosening her grip as she caught him up to date on things.

Full Bloom

In a lone castle on a hill, there grew a garden. All kinds
of flowers grew in this patch of earth, but none so rare as
a small bed of vibrant blue flowers, their hue crystalline
in nature. At one time, the allotment held a dozen of the
strange flora, but now only three remained. The stone
walls of a small courtyard hid the garden from the world—
reserving its beauty for one man. The man now knelt
to examine the blue flowers, his hand gently cupping
the petals of one. His dark clothing hid his somewhat
muscular build, and he kept his neat, ombre hair pulled
back in a ponytail. The strands started out black at their
roots and continued part way before fading into platinum
white strands that reached his waist. His fair skinned,
chiseled features appeared young, marking him to be in his
thirties. And yet, a wise aura permeated his countenance.
His handsome face and calm demeanor brought many
women to him, but he chose a life of solitude. The people
in the villages under his charge knew him as High Lord
Tsukuyomi SoulMirror, Head of House Shadow Veil.

A woman with bright red and obsidian streaked hair
stalked down the corridor towards the garden, agitation
radiating off of her in waves. Stranger than her hair were
her eyes: where the whites should be was stained red, her
irises orange flecked with small blood vessels. Rather than
the pale tones of a native Nocium or even a human, her
skin was stained a sickly fossil gray. Hiding beneath the
strands of her hair were mutilated ears, cut and scarred to

form tips. Slightly behind her, his expression as unreadable as ever, was the obscured StormShaper.

"I still do not see why I could not finish him before our return," the woman was complaining, her red lips formed in a pout. StormShaper said nothing as he held a vial filled with crimson liquid towards her.

"Timing, Marilyn," he informed the woman calmly once she had snatched the vial from him. "A tactician's closest friend— followed by patience." The woman huffed before crossing her arms. After a moment, Tsukuyomi entered the corridor. He halted upon seeing Marilyn and StormShaper.

"Have a good run?" his deep voice asked calmly. He surveyed her agitated behavior before striding up to her and gently tucking some of her hair behind her misshapen ear. Marilyn's agitation melted into an almost giddy grin under his caress. "I see you retrieved his blood."

"Of course, Master, would I fail you?" she purred, sliding a hand up his chest.

"Never," Tsukuyomi acknowledged. "I just finished a little man-to-man talk with him." His hand moved from her ear, sliding along her jaw and tilting her chin up so she met his gaze. "Was your fun interrupted?"

"It was," she pouted. "I ran into an old friend, but Mister Serious back there made us come back." She slid a hint of mock-seriousness into her nickname for StormShaper.

Tsukuyomi's thumb traced over her lips. "Perhaps I can make it up to you," he told her smoothly. "Who was this old friend?" He really only cared if the person would cause trouble when he finally made a move to collect Tristan. "Will this person impede us?"

"Andor's little demon," Marilyn noted, shrugging nonchalantly. "Only a threat if the king continues to loosen his leash."

Tsukuyomi nodded. "The boy is long overdue in his return to me," he commented. "How soon can you have him under your control?"

Marilyn cackled. "How soon does my lord wish it?" she questioned seductively, pressing herself against him.

"We will give him a couple days to recover enough of his strength to travel but not enough to resist efficiently. I'm sending StormShaper to retrieve him; I will not risk Nightshade's return being interrupted," Tsukuyomi told her.

"As you wish," she whispered, slipping away from him and down another hall. Her giggles echoed around her.

Unfazed, Tsukuyomi watched her as she left. He lifted his other hand to survey the blue flower he'd picked from the garden. Though his injuries would heal quickly due to the boy's natural abilities and the healing from his comrades, Tsukuyomi knew the lad needed to recuperate after the stress he'd endured from the powers warring within him. He would have his son back one way or another; it was only a matter of time and patience. His thumb stroked the flower's petals as Tsukuyomi studied it.

Without raising his gaze, he addressed StormShaper, "What is your assessment of Nightshade's skills? Did he fight well when you faced him?"

"Well enough," StormShaper mused. "Fighting in the wild has both done him favors and hampered his success. His style sacrifices strength for speed." He did not move to step closer to his master, his arms seeming to be clasped behind his back. "He is emotional when he fights, which leads to more openings, yet he fights well with constant movement rather than being restrained to a single area." The lord of the estate nodded his acknowledgment. He had expected such a report; however, he knew StormShaper tended to be a harsh critic even on himself.

"He'll improve with training. See to it that he returns without issue."

StormShaper gave a slight bow of acknowledgment, but he made no move to leave. "I doubt Marilyn's glib report of little interference," he noted calmly. "While a single gnat is little bother, an entire cloud can be quite the nuisance. She underestimates the aid of her acolyte and Arden's men during the last fight. I request permission for more than simple retrieval. While Marilyn retrieves your warrior, I wish to enter their camp."

Tsukuyomi turned the flower over in his hands thoughtfully. "The Demon of Andor may interfere, as you believe. There are other forces within the camp who can also impede the mission," he remarked coolly. "Very well. Cause a distraction while Marilyn ensures Nightshade's retrieval. His capture takes priority; I leave the rest to your judgment." Now he turned to look his warrior in the eyes—despite the Obscure shrouding the man —cold calculation in his gaze. "I know you won't disappoint me." StormShaper bowed once again, this time lower, before spinning on his heel and marching from the hall. Soon he was a blur, the clouds that had accompanied his arrival dispersing in his absence.

***

Tristan groaned as he forced his eyes open. His body felt stiff and sore but rested. He listened silently for anyone in the tent with him, sensing someone there. Shifting to look, Tristan recognized Alconai sitting beside him. From his hunched position and the sound of his breathing, the man appeared to be asleep. Tristan grunted as he attempted to sit up. It was only then that he realized someone had removed the rest of his leather armor at some point to allow him to sleep more comfortably. The cooler air sent chills along his bare torso as the blanket slipped down to pool at his waist. Instantly Alconai's breathing changed with the younger man's movement, and Tristan felt strong hands quickly steady him by the shoulders.

"Easy t'ere, lad," the man told him. "'Ow do ye feel?"

"Stiff," Tristan croaked. He ran his tongue around his parched mouth to wet it. "Where's Rose?" Tristan inquired softly. The last thing he remembered was her by his side as he slipped asleep. "How long have I been out?"

"I' be t'e next day, so 'bou' 'alf a day an' all nigh'. Yer sis'er's been in 'ere from time to time, too." Tristan nodded. He'd no doubt that Arianna had been worrying over him. Despite Alconai's warning, the younger man started to get to his feet. With the man's help, Tristan donned his under shirt and tunic, forsaking his leather trappings for now. Once dressed, Tristan stepped to the tent entrance. He felt Alconai stay close in case the younger man needed a steadying hand. Considering the state Tristan had been in the last time he woke and that Alconai knew nothing of the warrior's faster healing, Tristan couldn't blame the man for hovering.

Fresh morning air filled Tristan's lungs, the forest scent as familiar as it was foreign. Walking out into the camp, they found it already bustling with pirates going about obeying orders Amaya and Captain barked. Tristan's gaze wandered until he pinpointed Arianna playing happily near Solomon. He smiled at his sister's cheerfulness. Then Tristan continued to watch the rest of the camp.

"I think I can make it fine on my own now. Thanks," Tristan told his helper. He noted Alconai's uncertain glance at him.

"Ye sure?" the man asked. When Tristan nodded Alconai shrugged. "All righ'. But if'n ye feel like yer 'bou' to keel o'er, jus' give a 'oller." Tristan inclined his head once more and slowly trudged toward his sister. Before he could get past the next tent, Captain was in his face.

"Welcome ta the lan' of the livin'!" she laughed, patting his shoulder. "Ye're jus'n time fer food! If I didnae ken any be'er, I'd say ye planned it." She continued to laugh, driving him towards the seats around the fire. Solomon glanced up at the sound of her voice and reached over to nudge Arianna.

"See? I told you he would be well."

As Tristan was pushed through camp, it became rapidly apparent to him that Rose was not in the camp— though he could sense her nearby. The solitary soldier had thoughts upon thoughts whirling through her mind. She did not feel comfortable in a crowded camp. While the pirates had proven their worth as comrades, she preferred the isolation she had come to enjoy in her freedom. She had found a waterfall nearby and sat on the rocky shore of the river, listening to the steady thrum of the water. She closed her eyes as she thought, but older memories came to assault the new.

The pounding of the water became hundreds of hooves as the soldiers of the Calvary practiced formations in the open field. Jeremiah stood watching, his arms clasped behind his back as he evaluated each movement. Unlike the present day, this Jeremiah towered over the little Half-Drow slave who stood silently behind him. She paid no mind to the man, enthralled by the large beasts and the men in armor below their vantage point. Jeremiah smirked, glancing over his shoulder and down at her. There was warmth in his gaze that lived only in her memories now.

"What do you see?"

Rose frowned, glancing up at him. When he nodded, she looked back down and pointed. "Those ones are out of line."

He nodded. "Very good. You'll make a fine soldier, yet."

"Slaves cannot fight."

"Whoever said such a ridiculous thing?" Rose glanced back up at the man, frowning. He was an odd master, not like the first humans she served. He allowed her to speak openly, and often engaged her in conversation.

"All of the masters and handlers. Slaves cannot fight, unless in the arena."

"There is no law against such a thing; only if one were to kill their own master or fight outside of orders." Jeremiah was watching the horsemen again. He gestured to one of his commanders on another platform, bringing his attention to the lagging soldiers Rose had pointed out. "I shall teach you to fight. You have the potential to be one of the best."

"Can one be best if one is not their own?"

Rose's eyes snapped open when she sensed Tristan stirring. She reached her thoughts out to him, brushing her consciousness to his in case he did not wish to speak with her.

Tristan sighed with relief to feel the connection, Rose's steady presence a comfort in his constant world of chaos. He let Captain lead him to a log by the fire. As he moved, the stiffness slowly subsided, energy returning to his body. He recalled the warm presence that had healed him during his latest episode, wondering about it even as he stared into the fire. A sudden blur of limbs and fabric tackled him to the ground. Tristan grinned, hiding his pain as his back hit the dirt. His arms wrapped tightly around the girl now hugging his neck. Tristan rocked from side to side carefully, rolling Arianna slightly. He felt her body vibrating in her silent laughs as her joy washed over him. Her happiness even swept across his connection with Rose. Stroking her hair gently, Tristan remained lying on his back, his own chuckles vibrating his chest and shaking the little girl. Arianna gave him a peck on the cheek and then hugged him again. Relief, love, and pure joy cascaded over his consciousness from his sister.

"I take it you missed me," Tristan commented. He remained on his back for now as Arianna hugged him tighter in answer. Tristan's own fond smile had yet to disappear. It was probably the first time the crew had seen him look happy.

Jabez's eyes crinkled slightly at the edges, evidence of the smile hidden by his mask. Watching the kids caused him to glance at Alconai. The ninja hung back away from his sibling, much to his brother's disappointment; however, Jabez still felt uncomfortable around Alconai despite the younger man's declaration of forgiveness and attempts to be companionable. So Jabez just stayed near in case his brother needed him but didn't join him. Not yet. When Amaya caught his eye and arched an eyebrow at him, he averted his gaze and returned to keeping watch.

Amaya smirked at Tristan and Arianna. She glanced at Zatook and approached him. Nudging his shoulder with her hip playfully, she teased, "Now we just need to work on you, eh?"

Zatook, for his part, simply quirked an eyebrow at the woman he was beginning to label as 'odd.' He needed no 'work' or 'training.' Amaya bent in front of Zatook, her bell chiming with her movement.

"Look happy," she emphasized cheekily. "Seriously, ye always look like a sea gull just crapped on yer breeches." She straightened and winked at him before moving to help prepare for departure, her bell once more chiming with each of her strides. She wanted to get everyone back to the ship before anything else happened.

Zatook watched her walk away, as stoic as ever. He noticed Captain watching the pair for a moment before the girl flounced over to her other guardian.

Tristan felt Rose withdraw, leaving the siblings to their reunion. She paused where she now stood, having moved to rejoin the camp, staring back at the waterfall. Something tugged at the corner of her senses, but she was lost in memories. Long before Jeremiah and her training. Before her grandmother. Back to a small cabin. *A woman, ebony with starlight hair. A boy, more human in appearance yet with the pointed ears of a half-elf and the silver hair they all shared aside from their father. The silhouette of a man in the fields.*

Tristan paused with Rose's withdrawal and simply held Arianna for a moment. He did return to sitting on the log and shifted Arianna onto his lap so that she could continue hugging him. He considered asking Rose what was wrong, but he decided to leave her be for now. If she needed him, she would say something. Still, his concern filtered across their connection.

I sense magic that is not of our companions. She had felt the concern but chose only to address a portion of it. The past was the past, after all. *It is difficult to pinpoint.*

Tristan hesitated. "I'm not really all that hungry," he told Captain when the girl started to hand him a bowl of food. He gently placed a hand on Arianna's head. "I'll be back, all right? I'm just going to check on Rose. Will you stay and keep Solomon and Captain company?" The child hesitated, reaching up and clutching her brother's hand. She didn't want him to leave so soon; he just woke up. Tristan pressed his forehead to hers, rubbing it gently. "I'll always come back to you, and I'll do all I can to protect you. You trust me, right?" Arianna's innocent gaze peered into his eyes for a moment. She sighed but nodded and released his hand. Tristan softly ruffled her pigtails again as he smiled at her fondly. "I won't be long. And then we can play. Maybe we'll get to do a little exploring, too, if we have time." He pulled back enough to tenderly kiss her brow. Arianna beamed at him, kissing his cheek again. She then scurried to Captain to see what was for breakfast. Tristan's smile remained as he watched her scamper away.

"Ye prob'ly shoul'nae go alone," Alconai piped up. "I'll come wit' ye. Rose is some'ere in ta fores'. I finally managed ta ge' 'er ta take a break from watchin' o'er ye."

Tristan nodded. "I'll be all right. She shouldn't be far." He then moved outside the camp. He wandered through the trees as he concentrated on his connection with the Drow, using her presence to guide him. He had gotten a fair ways from the camp when his head and vision swam dizzyingly. Slumping against a tree, Tristan shakily brought a hand to his head. An unfamiliar sensation tingled along his bicep, trickling through the rest of his body. His blood seemed to warm in his veins, the heat pulsing through him and making his flesh feverish. A whisper flickered through his mind, pulling him in a new direction. Away from Rose.

Come. Come to me.

Tristan frowned as he tried to pinpoint the voice. *Who's there?* he questioned. His mind immediately flashed to his father. Was this one of his minions? Digging his fingers into the rough tree bark, Tristan struggled to stay in place. With a surprising show of mental strength, he pushed through the haze. *Rose,* he called, his voice strained across the connection. He shuddered. There was something… unnatural about this sensation…something evil.

Hush, Tristan…fret not, child. Come to me. The whisper was warm, gentle, like a beckoning breeze. Before Tristan could fully process what was happening, his body began to move on its own. Tristan focused once more on the voice as he fought against its hold in his mind. Worse still, he couldn't find Rose. His mind struggled in the haze blackening his vision. Feeling himself slipping more and more into darkness, he grasped desperately at his consciousness. He knew if he fell into that darkness that there would be no way back. Every instinct told him to fight. *Ssh, ssh, no need to fight...* The voice continued to lull him, pulling him deeper from himself. His head snapped up as the sound of a blade being drawn reached his ears. Rose stood there, one blade pointed at the ground and the other leveled at his throat.

"Release him." She could practically smell the blood magic roiling through him. To confirm her suspicions, the warrior's eyes were stained pure red.

"I think not." A woman's voice answered, an odd cackle to its tone as 'Tristan' straightened and shook out his arms. "This one is long overdue for his arrival. I suggest you stand aside, lest you die by this boy's blade."

"I refuse."

"Then you choose death, Tainted One."

Rose paused, her eyes flashing. "Whether I win or lose here, I will find you. And you shall die."

"Brave words from one quite so cursed. Tsk, tsk. Half-human and a slave? No wonder Keeshe—" The words were cut short as Rose leapt forward, lunging towards Tristan. If she could incapacitate him, they could purge the control.

She could just barely sense his mind now, the young warrior struggling fiercely against the control. But if this influence truly was a Drow Elder, then she doubted he had the necessary fortitude to break free alone. Whoever they were, she could sense their power was far stronger than the mage she had faced in Thorn-Drake.

***

Back at the camp, Zatook moved. In less than a blink, he was standing several feet away from his chosen tree, his blade in his hands and clashed against the sword that had almost embedded in Solomon's back. StormShaper's sword. The man had arrived moments before the clouds closed in around the camp, outrunning the constant warning of his presence. Solomon quickly turned and stepped back, pulling his own blades free. The obscured warrior chuckled.

"So, you sensed me after all, demon."

"Oi!" Alconai exclaimed, leaping to his feet and drawing his dagger. One of the pirates had lent him the blade so he wouldn't be completely defenseless. He blinked when he noticed someone else holding a dagger to where StormShaper's neck should be. Jabez's ice blue eyes glared calmly at the obscured figure. StormShaper chuckled once again, his voice deep and yet almost familiar. Lightning suddenly burst from him in several arcs, blasting the two men away from him and lashing out at everyone else. Zatook quickly righted himself, dashing back through the lightning. Shadows wrapped around him, catching any lightning and releasing it behind him. Lightning and darkness clashed as the two warriors began exchanging blows, flaring through the camp. But StormShaper was not there for a duel. He had a mission; lightning continued to arc through various parts of the camp as the wind began to howl. The clouds ripped open, rain drowning the camp in a wicked deluge. The pirates moved quickly, working to protect and salvage what they could; they knew when they were outmatched, and no one wanted to get between the men. Solomon had moved straight for Captain, using an arm to keep her behind him despite the disgruntled arguments the sprightly girl was trying to give above the sounds of the storm.

Every time the lightning tried to strike the camp's inhabitants or their belongings, the power never reached its intended targets. No one saw the deflections; it simply looked like the lightning snuffed from existence. While the rain continued, the winds' damage remained minimal as though wards protected the camp's equipment. StormShaper didn't seem perturbed by the odd happenings, though he did attempt to trace them. As the battle raged, the source remained elusive. However, Amaya now protected Arianna where Captain and Solomon stood. Daggers in hand, the first mate poised for attack, but she had yet to move otherwise. Jabez also resumed his own position, watching and waiting for an opportunity to attack StormShaper.

The sky overhead was roaring despite its subdued effect, feeding on StormShaper's furor. Neither warrior relented in their attacks; StormShaper was obviously unaffected by the storm, and Zatook ignored it completely. Lightning flashed overhead, and a bright blue light surged through the obscure where his eyes should have been before electricity suddenly flared from him, joining with that of the sky and hidden in the ground below. Lightning spiked through the camp, but it was the radial jolts from StormShaper that managed to make contact with the group. It connected with the energy in their bodies, surging through them with stunning force. Several of the pirates were knocked to the ground; Solomon had knelt as the arcs flared out, shoving one of his blades tip-first into the ground before their little group— the etched runes glowed with a strange energy, shielding himself, the first mate, the Moon Child, and little girl from the power and causing the lightning to split around them.

Jabez bodily tackled Alconai out of the way of the blasts aimed at the two men. Once more the ninja felt grateful for the leather in his own outfit as he felt the crackle of electricity in the air. Alconai threw a smirk at his brother. Jabez acknowledged him with a resolute nod. Standing and helping his brother to his feet, the eldest sibling gripped his blade and chain in a ready stance, but he didn't move. He knew from their last encounter that he couldn't hope to defeat StormShaper. Still, he would protect Alconai and Captain as best as he could. He glanced to the side when he heard Amaya growl.

"Damn brat," Amaya muttered, her eyes glaring daggers at the obscure figure. Energy sparked around her hand and blade, but she didn't seem injured. Amaya stayed put, trusting Zatook to handle StormShaper for now. The shadows swirling around Zatook kept the electricity at bay, solidifying whenever the energy lashed out. The ferocity of the battle increased, the two power sources saturating the air with their presences. "Oi!" Amaya called to the crew. "Scatter, or we're gonna be blasted to smithereens!" She scooped Arianna up and nudged Captain's shoulder before helping Solomon to his feet as well. Jabez followed Alconai as the younger man made for some cover in the trees.

***

'Tristan' leapt back to avoid Rose's first swipe, lifting a hand to catch her second blade. A dull sound accompanied the blow, and the Half-Drow found her blade stopped short. Instead of slicing into his hand, it had met his crystal. The twilight-hued substance slowly spread and took shape along his hands, stretching up to form talons around his fingers. A malicious grin spread across Tristan's face as the blood mage manipulated his powers through their connection. Rose quickly surrendered the secondary blade, dodging as his other hand came up to swipe at her abdomen. So, whoever this woman was, she was a close-range fighter when it came to weaponry. Like most blood mages, she no doubt preferred fighting from a distance with her magic. Rose figured her grip must be fairly tenuous if she wasn't trying to fight the same way through Tristan. That could give her an advantage.

Rose's eyes didn't leave the controlled Sun Child as he easily snapped her blade in half and tossed it to the side. She frowned, debating. The crystal was abnormally resilient, as evidenced by the difficulty Jeremiah had in escaping it. What good would the metal of her remaining blade be? Rose sighed. Best to fight magic with magic.

Tristan's eyebrow arched as he watched Rose relax from her sword-stance. "Oh?" the woman's voice taunted. "Surrendering already?"

"Hardly." Rose held out one of her hands wrist-up before slicing across her veins. As her eyes stained red, she sheathed her steel blade. Instead, crimson drained and then twisted, seeming to move of its own accord until a semi-translucent, crystal-like sword was grasped in her hand. The air around her shimmered as the star on her forehead lit up, and a veil of stardust covered the blade to strengthen it. She hoped it would be enough to match Tristan's crystal. The blood mage painted the lad's face with a contemplative look as if weighing the chance it just may be.

Rose didn't give her the time to consider it further. She shifted into a new stance, better suited for a single blade, before charging forward. Tristan quickly raised a hand to fend off her blows, but Rose moved with such speed that the puppeteer was left on the defensive. She couldn't control Tristan and fight at her best, it seemed. Good. Tristan had strong mental capacities, which could tilt the battle in Rose's favor. Hopefully she could incapacitate him before the mage gained a stronger foothold. The pair barely noticed that the sky had darkened overhead; they completely ignored the flashes of lightning as a steady downpour released around them. StormShaper. No wonder the camp didn't seem to hear the sound of a fight so close by. The obscured warrior must be creating a distraction. Rose would have to take Tristan down alone.

Could she? Her eyes narrowed as her blade continued glancing off of Tristan's crystal. The power of the stars seemed enough to reinforce it, but she wasn't really making a dent in his weapons, either. Her reputation wasn't exaggerated— the seamless transition between weapon styles attested to that. But she had mostly fought against humans and the occasional spar with Jeremiah. She hadn't known he was a dragon, mind, but it was a bit obvious to her that he wasn't human. Fighting Tristan felt similar to Jeremiah's human form. Thinking of her former master sparked an idea.

When Tristan caught her blade between both of his hands, she ducked beneath his arms and headbutted his abdomen. She heard the wind escape him as he staggered back; the crimson in his eyes fluctuated. So, pain could throw off the woman's concentration. Not a Drow Elder, then? Perhaps a matron in training, or a lesser priestess? As she wondered, her motions continued to flow. Surely she was Drow; Rose had never felt a human obtain this level of power over blood. She twisted her blade free with a quick flourish and tug as her momentum carried her down. She planted her hands as she turned the motion into a spin, seeking to trip the other warrior. Tristan's handler had recovered, however, and he quickly evaded the attack before slicing crystal talons along Rose's back.

"Is this the best you can do, spawn of T'puuli?" the voice jibed.

"Only a fool allows taunts to sway them," Rose hissed as she righted herself, wincing slightly at the sting in her back.

"Hmmm, and you are not a fool? Time will tell." The woman laughed. "The apple only falls so far from the tree, I'm told."

"Do not let Elder Keeshe hear such words. Or have you not yet heard I am of her line?" That hit a nerve. Tristan suddenly surged forward in a flurry of movement, his speed picking up as the mage tapped into more of his abilities. Rage and loathing painted his expression. "Who... is the fool... now?" Rose taunted even as she dodged and parried; she was completely on the defensive for the moment, but perhaps she could jolt the woman's control. If Tristan's fighting grew less restrained, she would no longer be able to spare breath and thought for banter. Then again, perhaps her opponent was easier to disparage then she initially thought. If such a glib comment could evoke this reaction, what would it take to imbalance her enough for

Tristan to regain himself?

She closed her eyes for the briefest moment, taking a deep breath as she allowed instinct to guide her before slipping into the familiar dance. She lost track of how often they circled or crossed the clearing, exchanging even blows and the occasional scratch. Tristan's Child powers never activated to heal him; could the mage not access a Shaddai-chosen gift, then? It would make sense by the Teachings. Though, that meant she should be careful; when all was said and done, he would need to be healed. If they were both too tired, the result could be fatal. But how to conserve her energy and goad the mage? Time stretched around them, yet she knew they couldn't have been fighting for more than a few minutes.

The way the woman spoke of Elder Keeshe, she must have studied under her. Yet she had not grasped the Drow's temperament control. Keeshe was full of hatred and rage, but she always kept a calm exterior anywhere other than her own chambers. Oftentimes, even there. Perhaps Rose could use that to her advantage. So far the pair was fighting fairly evenly; Rose had no doubt that would not last if the woman managed to take full control of Tristan. Rose would be held back from her concern for her comrade, whereas this witch would want her dead. Or, at least, close enough to deliver her back to Jeremiah or Keeshe herself.

The pair disconnected, Tristan flexing his hands as Rose slid a stray clump of wet hair back behind her shoulders. The rain was washing away Arianna's work, but there was little she could do to save the flowers. Her focus needed to be on the battle at hand. A steady shimmer of silver formed around her, just enough to keep the water from her eyes so she could see clearly. She let it hit her back, the mostly pure water helping to wash away the blood. She didn't want to spare energy for healing; she had fought with worse. She turned her attention back to Tristan, who was examining a talon.

"I wonder…" the words whispered across the distance as pure-red eyes rose to meet the Half-Drow's gaze. Curiosity spread to a slow grin. Rose's eyes narrowed.

"What are you planning, witch?"

"What would be the fun in telling you, Tainted?"

Rose sighed. Talking was little use at this point; she should conserve her efforts. But something in that expression gnawed at her. What was she missing? Well, she would just have to regain the mage's attention before any other foul plots could solidify in her head. Rose gripped her hilt tightly, sliding back into a fighting stance. She planted her feet, shifting her rear leg back a hair before pressing off at a run.

Some soldiers would holler at their enemy with every swing, every attack, but Rose was silent. She was breathing. She measured each step, each swing, each parry and counter. The crystal weaponry gave sharp sounds as they connected, reminding her of crumbling slate in a quarry or spar blades connecting. Sharpened magical rock against sharpened magical rock rang through the clearing as the two continued to match strengths, possessed warrior against tiring soldier. And she was tiring. Tristan's stamina was incredible on its own, but she knew the witch could also force him to fight at full capacity past the usual limits of fatigue. Technically, Rose could do that to herself; she was loathe to do so. The results and recovery threatened to be a catastrophe their group really could not afford were Tristan to slip from their battle and escape. It was a delicate balance, weighing the current battle against what could be.

Stardust-shielded blade met dark crystal claw with growing ferocity. Rose noted that her blade was starting to crack; with some surprise, she saw the same could be said of Tristan's crystal. She moved to press her advantage; reforming her weapon would be easier than the witch having to reform Tristan's crystal if the lad was still giving her trouble. That could be the opening she needed. She let a little more energy into her attacks, quickening her steps and strengthening her swings. It was a gamble, but she couldn't afford to play it safe for the entire battle. Crystal collided with crystal as she pressed, the mage losing ground in their current exchange.

Rose chanced a glance at the trees behind her opponent, noting with satisfaction a sturdy trunk nearby. If she could get the mage backed against it, she would have her opening. The mage seemed to realize what she was attempting. With a hint of desperation, Tristan shifted, his palm blocking Rose's next blow. Their weapons collided with such strength that both crystals shattered at the point of impact. Rose winced as shards of both hit her arm, but she was focused on her opponent. On reforming her blade, on swinging for Tristan's hand again in the hopes of gaining access to his blood.

She immediately stopped her swing when Tristan staggered back, reaching a shaking hand to his forehead. The red in his eyes faded slightly; was that all the opening he needed? Tristan's whole form was shaking as he backed up again, both hands on his head. If she moved to help, would it break his concentration? She watched, warily matching steps as Tristan backed against the tree, doubling over. He gripped his hair tightly, a slight growl escaping him. Rose didn't approach to reach for his blood, instead reaching for his mind. It was like approaching a brick wall.

Let me in, Tristan. Let me help.

Why? It wasn't Tristan's voice that answered. *Why are you fighting so hard for this one? Just let me have the delicious thing. We'll take good care of him...*

Rose scowled. *I know what it is to seek freedom, witch; I will not let you take him.* She stepped forward, reaching a hand towards one of the wounds she had managed to inflict earlier. Tristan's head snapped up, the wicked grin back in place.

"You let your guard down, Tainted," the woman's voice hissed just as pain seared along Rose's arm. She hollered in surprise, staggering back and quickly raising her arm to look. Shards of Tristan's crystal had embedded there, and now they were splintering and spreading, worsening her wounds and creating new ones. Rose tried to call on her blood, but she had to leap back as Tristan surged forward and swiped at her.

The witch wasn't giving her a chance to concentrate, tapping into more of Tristan's strength, his speed. Rose struggled to keep up; she had formed a new blade in her other hand, haphazardly blocking Tristan's attacks as she tried to focus past the pain spreading along her arm. She hollered as a furious string of swipes landed more blows, planted more shards of crystal.

I'm going to lose. The thought hit clear as a bell. The mage had found her advantage, and Rose was slipping. But she couldn't let the woman get away with Tristan. She mustn't. Rose growled as she moved to block Tristan's next swipe, but then hollered as he managed to knock her blade from her hand. Her wrist was numb from the jarring blow. She moved to jump back, to regain some distance between them, but Tristan matched her leap— only his was faster. He flashed right up in front of her face as his claws pierced her abdomen. Rose choked on the pain, blood and bile rising in her throat, reflexively grasping Tristan's shoulder. He leaned forward, the witch's voice whispering in her ear.

"The only freedom you will ever know, Tainted One, is death." Tristan grinned as he pulled his arm free and pushed her away. She could only stagger. Before she could fall, Tristan's foot connected with her abdomen where he had pierced her. The blow was powerful enough to send her flying before she crashed down into the river. Pain and darkness consumed her as the water closed around her head.

***

Lightning flared up from the ground encircling the camp, trapping them within its bounds. The energy didn't fade like normal bolts, instead flaring as a barrier. Captain's eyes narrowed; she slid to a stop in her run before she could collide with the power. She chewed on her lip slightly and flexed her fingers. She couldn't use the teleport trick like she had with Jabez, she simply couldn't handle that many let alone control where they landed. As Solomon caught up to her, she suddenly raised a hand to her head and swayed. Her eye was glimmering with power as Solomon caught her. Before he could even ask if she was all right, she bolted upright in his arms.

"I's a distraction! 'e's jus' keepin' us from Rose and Tris!" Zatook's eyes narrowed as her words reached him, but that was not all that changed. His irises stained a deep black while purple runes ignited within. His skin seemed to darken, as if the shadows themselves were seeping into his flesh. He was faster, stronger— more power flared behind his blade. StormShaper actually laughed as he increased his own pace to match. Finally, a challenge! He did not need to hold back with this one.

Stormie-boo, time to go. You have precious cargo to escort.

StormShaper's laughter faded as the warrior growled. He suddenly skidded into the dirt, locking blades with Zatook.

"It would appear my task is finished," he growled, bright blue blazing from within the enchantment once again. "Another time, then." The power blasted outwards, more intense than before since he had stopped holding back. A bolt of lightning dropped from the sky; instead of connecting to him, he merged with it and vanished into the clouds. Zatook staggered from the sudden loss of contact, but he turned the move into a pivot and ran for the river as the lightning barrier faded in its master's absence.

Jabez had frowned in concern at Captain's cry. He quickly darted after Zatook toward the direction of the river. As he sprinted, Jabez staggered slightly when an immense sense of fear lanced through his core, freezing his blood. Cries of alarm sounded behind him in the camp. So, it wasn't just him, but then what was causing this? The farther he got from the camp, the less the influence seemed to affect him until, finally, Jabez managed to push the emotion down altogether. For now, he chose not to ponder it and focused on finding his missing comrades.

Back in the camp, the immense fear catapulted through everyone. All the pirates cried out in alarm at the invasion of emotion and stared fearfully in the directions that Zatook and the lightning wielder had gone. Alconai frowned at the sensation but kept himself from panicking. He'd felt something like this before, a long time ago. To his surprise, Amaya barely reacted either as she cradled Arianna. The child curled into the pirate's arms, clutching her shirt and shaking with silent sobs. Alconai felt for the little one. Could she be causing this? It'd become apparent that she and her brother weren't normal humans, after all. After a moment, Amaya gently handed Arianna to Solomon before joining the search party herself. The little girl clung to Solomon now, half her face tucked against his neck while the other half revealed tear tracks on her cheek. Tristan said that he'd be back. She believed him, but she wanted him so badly. Her brother always kept her safe. Shakily, she began making the sign the group knew she used for Tristan's name. Her eyes pleaded with Solomon as the child continued making the sign.

Solomon sighed as he tucked the girl close, gently rocking her. "We will find him, Anna," he assured her softly. "Zatook has gone to help him even as we speak. Easy, child." He was moderately impressed that Alconai had managed to withstand the emotive assault. Amaya he understood, and he had experience with powerful empaths as well. But the minstrel was a surprise. He would have to ask the lad later; what other hidden talents did these siblings possess?

***

Rose lay on the bank a few miles from where she had faced Tristan. Her wounds screamed; the sand beneath was staining crimson with her blood. She knew the wounds should have killed her, but she also knew she couldn't die. Not now. Rose stared at the sky with a lifeless gaze. She was not going to give the blood-witch the satisfaction of having those last words affect her. She knew better. Rose winced as the clouds overhead continued to let loose their watery burden. Normally she loved the rain, but right now it only brought more pain. She closed her eyes, attempting to numb her body. As the rain began to fall harder, she cried out. There was no ignoring this. This was the worst she had ever been— it *hurt*. Still, she refused to lose consciousness. She could feel the cold embrace of death tempting her with eternal rest and peace, yet she struggled. Her entire body fired pangs of protest as Rose forced herself to her feet.

"Tri...stan..." she reminded herself in painful gasps. Rose managed to stagger forward a few steps before her legs gave way, momentum skidding her broken body in the sand. Rose hollered in pain but tried once more. "Tri...s... tan..." This cycle repeated for a while. Rose held herself up on all fours, coughing. She forced herself upright on her knees, then tensed as a cold hand steadied her shoulder.

"Easy, Child," a soothing voice cautioned. The owner of the hand stepped around the Star Child to reveal herself. Her skin was deathly white with a hint of ethereal blue. Her eyes were hollow, dark pits, yet deep within was a spark of light. Ink black hair flowed loosely around her shoulders and down her back. She wore a black gown that nigh-imperceptibly shifted into shadows further down. She was both terrifying and beautiful. Rose's eyes widened, and she instinctively jerked back, but the woman kept her grip. "Why do you struggle, Child? Why do you refuse my embrace?" The woman's voice held concern.

"M-my Lady…forgive…me…I…c-cannot…. die now." Rose shuddered. It pained her to even speak.

"What is so important," questioned the woman, "that you must endure this suffering?" Rose stared at the ground a moment, before looking the woman straight in the eyes.

"I love him." With that last gasp, Rose collapsed. The Celestial of Death held her gently, cradling the Half-Drow.

"Love," Lady Rin repeated with a distant smile. "Very well, Child." She placed a hand on Rose's forehead, reaching into her mind. *I will grant you the power you seek, but there will be a price.*

***

Zatook knelt by the Half-Drow, hand gently brushing her hair back. He had barely managed to find Rose. Her life force was gone. Tristan's life force had already traveled far from the forest. He had failed them. He had failed his mother. The Star Child was dead, the Sun Child was captured. Now what were they to do? He didn't glance up when he heard the others arrive. The pirates were silent as they took in the downed woman. They gave way when Captain arrived at a run, sliding onto her knees opposite of Zatook.

"…Oh Lawd, Rosie…" she sighed. "T'is i' gunna 'urt, love." Zatook frowned as she placed her thumb on the woman's forehead, sitting up straighter when the Star Child gasped. Zatook stared, stunned. How? He lifted his gaze to meet Captain's, but her expression told him it would have to wait. Jabez flinched back when Rose breathed. He honestly thought she was dead. Hadn't she been, though? He shook his head. It didn't matter right now. He stepped up beside Captain and touched a hand to her shoulder.

"We should get her back and healed," the ninja suggested. His gaze then swept over the area again, searching for any sign of the Sun Child's whereabouts. After all the promises they made about helping the boy and his sister stay safe, they let this happen. If— when —they got him back, would Tristan ever be able to trust them again? Captain nodded, but her gaze looked distant. She stood, jerking her head towards Rose. The pirates acted quickly, gingerly lifting Rose off of the ground and moving her back to camp. Captain glanced at Jabez over her shoulder.

"Tris is nae in t'e fores' anymo'e," she told him quietly. "T'ough ye prob'ly guessed as much."

Jabez nodded. He glanced at Zatook, considering the man's powers. "I get the feeling my tracking skills won't do us much good at the moment. Do you think you can find his trail?"

Zatook nodded but paused when Captain lifted her hand. "As much as I be wantin' to follow 'im, we ainnae in t'e condition. Ge' back to camp fer now. Le's get t'e ot'ers healed an' ge' some supplies. We migh' be needin' tha' shield o' Rose's." Jabez sighed but nodded.

When they reached the camp, Arianna was still clinging to Solomon. The girl had cried herself to sleep, but her hand clutched the man's vest. Amaya soon joined them with the rest of the crew. She worked with them to remake the camp as best as they could. Jabez watched all this with a sense of unease. His gaze strayed to Rose once more. He felt tempted to pull Captain aside and ask if she knew what happened to the Drow, but he had a feeling the pirate girl would address that in due time.

Bitter Reunions

Tristan had fought the control over his body throughout the fight with Rose. His struggles only intensified when he was forced to watch himself kick her into the river, anger boiling his blood and hardening his resolve. Still, it hadn't been enough. Even now, his body moved without his consent, racing across Aviyah. When StormShaper joined him, Tristan's heart sank with dread. Even with the landscape blurred, he knew where he was going. As dusk settled, the all-too-familiar castle loomed on the hill. He tried to turn around, to stop, to collapse, anything to keep from reaching that accursed structure.

Unlike the high lord's dark personality, the castle actually appeared rather beautiful and cheery. Beige masonry gave the architecture a light and pleasant look. The heavy gate opened for the new arrivals, and as soon as he raced across the path through the courtyard, Tristan's eyes took in the details etched into the trimmings of the castle fixtures, the sights familiar but not comforting. Stained glass windows added spots of decoration. Off to one side stood a closed-in garden where Tristan had spent time with his mother and his instructor Almas. On the other side lay the barracks where Tsukuyomi's human soldiers resided and trained. All these details Tristan recognized from his time living here. It had been his home. Memories of his mother and the friendly staff mingled sorrow with his dread, the recollections tainted by the presence of his father.

And then Tristan saw him. The power controlling him forced his body to a standstill halfway to the keep as Tsukuyomi strode with deliberate steps toward his wayward son. The sound of the gate shutting behind him tightened Tristan's chest with despair. He struggled against the power holding him to no avail, his body trembling slightly now with the effort. He watched helplessly and with growing dread as his father approached. Shadows of twilight magnified the dark and intimidating form of Lord Tsukuyomi. His silver eyes locked with Tristan's gaze, holding the young man's eyes with his commanding presence alone. The last time Tristan had seen his father, the man had delivered the blow that would kill his mother.

Tristan couldn't even flinch away as Tsukuyomi reached up and grasped his bicep where the younger man had felt the strange sensation earlier. With the grip closing around his arm, Tristan felt another sensation like something crawling around his arm and locking into place. This time when Tristan wanted to step back, his body did as he desired. He could still feel the power within his body, but for now it had released its control. Tsukuyomi's grip kept him from stepping farther away, though. The man's eyes flicked to StormShaper in silent dismissal. Once the man was gone, Tsukuyomi reached up with his other hand and gripped Tristan's other arm the same way.

"I regret that your stubbornness forced my hand, but finally you have returned to where you belong," he intoned solemnly. "Welcome home, son." Tristan glared at Tsukuyomi. Despite the man's almost heartfelt grip and his calm words, the Sun Child knew better.

"This is not my home. And you stopped being my father the day you killed my mother." This time when he pulled back,

Tsukuyomi released him.

"That was not the outcome I had intended, but there is nothing that can be done about it now," the man commented evenly. "You cannot escape this. We are bound by blood." Tristan's frown deepened. He knew his father wouldn't release him without some plan to keep him from running. Still, he decided to test it. Turning, Tristan made a dash for the gate. However, the closer he drew, the heavier his body felt and the more sluggish his movements became until he stopped just short of the entrance. He trembled as his body locked in place once more. How? Tristan thought back to his father's touch on his arm and the strange sensation. *We are bound by blood*, his father's words echoed in his mind. Blood magic? His mind flashed back to StormShaper cutting Tristan's arm and then retreating, the power that forced him to fight Rose, and the same power now holding him in place. He tried to summon his crystal or his Child powers, but nothing happened.

"A blood bond?" Tristan asked through gritted teeth. He couldn't even startle when his father's hand touched his shoulder and turned him to face the man. The hand then lifted Tristan's chin to meet his father's gaze once more.

"Yes. I will return your freedom and powers once I can trust that you will behave," the man stated. "Your disobedience to return has consequences, Tristan. As glad as I am to finally have you returned, as both your father and your liege, I cannot allow your actions to go unpunished. Be grateful that your sentence is a merciful one."

"Merciful? You forced me to fight my ally. You dragged me back here against my will after killing my mother," Tristan growled, "and you want me to be grateful? I couldn't be further from it."

"In time you will learn. Now, I have a guest to see, but we will continue our conversation later." He released Tristan's face and turned away, indicating for his son to follow him. Once it was obvious he would be given no choice in the matter, Tristan stopped fighting the control and his father released it, allowing the younger man to follow on his own. He caught a glimpse of servants as the main door opened for his father and him. Soon, Tristan found himself walking down familiar hallways. He remembered walking and playing in these halls when he was still a child. A part of him wondered if Instructor Almas still worked for his father. He doubted the man had stayed, though, once Tristan fled with his mother. The Sun Child watched his father's back as Tsukuyomi led him to the audience chamber. He instructed Tristan to stand off to the side while Tsukuyomi awaited his guest. It wasn't long before the person was escorted in by a servant. Tristan's eyes widened.

"Sir Jeremiah, welcome," Tsukuyomi greeted solemnly. "Allow me to properly introduce my son, Tristan. Tristan, this is Sir Jeremiah, a knight of great renown in the kingdom. Although, from what I understand, that title stands to change." His gaze met Jeremiah's levelly. "What news of the king?" Tristan's eyes remained fixed on the new arrival. What was the dragon doing here? However, before he could react, he felt his control seized momentarily to keep him still and silent. His eyes caught his father's pointed glance. The control remained even as Tsukuyomi returned his attention to his guest. Tristan's mind reeled. How did his father know the dragon knight? And what did Tsukuyomi mean about the king?

"To think the random boy from the forest held more interest than I at first believed." Jeremiah smirked at Tristan. "So, the elusive Nightshade is also heir. I see now why you sought him quite so fervently. Not unlike my own fallen star, so full of surprises." His gaze returned to Tsukuyomi. "As for the king, well...It seems Andor's treachery knows no bounds, and they sent a blood witch to kill him in light of our impending war. With no heir, the advisors practically begged me to take his place." The smirk slid to a full grin. "Marilyn is quite convincing, it seems. The people are none-the-wiser, and all the more ready to take on Andor regardless of their so-called demon."

Tsukuyomi nodded. "That bodes well. Of course, I will provide whatever support you require so long as our agreement stands." Tristan frowned as his gaze flicked between his father and the knight turned king. They had killed the king of Nocis and now wished to wage all-out war with Andor. But why? At the mention of Andor's Demon, Tristan's mind flashed to Zatook. Would he be forced to fight the man that had been helping him? And then there was the part of his father having his own goal. The boy's heart sank. He knew very little of what his father was planning except it was important enough to kill his mother over when she refused to cooperate. Tristan tried to struggle free of the control, but still he remained compliant against his will.

Jeremiah arched an eyebrow. "I gave my word, did I not?" he noted calmly. "Though... your blood-witch may have gone too far with the Star Child during her more recent," he hesitated, his eyes darting to Tristan, "acquisition." His gaze returned to Tsukuyomi. "Killing the Drow simply makes our predicaments more perilous— should she perish, we'll have to worry about her replacement in the cycle." Tristan felt his gut twist even as his heart sank into it. At the mention of Rose, the memory of the fight and him kicking her into the river left a sour taste in his mouth. He prayed for her protection and life. She couldn't die. Not by his hands; she was too strong for her life to end that way.

"I apologize for my blood-witch's overzealous nature. If the need arises, I will personally see to any precautions required," Tsukuyomi assured ambiguously. His gaze remained on Jeremiah, not even sparing Tristan a glance for now. Tristan, for his part, glared as best he could at his father.

Jeremiah nodded. "I should leave you to it, then. I have a war to prepare for, and I get the feeling your wayward ward still needs some taming." He smirked, turning to leave. "I can see myself out," he assured the pair, waving a hand.

Tsukuyomi waited until Jeremiah had gone before calling Marilyn. "Take Tristan to the solitary cell. I'll be there shortly." Marilyn hummed in response, hooking a finger in Tristan's collar and vanishing to the dungeon.

Tristan struggled against the control again but ended up with the same result as before. This was the blood witch that had taken control of him, he was sure. The woman who forced him to fight Rose. Anger blazed hot in Tristan's chest and eyes as he did his best to glare at her. Marilyn grinned wickedly when she felt his blood surge. She was confident that glaring was all he could do, but it still brought her joy that he wanted to keep struggling. She held up her other hand, gripping a see-through red stone tightly.

"You were sloppy, weren't you? Letting Mr. Thundercloud collect a sample for me..." Tristan barely managed to force a growl from his throat. Yes, he'd been sloppy, but he knew it wasn't entirely his fault. Circumstances had been stacked against him in that fight. Even so, he shouldn't have let StormShaper get a cut on him. He finally stopped struggling against the control for now. He wouldn't be able to break free, not in his condition. His body felt even worse thanks to the fight this blood mage forced him into with Rose. His eyes flashed when he thought of the Drow once more.

Marilyn cackled at him as she led him to a cell, shackling him in. "I made this just for you," Marilyn explained gleefully as she released her control. She giggled as he studied the barriers. He could hazard a guess about the runes painted in blood on the cell's floor and walls. Still, he struggled just enough to test them. Sure enough, they prevented him from calling forth his powers or using his strength to break the shackles. Despite the glare he trained once more on the witch, he knew trying to break free would only cause him to weaken more.

"Tough luck, kiddo. My, my, you've had a rough day. Finally woke up, left your sister, killed your girlfriend, and reunited with your father! You must be *exhausted*." She positively cackled now. Tristan's scowl intensified, his hands itching to drive a sword of crystal through the woman's face. However, even as he stood with his back straight, he felt just how drained he was. Still, he refused to allow his now trembling body to collapse with that woman still in the room. As for the woman's taunts, he was no stranger to mind games. And yet, he remembered the injuries his powers had inflicted on the Drow, remembered putting a hole through her torso. As much as he wanted to believe she was alive, doubt gnawed at him. Rose was strong; she had to be alive. And yet, even as Tristan tried to convince himself, he felt tears sting his eyes. As strong as

Rose was, a tumble in the river with her injuries could have easily finished her. Tristan closed his eyes to shut out his doubts.

"You didn't stick around to check for a corpse," he insisted, determination strong in his voice despite his trepidations. "Who's the sloppy one now, witch?"

"Oh? What's this, feeling in your heart of hearts she's alive? Then tell me— why hasn't she attempted to reach you, hm? I felt that little connection in your mind. Not there anymore, is it?" Marilyn laughed as she leaned against the wall. "Poor widdle Trissie, doesn't want to accept that he killed his widdle girlfriend."

Tristan shook his head. There could be other reasons she wasn't answering him. It was true he couldn't feel her connection anymore, but would he given the wards and barriers placed on and around him? Why would his father risk allowing that connection to remain? He snapped his tear-filled eyes open and glared at the blood mage.

"She wouldn't die that easily. It's just as likely my father or you are blocking the connection somehow. Why would he allow it to remain, after all? As for killing her myself, I'm not the one who fought and wounded her. That was your doing." He did his best to ignore the voice in the back of his mind reminding him that the blood witch wouldn't have had the chance if his mental fortitude had been stronger. Marilyn laughed louder, doubling over before raising herself back up and simmering to a chuckle.

"Face facts, Trissie-boy," she advised. "You're a curse. First your mom, now your girlfriend...Geez, you're unlucky with the women in your life. "

"I guess that's true," Tristan ground out, "because when I get out of these chains, I'm going to kill you." He met her gaze with fierce determination.

Marilyn laughed again, leaning her head back. "Ah, man, Trissie-boy, you're a hoot, a real riot," she told him cheerily. "But you forget—" Suddenly, her face was stone-cold, her hand holding up the stone as pain suddenly boiled through Tristan's blood. "I own you right now. For the Master, of course." Tristan shuddered with the pain, biting back a cry. He wouldn't give her the satisfaction. Another shiver ran through him when he felt a familiar, foreboding presence approach the cell. The aura shrouded everything in a veil of cold. Tristan remembered that feeling all too well, and he braced himself for his father's arrival. With a wave to Marilyn to release the torment and step back, the High Lord entered the cell, his merciless gaze locked with Tristan's azure eyes.

***

Captain pulled out the pot they had been using to cook, gathering a bunch of seemingly random ingredients before stewing them all together. An almost putridly sweet scent filled the camp as she worked, but the flighty lass seemed subdued. Her eyes occasionally wandered to the tent Rose had been set in. Solomon noted her gaze with a frown, but instead of moving to ask, he stayed with the little girl asleep in his arms and trusted Amaya to check in on their shared ward. Amaya approached Captain and peered into the pot. However, she didn't comment on the contents.

"All right, Captain. What's happened to Rose? No one here is buying that she wasn't dead just a bit ago," she commented.

Captain didn't say anything for a moment, watching the pot simmer. "She still is," the girl noted quietly. "Bu' I cannae le' tha' on. T'e crew's on edge as i' is from t'e Sto'm." She reached up to run her fingers through her hair. "T'e futu'e be 'azy," she admitted quietly. "I keep wonderin' wha' we're s'pose' to do wit' the Sta' Chil' a zombie. I sense Lady Rin's power clingin' to 'er, bu' I cannae tell how or wha' deal they may have struck. I cannae See Trissie, eit'er, an' yet..." She raised her gaze to the clouds. "I 'ave a bad feelin' about things." She took a deep breath, standing a little straighter and gazing back at her task. Amaya sighed but said nothing. Her gaze swept across the group. She noticed Jabez standing nearby, listening without partaking. He met her gaze for a moment before shifting it to the expanse of trees surrounding them.

"Whatever the deal, then, Lady Rin means to collect Rose afterwards. And we'll be back to square one," Amaya remarked, though she meant no disrespect by it. Her eyes strayed to Arianna sleeping in Solomon's arms, her gaze softening sadly.

"Aye, unless t'e Lady 'as somet'in' up 'er sleeve." Captain calmly ladled the purple stew into small vials. "T'e Sisters been takin' an interest in events lately, so she jus' migh'. T'ough I donnae see the Lady of Death cheatin' 'erself, ye ken?" She shook her head. "This is one o' those times where we'll jus' 'ave to wait an' see. Le's focus on gettin' Tris back first, ya?" She shifted her gaze to Zatook. "Find a map an' mark out where we need to be goin'. We're gonna need at least an idea of wha' we be up against." The warrior nodded, bowing slightly before moving off to do as instructed. Amaya's gaze darkened in contemplation, but she simply nodded. She then moved over to Solomon and gently stroked Arianna's brown ringlets.

"Don't you worry, Anna. We'll get your brother back," she told the sleeping little girl. Her gaze then shifted to Solomon. "How is she doing?"

"She is distraught," he answered honestly. "She worries for her brother— I doubt she will rest well until we find him." He glanced up to meet Amaya's gaze. "For now, I am subduing her empathic abilities. Hopefully, we won't have a camp-wide influx of emotions again." He couldn't help a slight smirk. "I suppose I should be thankful for all the practice Isabella gave me." He barely flinched when a bit of cloth hit the back of his head.

"I 'eard tha', Ol' man. Ye ken be'er than to call me tha'."

Amaya smirked for a moment at the banter. "Yeah...Zatook seems like he might be able to find our prodigal at least," she murmured. Her expression changed back to being more serious. "I've got a feeling we're in for one hell of a fight. And the only one who might have a clue as to what happened is currently unconscious." She straightened and moved to the tent where the pirates had placed Rose. Entering, she knelt by the Drow and gently touched a hand to Rose's brow. "Hey, Rose. We need a little help. Do you know what happened to Tristan?" she kept her voice low so no one would hear her.

Rose's eyes flickered but didn't open. She could barely lift a finger, let alone summon her voice. Instead, she contacted the woman's mind. *Blood mage.*

Amaya moved her hand to Rose's shoulder and rubbed it lightly. "We'll get him back," she told the girl. She then headed back out to speak with Captain. "Blood mage took Tristan, or so Rose said," she told the sprightly girl.

"Probably the same one that teamed up with StormShaper before, aye? That's at least part of what we be walkin' into."

Captain nodded, standing. "Tell t'e crew to ge' some rest. I'll take a peek an' see wha' I can fin'." She moved over to Solomon, sitting behind him and leaning her back against his as she rested her hands on her knees and closed her eyes. Before too long, the tell-tale rainbow shimmer flickered beneath her eyelids. Amaya gave the orders and then checked on Rose to make sure the Star Child was comfortable. She glanced at Solomon when she reemerged, smirking at the sight of Captain resting against his back. After a moment, she went in search of Zatook to make sure he'd found a map and was able to chart a course for the group to travel.

***

Tsukuyomi slowly approached his son. Despite his fear and the pain echoing throughout his body, Tristan straightened and faced his father bravely. Tsukuyomi towered over the boy like the Lord of Shadow he was.

"I had hoped you would have returned of your own volition, but as the years passed I concluded that your mother managed to convince you that I was the monster she believed me to be," Tsukuyomi said in an emotionless voice. The boy scoffed softly. Seeing his mother die at his father's hands had been all the persuasion he had needed. Seeming to guess his son's train of thought, Tsukuyomi continued, "I never intended to kill your mother. I truly regret that our disagreement escalated to such an extent, as it caused more problems than it resolved. All of this could have been avoided if she'd have let me use the Talisman of Ruin."

"So, when she refused to give you the object entrusted to her for safekeeping, you tried to force her," Tristan spat.

"Yes." His father's level answer sent ice down Tristan's spine. "However, I knew in the event of her passing, the Talisman would fall to another keeper unless she named a successor. Despite our differences, I knew my wife's mind. After she died, the less my search yielded results, the more certain I became of her course of action in her final moments." Tsukuyomi's hand reached out and gripped Tristan's chin lightly. His grip tightened when the boy tried to pull away. "With Arianna being too young and Reina's time running short, her best option was you." Tristan steeled his expression, not wanting to give anything away, but his father saw right through him. "Deny it all you want; I sensed the power within you during our mental encounters. Now, I give you the choice I once presented to your mother. As the Talisman's keeper, only you can summon it. You don't have to carry this responsibility. Just as your mother passed the Talisman to you, you have the choice to give it to another to be used. Either stand with me as you are meant to as my son and heir or, if your conscience won't allow you such, then give it to me so that I may remake the world into a better place."

"No," the young warrior refused. He wouldn't let his mother's sacrifice be in vain, and he wouldn't let his father use him as a puppet. He grimaced as his father's grip tightened on his jaw.

Tsukuyomi spoke coldly, "Keep in mind, I will not make the same mistake as last time. The decision seems simple enough when you are called to sacrifice your own life, but the bravado falters when your decision costs a life other than your own." Tristan's eyes widened, his heart dropping into his stomach with his father's words. Tsukuyomi released his son and stood tall as he regarded the boy with his level gaze. "Who will you allow to die for your stubbornness?"

Tristan fought to regain his composure. "They're not so weak," he insisted, praying silently to the Sacreds that he was right.

"It's not a matter of strength, but rather a matter of knowledge. And I know enough about my enemy to find their weaknesses. Even the mightiest man will fall if you pinch the right nerve." Tsukuyomi regarded his son as his words sank into Tristan's mind. "Who would you have die first? The pirate girl? The ninja? Or maybe your sister?"

Tristan's vibrant blue eyes flashed dangerously at him. "Stay away from her," he demanded.

"Whether any of them live or die is in your hands, Tristan," Tsukuyomi told him. He summoned a small mass of darkness in his hand. After a moment, the shadows fell away to reveal a diamond pendant clutched in the man's hand.

Ice ran through Tristan's veins when he saw the pendant, heart racing. "No. H-How...?" he breathed in horror. His father had created the pendant to bind Arianna's essence with the intention of controlling her. Tristan's mother had taken it with them when she fled with the children, and with her passing Tristan had hidden it in a place he had hoped his father would never reach. Had he truly failed so horribly?

"Where better to hide something so precious than in a

sanctuary forest guarded by elves and a seasoned Drow?" Tsukuyomi answered calmly.

"What did you do to them?" Tristan demanded quietly. The inhabitants of the forest that had helped him raise Arianna and taught him so much. Wise, patient Clo who had taken Tristan under his wing. They couldn't be dead.

"Your friends fought valiantly against me, but in the end they were no match for my power. I tore the forest apart and cut down anyone or anything that dared to interfere," his father told him.

"Why would you?" Tristan's mind raced as he stared at the diamond. Why would his father go to such lengths just to get his sister's pendant? Then, realization dawned. "You still can't find mine." His mother had hidden the one Tsukuyomi had made for Tristan years ago. "You wanted leverage because even with a blood bond, you wouldn't be able to force me to use the Talisman. And you have no guarantee that using my pendant would have yielded different results."

Tsukuyomi nodded almost imperceptibly in Tristan's peripheral vision. "You've always been astute, Tristan. And now, you must choose." He gripped the pendant in his hand.

"Stop it!" Tristan demanded instantly. Tsukuyomi continued to grip the pendent more tightly. Tristan watched in horror and pulled vainly against his shackles. If his father broke the pendant, Arianna's essence would scatter. She would die. "Please…don't!" he pleaded. He felt his father's hand grip his chin once more and force him to look at him. Tristan's expression changed to desperate anger as he met his father's merciless gaze.

"It's your choice, Tristan. Your sister's life or the Talisman."
Tristan felt defeat crushing his soul, the sensation so
unbearable he almost stopped breathing. The boy shook as
he stood frozen in his father's grip. For seven years, Tristan
had protected her. But now he felt completely useless. He
knew the right answer, but how could he give it knowing
the consequences?

The boy took a breath and quietly forced the most difficult
answer he'd had to give through his lips: "No."

Without another word, Tsukuyomi gripped the pendant
tighter in his hand. As he watched cracks form in the
diamond, Tristan felt warm tears slip from his eyes.
Desperation filled him as the lad fought to connect to
his powers to stop his father. Despite knowing it would
be in vain, Tristan threw himself against the chains. He
strained in his effort to break them. "You can't. She's your
daughter!" Tristan screamed. He couldn't just stand here
and watch his father kill his sister. He had to do something.
Anything. For a moment, he felt the familiar warmth of
his Child power run through him. If he could just channel
enough of it to break free.

A soft, tinkling crack robbed all warmth from Tristan's
being. He used his mind to call to the only person he could
think of even though he knew she would never hear him.
Rose! His eyes watched in horrified despair as the pendant
shattered. Tears spilled down Tristan's cheeks, his eyes
wide in stunned disbelief. A crushing pain stabbed through
his chest as a sob wrenched from his throat. "Arianna," he
cried softly.

***

Arianna slept soundly in Solomon's arms. Her features had relaxed from worried to peaceful during her slumber. The little girl's head lay on Solomon's shoulder with her face nestled in the crook of his neck. Her warm breath ghosted the pirate's dark skin rhythmically. Then stopped.

Ruin and Reckoning

Captain suddenly hollered, doubling over and clutching her eye. Though she did not look, she could See. She saw the spike of power from the Star Child, silver flares radiating from the tent as the Drow within arched in sudden pain and turmoil. She saw the look of confusion turn to horror on Solomon's face as Arianna's thread unraveled, her soul fading away. She saw Amaya, trying so hard to restrain herself and yet clenching her fists tight enough to draw blood. She saw the surprise and horror among the pirates. She saw Tristan, curled on the dungeon floor, shimmering dust covering the ground before him. She saw Lady Rin standing at the edge of their camp, watching. The Moon Child sucked in a breath, regaining control before shakily standing. Jabez helped steady her.

"This is grievous indeed," Rin whispered to the air, stepping into the clearing. The camp grew still as they registered Lady Rin's presence. The pirates slowly backed away from the Guardian of Death, uncertainty flashing across their features. Lady Rin strode past them all, gently kneeling before Solomon and holding out her arms. His grip on Arianna's lifeless body tightened a moment but then loosened. Lady Rin gingerly took the young girl.

"Have no fear: she will rest well in my embrace." She cradled the small girl in her pale arms before standing. Her gaze fell on Solomon before turning to take in Andor's stoic champion and the others before finally landing on Rose.

While everyone had been watching the dark Lady, Rose had slowly exited the tent. She stood at its mouth, gripping the cloth tightly. "Your duty awaits," Rin told her solemnly. "I grant you one final boon: you will feel no pain until your task is complete." Rose nodded before turning to glare at the others in the camp.

"Who will come?" the Star Child asked softly, but there was no warmth in her tone. She was a soldier once more. Zatook did not hesitate, Captain coming up alongside him. The pirates looked at each other uneasily, then at Captain. She shook her head at them.

"No' all o' ye. Some need to return t' t'e ship. Get 'er somewhere safe." She glanced at Zatook. "Ye can 'elp them ge' back, ya? Before takin' us?" He nodded. She turned to her crew again. "Pack up t'e camp; leave us enough to travel wit', take the res' back to the *Effervescence*." She moved to help, but also to split the pirates into two parties— those she was sending to help sail the ship, and those she knew could help in the fight. Tsukuyomi was a Nocium High Lord, after all. He would have regular soldiers to contend with on top of his powerhouses.

Rose watched them all a moment before turning to stare into the shadows. *Tristan.* She closed her eyes, willing her voice to reach him. *Tristan, we are coming.*

Jabez and Alconai stepped forward. Both men appeared stoic, their gazes hardened. Amaya remained rigid where she stood, indecision warring in her eyes with the anger roiling there. She stared off into the distance as though trying to kill something with her gaze. However, she finally turned and silently joined the pirates who were getting ready to leave for the ship. Jabez watched her in slight confusion, but he didn't question. Captain's gaze fell on Amaya, but she didn't speak. Solomon stepped up alongside Jabez, his expression inscrutable. As the pirates Captain had chosen to come with them stepped up to the group, Captain nodded to Zatook. The shadows in the camp flared upright and spun around the small group, encasing them in something like a bubble before sinking into the ground. When the shadows rose again and let the group free, they were deposited mere feet from the gatehouse. No one in the group was surprised to see the curtain wall closed to them, a heavy metal portcullis guarding the heavy wooden door behind.

"I would bet my left scimitar that he has more than what we see," Solomon noted calmly. Captain was eying the wall, her eyes shimmering beneath her bangs.

"Aye. T'e air above t'e wall be shielded by magic," she glanced over at Zatook. "Even yours. 'e's go' some strong wards aroun' for anything stronger than a 'uman. T'is keep coul' defend agains' a dang Celestial…" She reached up to rub her chin, but Zatook stepped past her in front of them all. He held his hand to the side, calling his blade from the shadows. "Oi." He glanced over his shoulder at the girl, his gaze level. Then he actually smirked, surprising her enough that she didn't protest further.

He could sense the power clinging to the stone, set against what he was and what others may have suspected him to be. But the man within the walls had missed a very key component to the Demon of Andor. To access the power, he knew he had to change. He had returned his gaze to the curtain wall. Shadows seemed to swirl around him as he concentrated. And then he shifted. No longer did the dark-clad warrior of Andor stand before them, his form growing and blackening as he transformed.

The creature he became was easily twice his human height
and broad, with gray-tinted purple skin covering most of
his body. His abdomen, chest, and face were black, as were
his forearms and hands. His stature was almost like that
of a gargoyle, and he boasted the bat-like wings to match.
His wings gleamed like gemstones or glass, black at the top
fading to a bright purple along the membrane. Horns now
decorated his head, a large pair curving forward, revealing
how he got the name of 'demon', while several smaller
spikes jutted from his forehead back in a line to disappear
under his hair. That was mostly the same, except now it
was a black that ombred into purple ends. Like his wings,
the horns shone like glass. The larger horns were a vibrant
purple at their base that faded to black, while the shorter
spikes were the reverse. Purple irises gleamed in contrast
to his pitch-black eyes and pupils as he tracked the wards
embedded in the stone. A newly formed tail lashed the air
slightly as he calculated. Even his clothes had changed; a
black metal pauldron had appeared on his right shoulder,
gleaming with purple magic. Metal shackles adorned his
ankles, and his feet were bare. He wore black leather pants
with armored knee covers, and a leather belt across his
waist. More leather straps formed a partial harness over his
otherwise bare chest. Purple leather tails, almost like one
would find at the bottom of an adventurer's coat, draped
around his legs.

Clasped in one hand was a weapon that was almost exactly
the same as his regular blade, only larger and made from
a black metal. Purple runes glimmered along the blade,
spelling out something in a language long forgotten by
most races. It was these runes on which he called, swirling
the blade before him and then slamming the tip into the

ground. Several cracks split away through the earth, and trails of purple runes sped from the cracks before swirling up and around the portcullis. Captain shivered as the odd chill from the runes reached them, taking a step back to ward away the feel. Solomon was watching in surprise; all of his years in Andor, and he had never seen this. The monstrous change, yes, but not this power with it. Even as calm as he usually seemed, Jabez stared in surprise at Zatook, but he didn't interrupt the man. Alconai gave a low whistle in reaction. He'd seen the man's shadow powers when he'd rescued Alconai and Captain from the jailhouse, but this was new even for what he knew of the legends surrounding the Demon of Andor. Rose watched calmly, waiting for an opening. She turned to Solomon, trusting Zatook to handle the castle.

"Once he gives us an opening, I'm finding the blood mage. I won't pay any mind to the bailey, so it will likely fill with soldiers."

Solomon nodded. "We'll keep them occupied," he assured her, gesturing to the pirates— a few were cracking their knuckles at the conversation, but most were staring at Zatook. Captain turned to them.

"Jabie, ge' in t'ere an' find Tris for us. I'll 'elp Alconai wit' his friend and t'e second mage while Rose goes for 'er quarry." She turned back to the palace. "As soon as we be in, we be fightin'. Ge' ready."

The chains of runes seemed to spell and move even as they wound through the metal. Zatook raised a hand, fingers spread wide before he clenched his fist. The rune streams convulsed, tightening and bending the portcullis like a human would wad up parchment, a grinding screech and crunch filling the air. Even as the metal was tossed aside, the wards were responding. More strings of runes branched off to tangle with the magic that could not be seen while those that had crushed the portcullis moved for the studded gate. Rather than crushed, this was ripped from its hinges like a fisherman's door in a heavy storm. The barrier protecting the air instantly attempted to cover the opening, but the runes latched around the edges and held it at bay. Oh yes, the master of the castle was prepared for many things. He was even prepared for what the world knew of the Demon of Andor.

But the world didn't know everything, and the King of Andor was a master of secrets.

Solomon and the pirates were the first to rush through, meeting a wave of Tsukuyomi's soldiers. Rose was in next, silver shining around her to fend off any projectiles as she sped around the soldiers racing into the bailey and smashed the inner gate open with her stardust. Captain walked through next, her power flaring around her in rainbow arcs. She quickly spied Finnegan and Lance, turning to walk towards them. Finnegan frowned, peeling off his gloves.

"Oi, Lance, I ken a challenge when I see one," he noted to the knight beside him, breaking off from the keep's soldiers with Lance on his heels.

Jabez nodded to Captain before dodging around Finnegan and Lancelot, following in Rose's wake as he dashed inside the castle. Quickly surveying the area, he calculated where the dungeons might be and started looking for an entrance. Might as well start at the bottom and work upward.

Zatook pulled his blade free, flaring large, leathery wings before flying through the gate. The runes let the barrier behind him free once everyone was in, and his eyes watched the life forces around them for his opponent. The man wasn't long in arriving, Zatook blocking a bolt of lightning with his blade. The bolt faded to reveal StormShaper, and their battle began again in earnest.

Alconai glanced at Captain and grinned. Then, he faced Lancelot. The knight he could handle. He hadn't journeyed over the lands without learning a thing or two about fighting; he'd come out of several skirmishes as the victor. Alconai pulled his hat down farther on his head, shadowing his eyes. He then stood waiting for his opponent. Captain took a step back, opening her sealed eye as she watched Finnegan. The blood mage stepped slightly behind Lancelot, letting the knight charge at Alconai and thrust a weaponized gauntlet towards his neck. Finnegan was drawing his dagger to cut open his arm, but a strange tugging sensation caused the dagger to disappear; it reappeared in Captain's hand, and she spun it leisurely. She trusted Alconai to hold off Lancelot while she hunted for the item that would free him. A grin spread across her face as she found the thread. She dashed past the fighting men, flashing into a teleport before appearing behind Finnegan. She deftly shifted to spin around, grabbing one of his pouches and using Finnegan's dagger to cut the tie holding it to him. She tossed the pouch over his head.

"T'e stone's in there!" Finnegan dodged as she aimed the dagger for his neck, glaring at her. Out of options, he reached a hand up to his mouth and bit on his fingers, *hard*. "Ick, mate. An' I though' you lot couldnae ge' any grosser," Captain commented as she pulled a face. "Where t'ose fingers been, eh?"

Alconai quickly disengaged with Lancelot, the entertainer holding his own surprisingly well against the man. He caught the pouch before ducking away from another blow.

"Snap ou' o' it, mate," Alconai told Lancelot. He dodged again as he rummaged through the pouch until he found the stone. Dropping the crimson rock on the ground, Alconai smashed it with his booted heel. He waited with bated breath to see if the man came to his senses, staying in a stance that would allow himself to easily dodge and defend if not. Lancelot staggered in his attack, reaching a hand up to his forehead and covering his eyes. He dropped to his knees, trying to process the sudden onslaught of... well, wherever it was that he was. He looked up, eyes clear of Finnegan's influence as he gazed around to try and piece things together. His brow knit in further confusion when he saw Alconai and the Doran girl. Captain weaved around the blood mage, avoiding the attacks of his now-taloned hands.

"Tsk. Afte' mis'r fun-'ouse face, ye be a walk in t'e park!" She laughed jovially, kneeing him in the abdomen after dodging under a swipe. The obscure figure crashed through the keep wall above where Captain was fighting Finnegan, landing a few feet from their battle. The large, gargoyle-like figure followed close behind him, teeth bared. They were only there for a moment, StormShaper flashing forward to renew their battle. They blurred with speed, disappearing around the corner of the keep.

Alconai tipped his hat to the bamboozled knight. "Glad to see ye're back wit' us. 'Fraid I donnae 'ave time ta explain righ' now, bu' 'elp me and Cap'n deal wit' bloody digits over t'ere, an' ye'll get yer answers sooner." He held out his hand to the man. His gaze remained on Lancelot even as Zatook came rampaging through the area. They didn't call the man the Demon of Andor for nothing.

Lancelot nodded, grasping Alconai's hand and letting the man help him up. Goodness knows he had questions, but blood mages took priority. Captain was on her opponent's shoulders now, her legs wrapped around his neck. She messed with his hair and giggled.

"Gid'ap, ye louseh 'scuse fer a 'orse!" She laughed as she threw her weight to topple the man over. Finnegan growled at her, taking control of his whip so that it split into strands before wrapping around her and tossing her at the two men. Alconai deftly caught Captain, spinning on his heel with the momentum before smoothly letting her back on her feet. Finnegan stood carefully, rubbing his neck.

"Bloody pirate."

"At yer service, mate," Captain chirped with a bow.

"A pirate, a minstrel, an' a knigh'. Ye're inna migh' bi' o' trouble now, lad," Alconai taunted. He then gripped the clasp of his cloak, sliding the two metal wheels slightly apart to release the garment. He yanked the drawstring through its loop in the fabric. Dropping the cloak to the ground, Alconai allowed the wheels to slide back into position and wrapped the string around the crease. Soon, he was armed with another yo-yo.

Lancelot frowned at the man. For some reason, just looking at that yo-yo gave him a headache. He turned to look at the mage instead. Captain had pulled one of her own daggers from her boot, Finnegan's dagger still in her other hand.

"So, lads, 'ho wan's to go firs', eh?" she teased, wiggling her eyebrows at the two men before taking the lead herself. She dashed forward, kicking against the ground to flip over Finnegan's head and land in a crouch behind him. She spun, swiping the daggers at his ankles. Finnegan jumped to the side opposite her swing's arrival, but when he went to slash her back in retaliation, talons met greaves as Lancelot blocked the attack. Alconai appeared on Finnegan's other side and whipped the yo-yo around, this one made of metal with flexible wire for string. He struck the mage's head with it, resulting in a resounding *thwack.* He then swung the yo-yo round again and caught it around Finnegan's knees. Pulling the wire taught, the minstrel slammed his heel into the mage's kneecap.

Finnegan let out a strained growl as his kneecap busted beneath the blow, trying to throw himself to the side, though it was more like a flail than anything. He quickly moved to roll from them, but Captain used him as a landing pad for her handspring before shifting into a grapple. Unable to lash at her with his taloned hand, Finnegan tried commanding the blood strips again. Lance intercepted them before they could reach Captain; even though the strips kept reforming, he simply continued to cut through them to keep them away from the other two. Alconai retained his grip on the yo-yo to help restrain Finnegan. However, Captain and Lancelot seemed to have things well in hand.

***

Tristan stared as his father released the diamond dust from his sister's pendant and let it sprinkle the floor. The boy's knees hit the stone floor hard when he collapsed in his crushing grief. Tears trickled down his cheeks in steady streams, his heart bleeding with the crystalline drops. It hurt to breathe. The grief crushed him more than any physical pain he'd ever endured. He hadn't heard Rose's thought, allowing his despair to convince him she had died at the river. He felt empty and yet overflowing at the same time. He blinked and shuddered when a hand suddenly gripped his chin tightly. Tristan didn't resist, allowing his father to tilt his head back and meet his gaze. Emotional anguish suddenly tore through him, magnified by his own grief. Thoughts filled his mind as one of his father's powers bore through him. Tristan's own memories worked against him to convince him of his shortcomings, wearing him down even further. He was weak. He failed to protect his mother, his weakness killed Rose, and now his sister had died on his watch. He wanted nothing more than to curl up and die. To slip away and join his loved ones. To stop fighting.

Tristan sobbed openly as the torture continued for a while longer, tearing apart his confidence and psyche. He barely registered when his father allowed Tristan to slip from his grasp, the boy slumping in defeat on the floor. He barely noticed the man leave. Instead, he lay down and tucked himself into a ball as he fought desperately to close off his mind, to shut down the voices telling him what he truly was: nothing.

In the dark cell, Tristan stared at the dust scattered across the floor. Still silently sobbing, he slowly reached out with his hand, searching for his Child power once more. The warmth came a little easier this time. He knew it wouldn't change anything, but he watched as the golden light stretched from his hand and engulfed the dust, gathering it slowly together. Once he had as much as he could save, he shaped the light into a new pendant as clear as glass. It glowed softly with his Child powers, the dust looking like tiny sparkles in the crystal. He drew the new pendant to him and held it close as exhaustion swept through him. His power dimmed until only what was in the crystal remained. When he felt the blood mage's power start to seize control once more, Tristan quickly tucked the crystal away somewhere safe on his person.

As the mage's power controlled his exhausted body to stand, the young man didn't even try to resist. What was the use? When the chains unlocked and the cell opened, he sped through the castle. The devastation he felt kept him from being able to fully focus on anything around him, his mind retreating into himself. A part of him silently prayed he would die in this battle. His now blood-red gaze never wavered, even as he passed Jabez in the hall.

***

Rose could sense her. The blood mage from before, the one who stole Tristan and knew Elder Keeshe. If she could take her down, the control over Tristan would vanish— as would any spells of hers keeping him bound. She blasted into a large hall, skidding to a halt as her eyes found the witch. Marilyn stood on a balcony overlooking the grand room, her face triumphant. It faltered when she saw who she was staring at.

"You're supposed to be dead."

"I am." Rose's eyes narrowed. That witch— she wasn't a Drow, but neither was she human. Not anymore. What had she done?

The blood mage wasn't sure what to think of Rose's response. Luckily, she didn't need to decide, as Tristan arrived in the Great Hall. *"Kill her."* Tristan charged at Rose, slashing at her back with a crystal sword. His eyes appeared dead as he fought her, no emotion even in reaction to the fact that Rose stood before him. He refused to believe his eyes. His heart told him he was hallucinating. No way she was alive; his father's tricks were continuing to torment him. Rose spun quickly, moving with ease despite the severe gashes beneath her bandages. She didn't even feel the wounds anymore, let alone the pain Lady Rin had taken. Good: she didn't need to worry about new wounds, so she could fight to her fullest. She caught Tristan's sword with one hand and placed her other hand on his arm. Red flared from her eyes in a small glow as her blood seeped through the bandages and over Tristan, winding around his limbs and tightening.

Jabez slowed to a halt once he reached the room where Tristan and Rose fought. He blinked at the young man. *Oh, no.* Thanks to his training both with the ninjas and Solomon, Jabez recognized the signs of someone possessed by blood magic: the scarlet hue of the younger man's eyes the greatest evidence. Jabez's gaze scanned the room, searching, before alighting on Marilyn and noting the vermilion stone she twirled in her hand. The mage's attention was still on the duel between Chosen Children, so she hadn't seen Jabez's entrance. Slipping into the shadows along the edges of the room, the ninja silently stalked closer to the balcony where the blood mage stood. He kept his eyes on her as he moved carefully to avoid drawing her attention. Fighting blood mages was tricky, even with his training. To make things more difficult, she would see him if he tried to scale his way onto the balcony. His best bet would be a surprise attack from his current spot, though that meant giving away his position. Calculating the distance, the angle, and the movement of the stone, Jabez let fly one of his throwing knives, aiming to release Tristan from the mage's possession. As it flew towards her, Marilyn caused Tristan's sword arm to swing back and thrust forward. She didn't get a chance to see what the Drow did, holding her other hand up so that Jabez's knife stuck through her palm and out the back of her hand.

"...hm...?" She stared at her hand in surprise, then down at Jabez. "Another party guest?" she giggled.

Jabez sighed. He had hoped to catch the mage while she was distracted by the fight, but apparently, she was more perceptive than that. Now that he had the blood mage's attention, he couldn't do much from his current location. He wasn't magic. Throwing stealth to the four winds, Jabez made a running jump for the bookshelves beneath the balcony. He leapt up the structures and then jumped up to the balcony itself. Once his hands touched the railing, he hoisted himself up and over. Pulling out his blade and chain, he faced the blood mage. Marilyn stood waiting for him, pulling the knife out with her teeth. The hole in her hand filled in and mended before Jabez's very eyes. She tilted her head, her bloodshot orange and red eyes examining him. "Not a very good specimen..."

Jabez quirked an eyebrow at her. "I'm not sure if I should take that as a good thing or bad," he said easily. He started twirling the chain in a circle to his right. The blade whistled as it rotated in the air. "Well, I'm known to have two left feet, but what say we dance anyway?" he remarked calmly. He let loose the chain, the blade flying for Marilyn's head. Marilyn simply watched him twirl, unmoving. When his sickle lashed through the air, she stepped to the side just a tad. The blade missed her head by an inch, digging into her shoulder.

"Is that all you can do? Sneak around, make snarky comments, and throw things? Hardly impressive, but what else should I expect from a simple human?" She reached up, ripping the sickle from her shoulder and tossing it back at him; the ninja caught the blade with ease. Blood streamed down Marilyn's arm before twirling and twisting into a thick whip that she grasped in her hand. As the blood stone vanished into her robes, Jabez's eyes flashed, noting the shifting bulge in her robes to see where the stone landed. Marilyn grinned at him, more than a hint of madness in her eyes. "But if you insist, I shall ensure that I step on each of your toes!"

Jabez spun the blade once more in an almost lazy circle, just fast enough to keep any slack from entering the spin. He made no sign that he knew where the stone rested. "Wow, someone who doesn't want my talents. That's a surprise— though I'll admit, a welcome one. Saves me having to do the rejecting," he commented dryly. Marilyn screwed up her face in a mocking smile and gave a short fake laugh before slashing her hand so that the whip flew through the air. The ends split, edges crystallizing like an elongated cat-o-nine aimed straight for Jabez's face. He stepped back, twisting his circling chain to his front. Blood shard connected with metal; while the chain's spin was interrupted, the whip instead moved again, twisting through the links. Jabez tested the tangle by pulling, but Marilyn matched the motion so that the coated chain remained between them. She reached her other hand up, using a finger to draw a tear under her eye— except rather than simply mocking him, she dug her nail into her cheek as she moved. She flung out her other hand, droplets becoming more shards. Jabez sidestepped the projectiles; he needed to get his chain loose. He had other weapons, but being locked like this limited mobility, and he didn't like the idea of the witch getting a new weapon. Judging by the strain on the chain, she may well break it. That was no simple feat for a blood mage, but then this mage seemed to be rather powerful. His eyes followed the crimson tangle to her arm; the whip was still connected. For this level of strength, did she need to maintain contact? He reached a hand to his pouches, clasping several small pellets. He flicked them out and at her, the little marble-like items erupting into smoke. As she waved her free hand to clear the air and cough, Jabez darted forward. Blood mages could heal even the worst of wounds, but perhaps this would get her to let go— he whipped out a blade and sliced it through her wrist. All of the blood along his chain went liquid, and he yanked his chain free as he pivoted and sprang back to his starting point. The whistle was his only warning, and he quickly slung his sickle and chain to block the one Marilyn had just made with her blood. Sure enough, as he looked, her hand was restored. She spun the red crystal sickle in a slow circle, mimicking his earlier movement.

"More cheap tricks," she mused, swaying slightly where she stood. "My, my. I really shouldn't be surprised. Your kind are always resourceful, if weak. Humans, that is." She grinned at him again, but Jabez just watched her levelly.

"From what I can see you're every bit as human, just more twisted with corruption than most."

All glee and mischief faded, pure loathing in its place. "I am *nothing* like you!" she screeched, darting forward and spinning the chain faster. The dance started in earnest then, the mage showing a surprising affinity for Jabez's chosen weapon. Metal blade clashed against blade-shaped blood shard, and their weighted ends crossed paths more than once. She didn't banter anymore, didn't laugh. Her face was rage and loathing, yet her movements were precise and calculated. She seemed to grow angrier with every one of Jabez's parries and strikes. Jabez had switched to more of a defensive play, focusing on keeping her weapon from reaching him. He knew: if she got his blood, this fight was over.

While Jabez kept the blood mage busy, Rose was left to deal with Tristan. His sword was currently stuck straight through her middle thanks to Marilyn, but she didn't pull away. Tristan's mind remained closed to her; his father had constructed barriers to keep other minds from influencing his son. *Tristan, you need to fight this.* Her voice was calm as she finished restraining him and tried to break his father's influence. The young man didn't bother replying to Rose as he simply stared at her. Even without his father's influence, even with his controller distracted, his mind refused to believe she was real. He struggled against the bindings, though only half-heartedly since Marilyn wasn't so focused on controlling him now. He didn't want to think. He didn't want to feel. He wanted to wake from this nightmare that started the night his mother woke him and took him from their home. He could do nothing to protect her when his father came after them. He failed to protect Arianna. He failed to break free of Marilyn's control and keep her from killing Rose. His father would get the Talisman one way or another and do Shaddai only knew what with it. Failure upon failure upon failure.

Tristan. Come on, listen to me. Rose touched a hand to his temple, strengthening her mental prowess with physical contact. *You've fought so hard, don't give in now. I know it hurts, Tristan. It feels like you can't breathe, like you can't go on. But you must. The world still needs you. Don't let Arianna's death be in vain.* Or hers, really, but she doubted that bit of information would help him right then. Besides, it's not like she knew when the Lady would come for her. Not really.

Two tears trickled from Tristan's eyes and down his cheeks. His gaze remained on Rose, unable to turn away while under another's control. It was his fault. Everything was his fault. *I failed her,* the thought came almost inaudibly. *I was supposed to protect her, and I failed. I couldn't keep from killing you. I can't help anyone. I'm a curse. I am nothing.*

Rose gently wiped his tears away before cupping his face in her hand. She leaned forward, touching her forehead to his as she gazed into his blood-stained gaze. *You didn't fail her, Tristan. You never failed. You fought for her, protected her as hard as you could. Failing would have meant giving up, letting your father win long ago.* She knew these words would not be enough to comfort him, but she hoped they could help at least a little. *She was happy. She loved you. She went quietly. Not a luxury many have, these days.* While they spoke, the magic in the blood wound around his limbs was fighting against the magic coursing through his veins.

Darkness wrapped around Rose then, ripping her from Tristan and slamming her against the opposite wall. Tsukuyomi stepped in between them. "Well, this is certainly interesting. You made a pact with Lady Death, I presume. You reek with her stench," he remarked in a smooth tone.

Tristan's gaze actually moved to his father when the man made his appearance. The sight of his father made the younger man want to shrink farther into his own mind, but something jarred his mental state. Information began filtering into him, slowly bringing him back to awareness: the solid floor beneath his feet, the sunlight cascading colors through the stained glass windows. Shifting his gaze, Tristan's eyes found Rose. No... She'd been there; he'd had her back. Was it all real?

Rose gasped as she was flung against the wall, but she did not stay there long. With a burst of silver light, she evaporated the tendrils holding her. "Tsukuyomi, I presume." Her voice was ice. Thin trails of blood hovered around her, and she glowed with a silver aura. She dashed forward, a warrior once more— silver coated her blades and trailed behind them like stardust as she slashed at him. With Marilyn distracted and Rose's influence, Tristan felt the control slipping. He now stared at Rose as if seeing her for the first time. *Rose?*

Marilyn paused when she sensed something change, but Jabez quickly pushed his advantage. He lunged towards her, overcoming the defensive range of her chain before bringing his blade up. He used a shorter length, spinning the blade rapidly and constantly changing direction to pepper her with cuts. He worked to wound her faster than she could heal, hoping to create an opening to aim for the stone. Marilyn dissolved her own chain, blood coating her hands and crystallizing into talons like the ones she had used as Tristan to fight Rose. She fell into his rhythm, parrying his swings even as she back-stepped from him and hissed. She hated fighting defensively, but she could feel the link between Tristan and his stone weakening. The boy would break free soon if something wasn't done. But she didn't have the focus she needed with Jabez keeping her busy. Dilemma, dilemma. Jabez refused to let up, meeting her parries with all the force he could muster. He was faster, more agile naturally, but magic flowed through her veins. The superior blood. She wouldn't lose to a human.

"I am going to kill you," she growled. "You will never be buried. No flame will sanctify your death. I will dance on your bones. Your blood will waste away to nothing, nothing. *Nothing*, do you hear me?!" She caught the handle of his blade, turning it against him and slashing him from shoulder to chest. Jabez cursed, shifting his feet and kicking off to get some distance. Marilyn seemed to blur, clawed hand slashing from his opposite hip to meet his other wound. She ducked down under the weighted end seeking her face, then leapt up so that their noses almost touched and sank her talons into his un-marred shoulder. She yanked his blade and chain from his grasp, tossing them to the side as he staggered away. "I won't even use your disgusting blood, your stupid human blood," she snarled, stalking towards him. "Perhaps I'll let my acolyte have it for practice. But he won't get to drink it, oh no." Jabez pulled free a kukri, a special curved knife, trying to hold a defensive stance against the pain. "That would be far too high an honor for pathetic, common blood like yours," she continued. Her slow and steady pace suddenly blurred; she was in front of him again, slashing wildly. No pattern existed in her erratic movements; she was impossible to read, but Jabez did what he could to parry or at least deflect. She was solely focused on him now, pure rage radiating off of her. Jabez could practically feel the heat from her gaze alone. He cried out as she dug talons into the first gash she had made; the blood mage whisked her hand back quickly, ordering a small amount of his blood to leave his body. "I will teach you the meaning of pain. I will not grant you a fast death, oh no, you get to *suffer*."

Jabez gritted his teeth as pain tried to seize his body. Through the agony, he tried to think. He wouldn't be able to beat her at this rate, but he didn't need to. He just needed one opening. *Shaddai, guide my blade to Your victory,* Jabez silently prayed. As Marilyn lunged for him again, Jabez fell back. One hand caught her shoulder to keep her from completely toppling on top of him, but the other used the butt of his kukri to punch her robes as hard as he could muster; he felt a satisfying crunch, and she screamed in rage. Jabez bent his knees, hands fighting to keep her far enough that he could plant his feet on her chest and kick. It was just enough to get him free; he quickly scrambled up and backed away several paces even as his vision swam.

In the main area below, Tsukuyomi disappeared in a swirling mass of darkness. Spikes of shadow erupted from every direction in his absence, aiming straight for Rose. Tristan watched in horror as she made no move to dodge or call her shield, her posture calm and resolute as she waited for the spikes. Memories flashed through his mind: his years with Arianna, the day they met Rose, and their time together until the present. Arianna's smile dominated all the images along with the memory of kicking Rose into the river after running her through against his will. A single sentence echoed through his mind, the memory of Rose's words: *I don't want you to leave.* Just as the shadows would have reached Rose, twilight crystal infused with sunlight encased the dark tendrils. The crystal froze the shadows before disintegrating into harmless dust. Tsukuyomi's sword blocked the one Tristan had made, his son suddenly before him, eyes burning with determination and fury. Sunlight radiated from the younger man as his Child powers surged against his father's darkness. The two men disengaged only to flash together in another spot. Steel and crystal clashed in resounding rings throughout the room, the battle moving faster than humanly possible. It was only a moment before Tsukuyomi found himself fending off another blade alongside his son's, this one radiating starlight. Rose and Tristan moved in tandem despite this being their first full battle together. The combined fury of the Star Child and the Sun Child filled the hall with blinding gold and silver light. Tristan watched as his father chose to shroud himself in shadow rather than combat the lights individually. Blades of sunlight and starlight clashed with steel and cut through shadow, but no matter what they tried, Tsukuyomi held his ground. His steel remained solid, his shadows reformed, and he did not waver. Tristan sent a wave of twilight crystal across the ground to amplify the lights' intensity. Even that seemed to barely faze his father. Why? How was the man faring so well against two light wielders? Then again, his father had been alive for longer than either him or Rose.

The flare of sunlight through crystal earned a howl from Marilyn, the blood mage staggering away from Jabez and raising the sleeves of her robes to shield her face. The ninja groaned, rolling back onto his front and forcing himself up. He needed healing, and soon. But he couldn't exactly get out of the room. The battle below would overwhelm him in his current state, and a dive out the window would end him. At least he had managed to break the stone. Not so bad for a weak human, he thought with a wry smirk.

Oh, aye. Even be'er when ye live to tell the tale, eh? I swear, ye make me do all t'e work 'round here.

Jabez closed his eyes, managing a soft, wet chuckle. *Someone's got to keep you on your toes. 'Sides, I can always count on you to have my back,* he teased in turn as the tell-tale rainbow flash surrounded him.

As Tristan and Rose tried once more to charge Tsukuyomi, shadows erupted from the man's form and actually cut through the light. They reached Rose and Tristan, throwing both youths back. His back impacting the floor forced the air from Tristan's lungs in a gasp, but he allowed the momentum to carry him into a roll back up to his feet. Even so, he swayed from the force of the blow coupled with his less than ideal condition from earlier. He glanced over to Rose to see her on her feet as well, her stance defensive and focused. Tristan readied his own blade, his confidence faltering as his gaze returned to his father to see the man seemingly unaffected by their efforts. Before he could dart forward, darkness spread out from Tsukuyomi's form like a tidal wave of shadow. Tristan watched in horror as the light around them vanished. He saw nothing now, only darkness. How could this be? The Sun Child gathered his light in an attempt to illuminate the area around him, but it only allowed him to see his own body. He could find no sign of Rose or his father, but he could hear them clashing still. He tried to follow the sound, to get back in the fight. As soon as he took a step, the shadows surged towards him, moving to restrain him. Tristan lashed out with his light and his twilight crystal, cutting through the shadows. Too many. There were too many, and he felt his body waning with exhaustion. Still, he refused to give up. He couldn't. Not with Rose so close. What could he do, though? It was obvious that he was no match for his father. Even as he fought them now, Tristan's horror grew as the shadows absorbed the light used against them. Even combining his light with his crystal barely held the shadows at bay. Of course. His father had years of experience. He probably knew how to counter all kinds of powers and fighting styles. So how much of a threat would two newly-realized Chosen Children be to him?

Another surge against him made Tristan stagger. The shadows used the opening to quickly coil around his limbs and tighten, holding him in place. Tristan struggled against the restraints, summoning his crystal and light to no avail. He was reaching his limit after already pushing past it once. Despair and desperation pressed in on him like lead weights. The sensation only heightened more when Tristan thought he heard a cry of pain or rage off to the side. Rose. Fear froze the blood in his veins. Would his father kill her? Tristan still saw and felt vividly that horrible moment he'd kicked Rose's bloody form into the river. The memory filled his mind now along with the more recent memory of his sister's death. His mind also flashed back to seeing his mother die at his father's hands. All this for that stupid talisman. He knew he shouldn't, but what more could he do? Now along with the fear, Tristan felt his anger blazing through him like an inferno. If his father wanted that power so badly, then Tristan would give it to him— though not in the way his father wanted.

Rage filled Tristan with fire even as an icy power resonated through him, clashing with the warmth of his Child power. The shadows suddenly froze into a familiar dark crystal. However, red veins laced the substance before the crystal disintegrated, the shadows disappearing with it. The red veins pulsed along the exposed parts of Tristan's body, disappearing into his clothes.

Rose was staring at him, first surprise and then concern flashing across her features. Tsukuyomi had stopped as well, frowning at the spectacle that was his son. Marilyn leaned over the balcony to watch, arms propped on the railing and chin in her hand as she pouted about her loss. But she wouldn't flee unless Tsukuyomi did; neither would she intervene unless he ordered. The ninja wasn't worth chasing right now; she would find him again when she felt like it.

Anger emanated from the Sun Child, the light keeping his father's powers at bay. Tristan suddenly dropped to one knee and slammed his hands on the ground. Dark crystal spread throughout the castle like twilight ice. The red veins and pulsing sunlight glowed throughout the crystal, magnifying the powers until the whole structure began to break apart. Tristan grimaced as the red veins and his sunlight started to oppose each other, but he kept his focus. He needed to flush his father out if he hoped to end the man before he could hurt anyone else.

***

Captain was wiping the blade of her knife clean, Finnegan's corpse on the ground behind her. Alconai had Jabez now, and Lancelot was helping treat the ninja's wounds as best they could on the fly. Captain had tossed them a Concoction as well, though she had only been able to make a few weaker ones before things went sour. She turned to check on Sol and the boys. A fair amount of soldiers lay sprawled within the wall, the pirates still fighting to keep the remaining soldiers at bay. Unlike the blood mage, they weren't actually trying to kill the soldiers— the lads were just doing their jobs and serving the High Lord. Solomon took a step back to check on Captain, letting a couple of the crew fill in for him. He frowned when he noticed a red glow, pulling up his medallion. His eyes widened, and he turned away from the soldiers to run.

"Get to cover!" he yelled, grabbing Captain's arm as he reached her without stopping; she fell into his pace quickly, sensing the urgency. The pirates had turned to flee, as well, leaving the confused soldiers in their wake. Lancelot and Alconai got Jabez up between them and followed. Alconai had no idea what was going on, but even he could sense the powerful energy within the castle. When the soldiers saw Lancelot running from the castle, they gave up on the pirates, grabbed their downed comrades, and followed suit. A large shadow flew over and past them before the gargoyle form of Zatook landed in front of them. As they ran past, he twirled his blade before slamming it point-down into the ground. Shadows and a dark purple magic sprang along the earth and rose in a shimmering barrier wall.

***

Rose ran to Tristan's side, her stardust shimmering along her form as a protective layer. She joined him on her knees, wrapping her arms around him as her starlight shield spread to cover them both from any falling debris.

Tristan sensed the absence of his father's presence. Tsukuyomi had left the castle, taking some of his most trusted followers with him, including the blood mage. Now that the threat of his father was gone, Tristan tried to recede the Talisman's power. Instead of obeying him, however, the destructive energy continued to increase and spread. Panic quickly replaced the young man's rage as he felt the corruptive power flare, like a crack in a dam slowly getting bigger as more and more water pushed against it. His mind quickly recalled that there would be servants working in the castle: innocent people who had no part in Tsukuyomi's plan aside from caring for his estate.

Tristan curled in on himself tighter despite feeling Rose's arms and power around him. He kept his head down, grief and physical pain crushing his spirit. He wanted to reach for her and pull her to him, but he feared what might happen now that he'd tapped into the Talisman's power. He'd known it was dangerous, but in his anger and

274

desperation he'd given in to the temptation. Now it was as if Rose and he huddled in the center of a lake of blood and sunlight. The corrosive power possessed a feeling of ending as it leeched off Tristan's emotions. All the things he'd buried deep down inside himself now swelled. He shook with emotion, fatigue, and pain as he fought to bring the Talisman's power back under control. Agony seized his body the more he tried to pull the force back, the red veins pulsing angrily along his form. What could he do? He could barely think through the turmoil plaguing him. He was vaguely aware of the crystal and Talisman powers spreading throughout the castle. People were going to die because of his stupidity, and his best efforts to rectify his mistake weren't going to be enough.

You're not alone, a gentle voice cut through the anguish in Tristan's mind. Warmth enveloped him as though arms embraced him alongside Rose's. A new power resonated with his, strengthening him and aiding him in pulling and holding the Talisman's power at bay.

***

A presence touched Zatook's mind as well. *There are people in the castle who need to get out. She'll help, but it will take the two of you. I am helping Tristan hold the power back for now, but his strength is already exhausted. Please, Zatook.* The voice in the shadow warrior's mind resonated with warmth and gentleness not unlike that of a mother.

As the voice finished speaking, a flash of light darted into the castle despite the overflowing power. Barely seconds later, people started appearing outside the castle, carried there through what appeared to be bolts of lightning.

The gargoyle did not so much as flinch when the voice reached him. Between the Moon Child and his master, Zatook was used to being contacted through telepathy or telepathy-like spellcraft. He did not question, reaching through the shadows of the castle to find those the lightning streak did not, teleporting them through in either groups or singles as he found them. He flinched slightly with the effort of holding his barrier and working to help the other presence rescue the inhabitants.

Once all the people were relocated safely outside, the lightning struck the ground just beyond the castle. Instead of leaving a burn mark, the bolt shaped into the figure of a woman. Her pure white silhouette appeared wisp-like in nature, billowing and stretching like flame. Blue and purple tattoos decorated her skin to form a more solid shape to her body and give her a sense of modesty without smothering her raw form. Her vibrant blue eyes shone like gemstones as she regarded Zatook a moment, giving him a slight nod of acknowledgment. She then turned her gaze back to the castle.

***

Inside the stone structure, the Talisman-infused crystal once more began to creep across the stonework. Tristan shook horribly as he felt his body threatening to collapse with the strain.

"I can't hold it. I'm sorry," he whispered despairingly to Rose and the voice in his mind. He just felt Rose's arms tighten around him.

You did well, Tristan, the voice assured him. He felt the presence receding slowly. *They are all safe. You don't have to hold it back now.*

Tristan didn't reply, pain and fatigue overwhelming him like a tidal wave. The Talisman's power burst forth in a blinding, deafening, earth-trembling blast. Outside, it looked as though blood flowed through and over the stone before crystallizing the structure. Then, it erupted. The shattering sound of glass reverberated through the air as all the crystal blasted into shards and hurtled across the landscape, destroying the castle. Rose leaned against Tristan, holding him close. She didn't try to contain his power, letting his grief flow through the castle. She could just barely sense a strong power outside, and she trusted that to protect the area around the castle. Tristan didn't move as he allowed his emotions to fuel the Talisman and let the power rage, unable to control it and in too much pain to try any longer. He barely even registered the new presence outside the castle. Finally, he slowly, shakily slipped his arms around Rose and hold her close, grateful for her presence despite his fear of hurting her further.

***

As the power eradicated the castle, the wisp woman held her arms out to the sides, and the blue and purple tattoos shot out like flaming vines. They encompassed the area, absorbing the power straining against them and feeding it back into the woman's body. Zatook stared at the brilliant form, watching her contain the raw power with seeming ease. Since it was no longer needed, he pulled his sword free and let the barrier fall before morphing back into his human form. He tensed as he did so but showed no signs of pain. Something about the glowing figure seemed familiar to him, but he couldn't place it.

"Wha' ta finkle feat'ers is tha'!" Alconai yelled over the roar of power. He stared at Captain since it was too bright for him to look at the blast. He hoped Tristan and Rose made it out beforehand. Jabez's skin crawled as he felt the power of the blast wash over them. All this from Tristan? What the heck happened to the kid? And who was the woman managing to contain the power?

The woman's arms shook slightly as her body strained with absorbing the raging power. She held her ground even as her face grimaced in pain and determination. The billowing wisps of her hair whipped about her from the force of the vortex she worked to contain.

***

The blast finally faded. Tristan gasped for breath, shaking from the strain the raw power had placed on his body. The sword that had pierced Rose had disappeared once Marilyn lost her control over Tristan, so there was nothing in the way for the young man to hold her close. He barely managed to shift and curl his body around her as if to protect her. Everything seemed to grow deathly still. Tristan stared over Rose's shoulder at the ground now with weary, empty eyes. His whole body trembled from exhaustion and a jagged pain that surged through him. Tristan's warm light weakly spread over Rose as he subconsciously attempted to heal her wounds. His body shook even more as he tried to push it past its limits to tend to the Drow in his arms. His vibrant blue eyes continued to stare blankly at the ground. He moved automatically, feeling completely drained. He didn't even realize the Drow had slipped unconscious before the blast faded.

***

Captain was staring at the sky, but all she had to say was a soft "Oi yosh." Solomon shook his head in response to Alconai.

"I do not know, though I could almost sense Tristan's power mingled with the new one."

Once the power dissipated, the woman retracted her own. As she stood there her white silhouette continued to billow like flame. Her arms dropped to her sides while her gaze landed on Tristan and Rose, but she said nothing. Despite seeming to stand strong still, those with keen eyes caught the subtle tremble in her stance. She took a step to steady herself as she watched the proceedings for a moment.

Alconai emitted a low whistle. "Wha' in blazes is tha' lad?" he wondered in amazement. He glanced back at the crater where the castle once stood. "Can ye tell if'n he survived?" His eyes then caught sight of the woman who had been holding the blast at bay. "I be damned. I believed t'e stories about Celestials, but I ne'er though' I'd see t'em in person. First the Lady of Death and now this one." His attention snapped to his brother and gave him a disapproving frown when Jabez pushed himself to his feet. "Oi, ye were bleedin' jus' a moment ago. Let someone else handle t'ings for a bit, aye?"

Jabez shook his head carefully. "I...I want to see for myself that they're alive," he answered, sounding tired but determined. He winked at his brother. "Don't worry. I won't push myself." Alconai sighed but didn't argue for now.

"The Sun Child, yet something more, it would seem," Solomon answered simply. He looked to Zatook as the light faded. "Go with Jabez to collect our comrades, would you?

Take a couple of the lads in case you need extra hands. I'll see to our Celestial helper. Alconai, help Captain find a place we can set a small camp. Whoever doesn't go with Zatook can help. I doubt we shall be journeying far tonight." He nodded to them before taking off towards the white form. He didn't address the lad's awe about Celestials yet. There were things to be done. Lancelot rubbed his arm awkwardly; he still had no idea what was going on, so for now he stayed near Captain and Alconai.

Alconai nodded at Solomon in understanding. Considering their travel companions thus far, the minstrel wasn't surprised to learn there might be something more to Tristan than initially perceived. He'd known there was something strange about the younger man, but he hadn't been with the group long enough to get the full story. And what a story they had to tell. Later. For now, he nudged Lancelot to follow their comrades.

"We'll be exchangin' stories la'er, I be wagerin'," he told the knight.

Lance nodded, though his eyes were following the Demon of Andor and the injured man. "I'm sure we will, but I gather I'll be more helpful to our friends investigating the damage." He glanced at the pirates already moving to obey the russet-haired girl. "Stories indeed…" He shook his head, smirking at Nai and moving after Jabez and Zatook. He didn't fully understand what had happened yet, but he knew he had been stationed here. If there were survivors, they would want a friendly face.

Jabez nodded to Solomon's suggestion and headed for the empty space left from the blast. He gestured for Lancelot and the pirates to check on the rescued people now standing a decent distance from the area before turning his attention back to the Sun Child and the Star Child. From what he could see, Tristan and Rose seemed to be alive at least— albeit shaken and bloodied. As the ninja neared, his keen eyes swept over the pair. The boy looked awful: pale and drawn. The empty gaze in Tristan's eyes worried Jabez. A frown settled beneath his mask when the lad continued healing Rose even though his golden light seemed to be doing nothing. The man sighed. Perhaps the lad had worn himself out too much for his power to have any effect. Once he reached the pair, Jabez gently touched Tristan's shoulder, but the boy didn't acknowledge him.

Zatook wasn't far behind. Now that they could take time to assess the damage, even he looked a right mess. His clothing was tattered in several places, revealing the deep scars that laced any portion of his skin that was visible; some could have easily been battle wounds, yet even more Xs crossed his flesh as well. His shadows were already working to take the place of any missing cloth. He took one look at Tristan before reaching down and as gently as possible knocking the kid out— right now, the kid needed to rest. Tristan collapsed when Zatook pinched the nerve in the boy's neck. The younger man looked extremely pale and haggard, like power hadn't been the only thing surging out of him. Jabez glanced at Zatook and then turned back to Rose. He gently removed her from Tristan's now-limp grasp and gathered her in his own arms, trusting Zatook to carry Tristan. He grimaced slightly, his own newly treated injuries protesting, but he managed to carry Rose as he walked with Zatook to rejoin Captain. His gaze strayed once toward the woman Solomon approached, but he didn't stop.

The being shifted her gaze to Solomon. She inclined her head in greeting but said nothing for now. Solomon nodded his head in return, reaching into his pouch to procure one of Captain's Concoctions.

"I had wondered if you would be joining us this evening," he noted calmly, seeming to know the apparition. "I have the others finding a spot to camp. You should join us and rest, at least. That was quite the display."

As the woman reached for the Concoction, Solomon noted the white energy that made up her hand and forearm was now black as though burned. Red veins laced up the limb, pulsing with dark power. Shakily, the woman took the Concoction with a chuckle. "Nothing gets by you," she intoned casually. The outline of a mouth became barely visible when she spoke. "Packed a bit of a punch." As she unstoppered the bottle and downed the contents, Solomon saw that the damage extended to both the woman's arms. Once she finished drinking, she sighed as she watched Jabez and Zatook carrying off their charges. "I suppose I might as well join you. Perhaps I can alleviate the many questions the group is sure to have after all this." She motioned for Solomon to lead the way, indicating she would follow.

Solomon nodded. "Very well." He moved for the camp that Alconai and Captain had started scrounging together. The pirates had been carrying the supplies they kept, and now they worked to set up a few tents and bedrolls. They handed off a few in surprise when some of the crew who had been with Lance ran over to the camp and explained about the survivors. Zatook had laid Tristan on one of the bedrolls, Jabez laying Rose on another beside him. The ninja soon found himself ushered to an empty bedroll by a glaring Captain.

"I know my limits, and I was careful," Jabez told her, his tone soft but teasing.

"Oh, aye. An' I ken jus' 'ow much ye like to be pushin' t'ose limits, too," she teased yet chided right back. "Which is why ye be sittin' now. I donnae wanna see ye up an' abou', ye hear me? Jus' 'cause I ainnae go' a plank on land donnae mean I cannae be thinkin' of somethin'!"

Jabez chuckled softly as he gave her a tired salute. "Aye, Captain." His gaze then shifted, as did the rest of the group's when Solomon returned with the woman in tow. Alconai stared at her in awe.

"Milady, 'tis an honor. And thank ye for your swif' intervention," the minstrel greeted, sweeping into a bow. His gaze immediately caught sight of her arms, but he said nothing for now despite the concern that flicked across his eyes.

The woman snorted. "Oi, oi, don't you start that bowing nonsense. Despite what the tales say, we're not gods. Neither am I anyone of import for ye to be groveling." Her voice sounded familiar. "I'm sure you've got questions, and I'm here to answer what I can. Oh, yeah," she added evenly, the white silhouette fading to reveal the form of Amaya, "surprise."

To be Continued

About the Authors

Carissa Barker-Stucky

Carissa lives in Missouri with the love of her life and their multitude of pets— two dogs, five cats, and a rabbit. Though her characters seem to have a will of their own, somehow she's managed to wrangle them into something resembling proper stories. She also dabbles in graphic design and other art. Nothing inspires her more than a cup of chai or frozen matcha and a purring kitty on her lap.

When Carissa's health changed her life course, she started to focus more on this series with one of her best friends. She also takes any opportunity to encourage awareness regarding Dysautonomia and the illnesses associated, such as her own Postural Orthostatic Tachycardia Syndrome. The curious can find more information from Dysautonomia International, the leading nonprofit resource regarding this health condition.

Kimberly Glassco

Kimberly lives in Missouri with her canine companion and her overabundant imagination. From the wildernesses of her childhood backyards to the lined paper of her notebooks, Kimberly loves exploring and storytelling. And now, she's excited to bring others along for the journey. Her inspiration stems from her love of all things Celtic, fantasy, and magic. Just give her a blank piece of paper, some epic music, and a cup of pumpkin spice chai, and she'll have a new tale to tell in no time.

While working a full-time job to pay the bills, Kimberly has constantly felt God's calling for her to write at least on the side if not eventually full-time. To that end, she has been focusing on writing this series with one of her best friends. They have so many stories to tell and so little time in a day to work on them.